A BURGER, FRIES, AND MURDER

A Food and Wine Club Mystery Book 3

CAT CHANDLER

Five Sisters Publishing

BOOKS BY CAT CHANDLER

The Food and Wine Club Mystery Series:

A Special Blend of Murder

Dinner, Drinks, and Murder

A Burger, Fries, and Murder

Champagne, Cupcakes, and Murder (Coming June, 2018)

The Ricki James Mystery Series:

One Final Breath (Fall, 2018)

One Last Scream (2018)

Be the first to receive notification of new releases, and receive a bonus chapter. Subscribe to the mailing list here:

http://eepurl.com/dhGQYr

CHAPTER ONE

"WHO MEETS AT EIGHT IN THE MORNING," JENNA grumbled to herself. "The ever-cheerful breakfast fairies?"

The computer geek and website designer pushed her oversized, black-framed glasses higher up on her nose. Grabbing her laptop and several file folders from the passenger seat, she balanced them in her arms while she unfolded her legs and scooted out of the car, shoving the door closed with one hip. She was dressed in a baggy sweatshirt and sweatpants, which was her usual morning attire. Her long tight mix of kinky dark curls was doubled over and pulled into a rubber band on the top of her head. The loose ends hung to her ears. An unruly strand had escaped its bond, and she impatiently blew it out of her eyes. She sighed when it simply flopped back down, blocking a good piece of her vision.

Jenna knew she looked like she'd just rolled out of bed, which was close to the truth. But Eddie Parker would have to take her "as is", if he was going to demand a meeting at this ridiculous hour of the morning. Everyone knew that programmers stayed up late at night, so you'd think the man would have been polite enough to agree to something around elevenish. At least that wasn't the crack of dawn.

Good thing for him that I can't afford to turn away any clients. Not at the moment, anyway. But with her little business starting to take off, especially with the huge client she'd picked up earlier in the year, that might change in the very near future. And then Mr. this-is-the-only-time-I-can-spare-Parker would have to adjust his schedule to match hers. Which would be strictly afternoon and early evening appointments only. Jenna gave a silent decisive nod. She'd tried to talk Eddie into meeting her last night, but he'd claimed he already had another business meeting, so she'd had to settle for this morning before the rest of the staff arrived for work.

But three hours before the diner opened? How much prep time did it take to produce burgers, fries, and a couple of other specialty fast-food items? Jenna glanced around the completely empty parking lot. Since Eddie lived in the apartment complex only two blocks away, he didn't need to drive to work. Jenna assumed he was most likely waiting for her inside. Which meant early morning hour or not, she needed to get a move on.

She juggled the laptop and file folders until she had a firmer grip on them as she walked under the faded striped awning shading the walkway in front of the diner. She'd brought the folders to show Eddie his payment history, which was dismal, and ask if he'd please settle his entire outstanding balance, which was unlikely. But at least she might be able to pry a good chunk of it from him. She hoped so. She had bills to pay.

Her budget was still pretty tight, even with the pickup in her business and the huge rent break she was getting from Maxie, her colorful and eccentric landlady. Jenna also liked to eat on occasion. Her favorite meal was a carryover from her college years, and a perfect fit for this particular client. She loved to dig into a burger, fries, and a soda. Although now that she'd reached the lofty age of thirty, she'd become more health conscious. Which meant she usually substituted bottled water for the soda. But the hamburger was not negotiable. No matter what one of her best friends, Alex Kolman, who was now Dr. Kolman, said about it.

And her favorite hamburger joint in town was Eddie's Diner. *If he's too tight with his money to pay me in cash, maybe we could trade for free meals for life.* Jenna grinned. If Eddie offered that deal to her, she just might take it.

She'd reached the front of the building and leaned forward to peer through the glass window on the upper half of the old door. The inside of the diner was dark. Jenna glanced at her watch and frowned. It was just a minute or two after eight, so she wasn't early. And Eddie Parker had better not be running late. If she'd dragged herself out of bed at this horrifying hour, then he'd better have done the same.

Impatiently shifting everything she was holding to one arm, she raised her free hand and rapped loudly on the door that was only partially covered with peeling green paint. There was no movement or sound from inside.

Getting more annoyed by the second, she tried knocking louder, thinking Eddie might be in his back office. Another minute ticked by and still nothing. Out of frustration, the tall, thin website designer twisted the door handle then took a quick startled jump backward when it easily opened.

Jenna cautiously stepped up to the threshold and stuck her head inside. "Hello? Eddie? Are you here?"

No greeting came back to her.

I wonder if he forgot to lock up last night?

She immediately rejected that notion. Eddie had told her himself that he always locked up, and the last thing he did every night before going to bed was to take the short walk back to the diner to make sure it was secured. Every dime he was worth was in the slightly rundown eatery, which he'd built all by himself into a popular hangout for the local townspeople. And he owned it pretty much outright. A story he proudly related to anyone at the drop of a hat. She'd never asked what he meant by "pretty much".

And Jenna could appreciate that. Building any sort of business wasn't easy to do. But right now, she was wondering exactly where this self-made hamburger king was?

"Hello, Eddie? It's Jenna Lindstrom," she called out again, stepping into the diner and closing the door behind her. "We had a meeting set up for this morning. Are you here?"

Nothing came back but a slight echo of her own voice. Frowning, Jenna walked across the checkered-tile floor and around the wide counter spanning the entire back of the diner. She set her laptop and folders on the dull vinyl surface, right next to a cluster of sugar dispensers.

With her hands on her hips, she carefully looked around. Everything seemed to be in order. The tables scattered across the room all had chairs stacked on top of them, the floors looked as if they'd been mopped, and the counter was wiped clean.

The cash register sat on the shelf running along the back wall, and it didn't look disturbed. Jenna smiled. It was the type that used to be common in every establishment that did any kind of cash business. Sturdy, with push buttons, it harked back to an earlier time and was a far cry from the electronic registers found everywhere today. And even further from the swipe-and-pay cell phone apps that were becoming popular. But that was no surprise. Eddie wasn't into spending money unless it was necessary. Or into any technology, for that matter.

Shaking her head at what a dinosaur her favorite burger maker was, Jenna headed for the swinging door that led into the back of the diner. She walked through the kitchen toward the very rear of the establishment where she knew Eddie had his office. The narrow cramped hallway wasn't lit, and there wasn't any light coming in from anywhere except the kitchen behind her. Feeling her way along the wall, she stopped at a door three-quarters of the way to the end. With a bit of patting around the general vicinity of where the doorknob should be, she managed to locate the handle, frowning when it too turned easily beneath her hand.

Eddie must have been in a big hurry to leave after his meeting last night, Jenna decided. The interior of the office was completely dark. And even though it was obvious Eddie wasn't in there, Jenna's fingers ran along the wall until she found the light switch. When the small space lit up to broad daylight under the 100-watt bulb hanging from a cord in the ceiling, her eyes opened wide behind the lenses of her glasses.

Papers were strewn all over the floor, and the desk chair was tipped over on its side. All the drawers were open, and so were the doors to the overhead cupboards. Jenna took another slow look around before carefully backing out of the office.

Something was definitely wrong. As her other best friend, Nicki Connors, liked to say, this whole scenario just wasn't adding up. Every door she'd tried was unlocked, and now the office had been trashed? It had the earmarking of a break-in. And Eddie was nowhere to be found.

Jenna stood perfectly still, holding her breath and tilting her head to one side, she listened for any telltale sounds. But she didn't hear a thing. Sucking in a big breath of air, she did a quick trot back down the hallway. As she passed the counter, she reached out one long arm and grabbed her computer and file folders and kept going right out the front door. She didn't take in another breath until she was sitting in her car, her heart pounding wildly as she pressed the button for the door locks. The comforting loud snap of them sliding down had her closing her eyes in relief. At least no one was going to jump out at her from one of the dark corners in the diner.

She stared out the front window of her Honda as she dialed the number for the local police station that was barely a mile away. *I guess it says something about my life that I have the police on speed dial.* She tapped a finger against the dashboard as she waited for someone to answer the phone.

"Soldoff Police Department. How can I help you?"

Jenna let out another long breath of relief. "Fran, is that you?"

"Who else would it be?" the raspy voice on the other end of the phone responded. "Who's this?"

"It's Jenna. Jenna Lindstrom."

"Why, hello honey. You sound a little shaky. Something wrong, or has your friend Nicki discovered another body and you were elected to call it in?"

Jenna let out a giggle that sounded hysterical even to her own ears, and Fran must have thought so too.

"Do you need me to send one of the boys out to your place, Jenna?"

"Get a hold of yourself, Lindstrom," Jenna said under her breath. She closed her eyes and chewed on her lower lip, concentrating on slowing her breathing and hopefully the painful pounding in her chest. It was only a break-in. Nothing serious.

"Jenna! Can you hear me?"

The sharp crack in Fran's voice had Jenna's eyes snapping open. "Yes. Yes. I'm sorry, Fran. I'm fine. And I *do* need you to send someone out here. But I'm not at home."

"All right." Fran's voice came down several notches. "Where are you, honey?"

Jenna smiled at the homey endearment. It did more to calm her than all those yoga breathing exercises Alex was constantly harping about. "I'm at Eddie's Diner. I think someone broke into it."

"Someone broke into Eddie's?"

Jenna certainly couldn't fault the surprise in the police clerk's tone. Eddie's Diner wouldn't have been her first pick to rob either. At least not if the burglar actually wanted to walk away with something of value.

"I had a meeting scheduled with Eddie, but when I got here, the door was unlocked, and his office was trashed," Jenna said. "And I don't see Eddie anywhere."

"Okay," Fran said slowly. "Now honey, I want you to walk out of there and get someplace safe. Maybe lock yourself in your car."

Good idea, Jenna didn't mention that she'd already done that. "Okay, Fran. I'll sit in my locked car and wait for someone to come."

"You do that. And I'll send one of the boys out right away."

For the first time since she'd pulled into the wide gravel parking lot that was a good deal bigger than the diner itself, Jenna grinned. She wondered how the definitely middle-aged chief would feel about being called "a boy", although the description fit his young, and only, deputy pretty well.

"I'll be here." Jenna pushed the disconnect button on her cell phone. Setting it on the dashboard where it was within a quick and easy reach, she took a slow look around, wondering where Eddie was. It could be that his appointment the night before had run long, and the diner owner had overslept this morning. Mentally chastising herself for not simply calling Eddie and asking where he was, Jenna picked up her cell phone again. Scrolling rapidly through her contacts list, she found Eddie's number and hit the call icon.

She was still holding the phone to her ear, listening to it ring for the tenth time, when a police cruiser came racing into the parking lot, spitting up gravel and dust as it slid to a stop next to her Honda.

Rolling her eyes at the overly dramatic entrance, Jenna was still shaking her head when she got out of the car. She stood inside the opened door, turned, and leaned her forearms on the roof. She looked over at the deputy who'd leaped out of the cruiser and stood with his legs braced apart, ready to take on a whole gang of bad guys.

"Hi, Danny." Jenna lifted one hand in greeting before letting it drop back onto the top of her car.

"Are you all right? Fran said you were at the scene of a crime, waiting for assistance." The deputy, with his brown hair, brown eyes and clean-cut good looks, imitated an owl as he swiveled his head around to look over the gravel lot.

Jenna rolled her eyes. "What I'm doing is sitting in the parking lot of the local diner that I'm pretty sure was broken into last night."

Danny's shoulders relaxed, and he stuck his thumbs in his belt. "Eddie's? Not much to take in there besides helping yourself to the ice cream machine and some soda. Probably kids. Where's Eddie? Is he inside?"

"I don't know where he is. I haven't seen him, and he isn't answering his phone."

The deputy looked from the diner back to Jenna. "How'd you know there was a break-in? Is the lock busted?"

He didn't wait for an answer but walked over to the door and squatted in front of it. Jenna had followed behind him, so she stopped and waited while he examined the lock.

"Doesn't look busted," he commented, easily rising to a standing position in one fluid motion, reminding Jenna that she'd heard Danny had been quite an athlete back in his high school days. Not that those were all that far behind him.

"I didn't think so either," Jenna said. "It was unlocked when I got here."

Danny glanced over his shoulder at her. "Maybe you should wait out here while I have a look around."

"Oh I don't think so, Deputy." Jenna shook her head. "I'm staying right with you, and that very big gun you have on your hip."

He grinned at her. "I thought you didn't like guns."

Jenna gave an exasperated snort. "Usually I don't. But since you have one, I'm sticking with you. I wouldn't want you shooting me by mistake."

"Funny," Danny muttered as he pushed open the door and stepped inside the diner. He stood looking around, his thumbs back in his belt.

"I'm not seeing anything here that indicates a break-in, Jenna." He shrugged. "Maybe your imagination got away with you because Eddie forgot to lock up."

"Forgot to lock up, forgot about our meeting, and trashed his own office?" Jenna's eyebrows shot up. "Not likely." She gestured toward the swinging doors. "Go have a look for yourself."

"You stay here." Danny pointed a finger at her. "And I mean it this time. Stay here."

She grabbed a chair from the nearest table, turned it over and set it onto the floor. Plopping into the seat, Jenna crossed her arms. "Sure."

He chuckled as he walked across the tile floor and disappeared through the doors leading into the back. Jenna thought he'd be gone for a while and was considering getting her laptop out of the car, when she spotted him through the cutout window which served as a pass-through to the kitchen. He was walking slowly with his head bent.

Tapping a finger against the tabletop, Jenna watched him in silence for a second or two before her curiosity got the better of her. "What are you doing?"

"Following some blood smears, I think," Danny called

back. He didn't raise his head or spare her a look, but just kept his slow walk toward the far corner of the kitchen.

"Blood...?"

Jenna was on her feet in a flash and headed for the kitchen. She came up behind Danny just as he stopped in front of the huge metal door that led into the diner's walk-in freezer. She looked at the floor. The trail of dark red splotches ended there. One hand flew to her mouth and her eyes got as big as saucers as she and the deputy exchanged a horrified look.

"You don't think..." Jenna couldn't finish saying it out loud. Eddie couldn't be in the freezer, could he? She swatted Danny's shoulder. "Just don't stand there, he might be trapped inside."

"Right."

Danny cleared his throat before grabbing up a dishtowel lying on the counter next to the freezer, then using it around his hands as he took hold of the wide silver handle. He pulled it down until Jenna heard the distinct sound of the door unlatching. He tugged it open enough for both of them to peer around its edge.

"Oh no," Jenna breathed.

She had to lock her legs in place to keep them from buckling beneath her. A body was sprawled out in front of them, his face up and eyes staring up at the ceiling. The hefty, dark-haired man was wearing a plaid shirt that was part of the diner uniform, with the name "Eddie" embroidered on the front pocket.

Danny walked forward and knelt, placing two fingers against the side of Eddie's throat. He counted off a good ten seconds before straightening up and leaning back against his heels. He glanced over at Jenna, his mouth pulled down at the corners, and shook his head.

"It's Eddie." He looked at the body. "And there's more blood on the floor around the back of his head."

The deputy pushed himself up to his feet and walked backwards until he was again standing in the kitchen next to Jenna. "I have to call this in."

He latched onto Jenna's arm and pulled her along with him. Once they were outside in the fresh morning air, he steered Jenna towards the Honda. "I want you to sit in your car while I call Fran and have her track down the chief. He's out handling a domestic dispute, but Fran will know how to get hold of him pretty quick. You should stay here on the scene until the chief arrives. He'll want to talk to you. Are you okay?" He studied Jenna's face. "You don't need to lie down or anything like that, do you?"

"No," Jenna croaked out. "I'm fine. I'll sit in my car and stare out the windshield."

"That's good." He took the key from her hand and unlocked the car. "Get in now. That's right." Once she was behind the wheel, he handed the key back to her. "Play the radio. That should help." He shut the door and did a quick-step over to his squad car.

While the deputy was talking rapidly into his radio handset, Jenna blinked once and then twice before giving her head a good shake. She wasn't cut out for stumbling across dead bodies. But she knew someone who was. Picking up her phone, she punched in a number she'd memorized long ago, breathing a sigh of relief when it was answered on the third ring.

"Hello?"

"Nicki, it's Jenna. I think we're going to have to have another informal gathering of our little club."

"Which little club, Jenna? And what are you talking about before nine in the morning?" Jenna heard the yawn come through her earpiece. She couldn't fault her best friend for that. She'd have done exactly the same thing if she hadn't just seen a dead body.

"Wake up, Nicki, and get over to Eddie's Diner right now."

There was a brief pause and then the sound of laughter. "I'm not in the mood for a hamburger for breakfast, and you shouldn't be having one either. Come on over and I'll make you some eggs."

"I'm not home and I'm not finagling for you to make breakfast. Believe me, I'm not hungry. I'm at Eddie's Diner and so are the police, since Eddie's dead and all."

"What?"

"Just get here." Jenna disconnected the phone and ignored it when it began to ring again. She didn't want to waste any time with more explanations that she didn't have. She just wanted Nicki to get here. And soon.

CHAPTER TWO

NICKI HELD HER PHONE OUT AND STARED AT IT IN confusion before narrowing her eyes. She rapidly punched in seven digits then put the device up to her ear and waited.

"Come on, Jenna. Pick up. This isn't funny," she breathed, waiting.

Ten unanswered rings later, Jenna's voice mail kicked in. Nicki didn't bother to leave a message. Disconnecting the call, she turned and faced Maxie and Suzanne. The two women had stopped by to help plan the gourmet cooking classes both of them had talked Nicki into giving.

Maxie, the older of the two and Nicki's landlady, was staring at her with concern in her eyes.

Nicki considered herself very lucky to be one of the few select tenants in Maxie's "artists' colony" that she had built on the far end of her large property. The well-known genealogist rented out the townhouses, which were built in pairs, for a reduced rent to anyone she deemed "a fellow writer or artist". Since Nicki wrote freelance articles on the food and wine events in the valley, plus a series of novels featuring

Tyrone Blackstone, superspy, Maxie had been happy to welcome her into her little community.

Nicki was not only grateful to have such a fabulous place to live for much less than the going rent in the area, but that Maxie had generously offered the townhouse that shared a wall with Nicki's to her friend Jenna. And her silver-haired eccentric landlady had been thrilled to get free help with her genealogy website.

"Is Jenna all right?" Maxie's stare was fixed on the phone in Nicki's hand.

"Did she just say someone was dead?" Suzanne's jaw had dropped down to her chest and her question ended on a squeak. Like Nicki, Suzanne was a member of Maxie's club called The Ladies in Writing Society, and always went along with whatever it was that Maxie dreamed up for the club members to do. Which included gourmet cooking classes.

"I mean, she was talking pretty loud, so I could kind of hear her. But I don't think I got it right." Suzanne's voice went even higher. "Did I?"

Nicki's hazel-eyed gaze returned to her phone. "I'm not sure what Jenna was saying."

She looked over at Maxie. Her unflappable landlady, with her perfectly coiffed hair, was dressed in one of her signature flowing caftans in a variety of soft greens, and cream-colored capri pants paired with matching sandals. She was sitting next to Suzanne, on a tall stool at the kitchen counter. A complete silence fell over Nicki's newly renovated kitchen, which made the next high-pitched squeal out of Suzanne that much more jarring.

"I can't deal with another dead person," the blonde middle-aged woman declared. "Not after what happened to Catherine. That was only six months ago. I can't go through that again."

Catherine had been Suzanne's best friend. Nicki had had

the bad luck to find her face down in a plate of pasta at her own dining room table. Like Suzanne, Nicki was having a hard time adjusting to Jenna declaring that another body had turned up.

She cleared her throat and nodded. "That's what Jenna said." Nicki winced at the even more shrill screech from Suzanne.

Maxie slapped her palms on the counter's quartz top. "Oh do stop that silly noise, Suzanne. Now isn't the time for theatrics." She folded her hands on the smooth surface in front of her. "Exactly what did our Jenna say, dear?"

Nicki let out a long slow breath. "She said we needed to get our little club together, that the police were at Eddie's Diner, and that Eddie is dead."

"Eddie?" Maxie's eyebrows winged upward. "Eddie Parker? Why is Jenna at the diner?" Maxie glanced at the oversized clock hanging on the wall. "Even for Jenna this is a bit early for a hamburger, isn't it?"

"I have no idea, but I'm sure going to find out." Nicki quickly untied her apron. Throwing it on the counter, she looked around for her purse.

Suzanne's head snapped back and forth between the two women. "Your little club? Is that you and your friends who work on the murder board in your office whenever someone's been killed?" At Nicki's frown, Suzanne's shoulders hunched forward. "Maxie told me about it."

"Because you asked what it was, dear, after you poked your head into Nicki's office." Maxie reached over and patted Suzanne's hand. "You've met Jenna. She has a bit of a dry wit. I'm sure she didn't mean anything about a club."

Nicki rolled her eyes when Suzanne looked disappointed. What happened to being upset over her best friend turning up dead? Deciding she must have left her purse and car keys on the hallway table, Nicki stepped around the large kitchen island and headed for the front door. Both Maxie and Suzanne trailed after her.

"So you don't think Eddie was murdered?"

Nicki ignored the bottle blond, leaving it to Maxie to deal with Suzanne. She frowned at the empty hallway table and made a detour into her home office.

"Eddie spent his life eating hamburgers, dear. While he does make the best ones in town, they aren't very good for your arteries. He likely had a heart attack, or stroke, or something else along those lines," Maxie said.

Spotting her purse lying on her desk, Nicki sprinted over to it then turned and headed back toward the front door. Maxie and Suzanne could debate what caused Eddie Parker's demise as much as they liked. Her biggest concern was getting to Jenna and making sure her good friend was all right.

She and Jenna had moved out to California together, leaving Nicki's hometown of New York City behind. There were too many memories of her mother there. The good ones of the wonderful times they'd had together, were overlaid by the final one of finding her only parent dead on her doorstep. She'd been robbed of her valuables and left in a crumpled heap for her daughter to find.

Jenna and Nicki, along with doctor Alex, were more family than simply friends, and when Alex had taken a residency at a hospital in the wine country of Northern California, her two "besties" had been happy to follow along. Now Alex was living in Santa Rosa with her fireman fiancé, Tyler, while Jenna and Nicki had adjoining townhouses in Maxie's "artists' colony". Their rent was a bargain, thanks to the fact that Maxie Edwards was their landlady.

Nicki stepped out the townhouse door, waving a hand over her head.

"One of you please lock up when you leave."

"That will be you, Suzanne," Maxie said, following close on her tenant's heels. "I'm going with Nicki."

Suzanne stood on the doorstep, sputtering. "But what about planning for the new cooking class? It's in three weeks, and the flyers have already been distributed all over town."

Nicki turned and walked backwards as she continued toward her car. "You pick out the first menu. My cookbooks are in the cupboard next to the refrigerator."

"I'm driving. My car is faster and more reliable than yours," Maxie declared, heading for the sky-blue Mercedes. It was parked right behind Nicki's sad little Toyota that had definitely seen better days. "And I doubt anyone would give me a ticket for speeding, dear. It's almost expected of me."

Not wanting to waste any time arguing with her landlady, Nicki switched directions. "Who's left to give you one? I'll bet the entire Soldoff Police Department is at Eddie's Diner."

Nicki quickly got into the car and snapped on her seat belt. It had barely made a "click" before Maxie pulled away from the curb and took off down the long curving drive, heading for the main road and the ten-minute trip into town.

When they pulled into the parking lot, Nicki spotted Jenna leaning against the hood of her little car. The minute Maxie stopped the Mercedes next to it, Nicki had the door open and was out in a flash, rushing toward her friend. The two women met in a hug, with Jenna bending over to completely engulf Nicki's petite five-foot two frame.

Once she was sure her friend was fine and in one piece, Nicki stepped back and held her at arm's length. "Why are you here at this hour of the morning? And what happened?"

Jenna drew in a deep breath, smiling as Maxie came up and gave her a quick kiss on the cheek. "I'm here because I had a meeting scheduled with Eddie."

"You never have meetings in the morning." Nicki frowned. "But it doesn't matter. What happened?"

"Well, I pulled into the parking lot, which was empty. And then I found that the front door to the diner was unlocked." Jenna related everything that had happened since she'd arrived. When she was finished, she pointed toward the diner. "So Danny's inside securing the crime scene. At least I assume that's what he's doing in there. And I'm out here, not sitting in my car the way he ordered me to. I don't take orders from kids. Not even deputized kids." Jenna crossed her arms and nodded, making another long strand of kinky brown hair slide out of the rubber band on top of her head.

"He may not look it, dear, but Danny's twenty-six," Maxie said. The strained note in her voice had Nicki glancing over at her.

"Is something bothering you?"

"Aside from the dead guy?" Jenna added, her tone dry as she went back to leaning against the hood of her car.

The older woman bit her lower lip as she cast a glance at the diner. "Are you sure Eddie was murdered?"

Nicki put an arm around Maxie's shoulders. "As Dr. Alex would say, that's for the coroner to decide. But if he was bleeding from the back of his head and left in a freezer the way Jenna said, he probably was."

"Maybe he slipped on some ice and fell and hit his head."

Jenna and Nicki exchanged a look before Nicki gave Maxie's shoulders a gentle squeeze. "That's possible too."

"My Mason is not going to be happy about this at all," Maxie said, referring to her husband who was the former police chief of Soldoff, and now spent his retirement looking after the gardening in the square that was the centerpiece of the town.

"Why would Eddie's death upset myMason?" Nicki asked. Since her landlady always referred to her husband as "my Mason", the entire town had adopted that as his nickname, rolling it together to make one word.

Maxie leaned in closer to Nicki and lowered her voice to a whisper. "My Mason loaned money to Eddie several years ago to help keep this place afloat during the recession. The tourist industry fell off, and people weren't eating out as much, not even fast food. Eddie was struggling to keep his doors open."

"Oh." Nicki blinked several times, wondering if Maxie was worried about losing the money, or her husband coming under suspicion for the diner owner's murder because of something having to do with the loan. And if Jenna's description of what she'd seen was accurate, the coroner would definitely be recording Eddie's death as a homicide.

Her thoughts were interrupted when a second police cruiser pulled into the parking lot. From the large build and thinning hair sprinkled with gray, Nicki knew that Chief Turnlow had arrived.

She dropped her arms to her side since she was positive he wouldn't appreciate a friendly wave under the circumstances. And especially not from the person he considered the town's biggest snoop, although he usually accompanied that assessment with a fatherly shake of his head. Even so, Nicki had a feeling he was going to be less than thrilled to see her standing there, just several hundred feet from his crime scene.

"I guess Fran was successful in getting hold of the chief." Jenna shrugged at Nicki's questioning look. "Danny said he was out on a domestic dispute."

"Probably the Tipple house again," Maxie said. "My Mason must have made a trip there at least a dozen times in the last year he was chief. Their fights usually started over their dog."

Nicki sighed. "Well that isn't going to put him in the best of moods." Accepting the inevitable lecture, she pasted a smile on her face and nodded as the head of the two-man, one-woman police department in Soldoff got out of the car and looked over at their little group.

He started across the parking lot and was already frowning before he reached them.

"Maxie, how are you?"

"I was fine, Chief, until I heard this sorry news." Maxie pointed a finger, with its nail polished in a pink coral, toward the diner. "This is very upsetting."

Chief Turnlow nodded his agreement as he shifted his gaze to Nicki. "Why am I not surprised to see you here, Ms. Connors?".

"Because you knew one of my best friends found the body?" Nicki's voice was pleasantly sweet as she lifted one eyebrow.

The chief snorted and shook his head again as he turned to Jenna. "Is that right, Jenna?"

"Sort of." The tall brunette pushed her eyeglasses higher on her nose and squinted at the chief through the lenses. "I thought it was just a break-in when I called Fran. It was your deputy who followed the blood trail to the freezer."

Turnlow's mouth thinned out into a straight line. "Blood trail?" He looked over at Nicki. "You don't look surprised, so I'm assuming you've already heard all about it?" He blew out a deep breath when Nicki nodded. "Well, everyone might as well come in and wait your turn to be interviewed." He smiled at Nicki. "And against my better judgment, I'm going to put your observation skills to use. We'll see how accurate your friend's account was."

He inclined his head toward the diner and strode off in that direction. Nicki linked one arm through Jenna's and the other through Maxie's as they walked along after the chief.

"I hope this won't take too much longer," Jenna said. "I can't say I'm fond of spending time close to a dead person."

She gave Nicki a sideways glance. "Now I know how you felt when you found Catherine."

"And that winemaker," Maxie added, grabbing Nicki's arm a little tighter when her sandal slid across the loose gravel.

Not to mention my mom, Nicki thought, but she only gave a small shrug. "Someone would have found them eventually. I'm just the one who happened to come along first." She gave Jenna a nudge in the side. "Just like this time when you happened to be the one who came along first. But better you than one of the teenagers Eddie hired."

"I guess so," Jenna reluctantly agreed.

Nicki kept urging her forward. The closer they got to the diner, the slower Jenna's feet were moving. Worried that her friend was affected by the shock of what she'd seen more than she was letting on, Nicki stopped at the painted green door that was propped open.

"You know, we could just go down to the station and wait for the chief there. We don't have to sit around here."

When Jenna turned wide eyes on her, Nicki gave her an encouraging smile.

"Should I call a lawyer?" Jenna asked in a small voice.

"What? Why?"

"Because I was the one at the scene of the crime all by herself. Maybe the chief thinks I killed Eddie." Jenna looked at the ground. "He did owe me money."

"How much money, dear?" Maxie asked calmly.

Jenna shrugged. "About eight-hundred dollars and some change."

"I don't think the chief believes you're a suspect at all," Nicki firmly stated. "And if he does, I'll certainly set him straight on that."

"If Eddie was killed over owing someone money, there might have been a long line waiting to do him in." Maxie sighed. "Including my Mason, and for a great deal more than eight-hundred dollars, dear. I don't think you have a thing to worry about."

"Right." Jenna straightened her shoulders and lifted her chin. "I didn't have anything to do with this, so let's go in and get this over with."

Thinking she'd have a private chat with Chief Turnlow and let him know he needed to reassure Jenna that she wasn't a suspect, Nicki grabbed Jenna's hand and pulled her through the doorway and into the seating area of the diner. Nobody else was visible, although she could hear voices coming from the kitchen.

Nicki walked over to the only table with a chair next to it, instead of on top, and pointed to the empty seat. "Jenna, why don't you sit here, and I'll get another chair down for Maxie."

As she lifted a second chair off the table, Jenna sat in the vacant one and stared at the tabletop. Nicki shot Maxie a worried look. The landlady returned a slight nod before sitting next to Jenna and putting a hand on her shoulder. "As long as we're here, maybe Nicki can figure out how to work those machines and make us all a cup of coffee."

"I'd like that," Jenna said quietly.

With concern for her friend riding high in her mind, Nicki looked over at the back counter. Calling out a "coming right up", she moved toward the drip coffee machine. She opened a few drawers until she found the filters and the coffee. Working quickly and efficiently, she measured out coffee, filled the pot with water and poured it into the machine. As it started heating up to brew, Nicki leaned over the counter. The pass-through window gave her a good view of the kitchen, including the back corner where the freezer was located. Danny was standing by the door talking on his cell phone. Since the chief was nowhere in sight, Nicki assumed he was in the freezer with Eddie Parker's body.

Just then Chief Turnlow stepped into the main kitchen.

He shook his chest and shoulders as his hand rubbed up and down along one of his arms while he listened to whatever Danny was telling him. Nicki held her breath trying to hear what they were saying but couldn't make out the words. When the chief started to walk across the kitchen, Nicki faded back to the coffee pot and poured two cups. Carrying them over to the table where Maxie and Jenna were sitting silently, she set a steaming mug in front of her longtime friend.

"Here you go. It's not perfect, but it's hot."

"I'm sure it's fine, Nicki." Maxie looked past her and smiled. "Hello again, Chief. Jenna's worried that you think she might have killed Eddie. Do you?"

Nicki coughed loudly. Leave it to Maxie to throw a direct question out at the chief.

"I suppose I should," the chief said, ignoring the glare Nicki shot at him. "And just might do that, as soon as I eliminate every other person in the county."

Jenna's eyes went wide behind her lenses. "What?"

The chief smiled at the tall brunette who was sitting with her hands clasped together so tightly her knuckles had turned white.

Nicki's shoulders relaxed, and she winked at Jenna. "See? I told you he didn't think that."

The chief's gaze shifted over to her. "Your friend here would be more likely to turn off someone's website, or hack into their personal email, than whack someone over the head." He studied Nicki for a moment. "And you'd probably make them into a villain and kill them off in a very creative way in one of those spy novels you write. A knock on the head just wouldn't do it."

"Gee. Thanks, Chief. I think."

The former Los Angeles homicide detective turned small-town police chief, looked back at Jenna. "Danny's going to

come out and take your statements then you'll be free to go."
He stared at Jenna for a moment, frowning. "Why don't you
give your car keys to Nicki and she can take it back to your
place after she's wheedled a look at the crime scene. I'm sure
Maxie won't mind driving you home."

"Of course not," Maxie immediately agreed. "I'd welcome
the company. Maybe we could throw together a bite to eat
while we wait for Nicki's report."

Jenna silently nodded and dug her car keys out of her
purse. Without a word, she handed them over to Nicki.

The chief leaned over and patted Jenna's shoulder. "It'll be
all right Jenna. After you give Danny your statement, you just
go home and get some rest." He turned and nodded at a very
worried Nicki.

"Let's go, Sherlock."

CHAPTER THREE

NICKI STOOD JUST INSIDE EDDIE'S OFFICE, HER HANDS ON her hips as she slowly looked around. She and the chief had gingerly navigated the narrow hallway, carefully avoiding the blood smears that were trailing its length all the way to the entrance into the kitchen. Nicki hadn't been able to control her wince at the smeared outline of footprints in the blood in several places.

"Looks like one of those beach sandals," the chief had commented over his shoulder.

"Like Jenna wears. But she said that the hallway was dark when she went to Eddie's office, so she couldn't have known there was blood on the floor," Nicki had countered.

"Which makes sense. This looks like it was disturbed after it was pretty dry, which fits with Jenna's story." The chief's head had been bent down as he'd studied the floor while he walked along.

Now standing beside her and looking through the open office door, Chief Turnlow's gaze swept across the room. "So what do you think, Sherlock?"

Nicki took a step inside. Papers were scattered over the

floor, and every desk drawer was open. So were the doors to all the cabinets on the wall over the desk. It almost looked as if someone had been searching for something. Almost. Nicki frowned.

"Something bothering you?"

She glanced over at the chief. He'd also come further into the room and had the same frown on his face that she did. "Probably the same thing that's bothering you." She pursed her lips. "It's the neatest trash of a room that I've ever seen. Jenna's desk is a bigger disaster than this."

Chief Turnlow crossed his arms and gave the floor a pointed look. "Seems like a mess to me."

For the first time since she'd answered the phone call from Jenna, Nicki laughed. "I doubt that, Chief." She waved a hand at the cupboards. "The doors are open, but even from here I can see that the contents haven't been disturbed." She lowered her finger to the desk. "And I'd bet that's true of the desk drawers as well, since I don't see anything on the floor but papers. Not even the stapler and that hole punch ended up on the floor. They're still on top of the desk." Finally, she pointed at the floor. "And all those papers look like they were carefully dropped, rather than tossed around." She finished by shifting her gaze to the file cabinet against the wall to their left. "And if someone was searching the office, they must have known whatever they were looking for wasn't in the file cabinet. It doesn't look as if it was touched at all."

"The safe wasn't either." At Nicki's puzzled look, Chief Turnlow pointed to a closed door next to the desk. "It's in there. It's old, but still a solid piece of hardware. And there aren't any marks to indicate someone tried to get into it. But I've called in a forensic team from Santa Rosa to dust it for prints."

Nicki's brow furrowed in thought. Why would someone

make it look as if the place had been searched? And not very convincingly at that.

Danny stuck his head around the doorway. "One of the employees just showed up and wants to know what's going on, Chief."

"Who is it?"

"Roberta Horton. She's the waitress and cashier here."

His boss nodded. "And Eddie's girlfriend, according to Fran."

The young deputy grinned. "I'm not much for gossip, but Fran's right. They've been dating ever since I can remember."

"Is that a fact?" Chief Turnlow looked over at Nicki. "Do you know Ms. Horton?"

Nicki shook her head. "Only to say 'hi' whenever I've picked up a burger." She shrugged. "Jenna might know her. She's spent a lot more time at the diner than I have."

"So you were the last one to see my Eddie alive?"

The loud accusation rang down the hallway.

"Oh crap." Danny disappeared as Nicki made a leap for the doorway.

"Don't step in that blood," the chief barked out as Nicki did an awkward, but quick, hop-and-step back toward the main dining area where she'd left Jenna and Maxie.

"Jenna never saw him alive, so just take that finger out of our faces, Roberta Horton." Maxie's tone wasn't as shrill as their accuser's, but every bit as hard.

Nicki raced into the dining room just as Roberta took a step away from the table, her glare fixed on a frozen Jenna. Danny reached Roberta first and planted himself in between her and the table, blocking the snarling woman's view of the two women sitting there.

"Calm down, Roberta. Eddie was already dead when Jenna got here." He stepped to the side, matching Roberta's movement when she craned her neck to see around him, effectively keeping the woman's glare out of Jenna's sight.

Short and stocky, with brown hair pinned up into a messy bun on top of her head, Roberta stood rigid with her fists clenched by her side. "How do you know that? You have no way of knowing when that nerd got here."

"We know that because he was killed in one place and moved to another. Something Ms. Lindstrom wouldn't have been able to do in the short time she was here before she called us." Chief Turnlow pinned his stare on Roberta.

She took a step backward but stuck her lip out. "You don't know how long she was here. Did someone tell you when they saw her pull into the lot? She could have parked her car somewhere else, sneaked over here and killed Eddie, and then driven back looking innocent as you please." She walked around Danny and narrowed her eyes on a silent Jenna. "Is that what happened? I'll bet that's what happened all right."

The chief cocked his head to one side. "If you don't calm down, Ms. Horton, I'll have to have Deputy Findley take you to the station and question you as a person of interest."

"Me?" Roberta screeched. "I wasn't the one to find Eddie dead."

Chief Turnlow shrugged his broad shoulders. "But you were one of the last ones to see him alive, unless you're going to tell me that yesterday was your day off?" He raised an eyebrow.

Roberta scrunched up her slightly pudgy features, narrowing her eyes into small slits. "No, it wasn't my day off, Chief Turnlow. But I left early because I had a date. So I wasn't the last one who saw him alive."

Nicki kept her frigid stare on Roberta as she stepped up and put a protective hand on Jenna's hunched shoulder.

"Maxie," she said, without taking her eyes off of Roberta.

"Why don't you and Jenna go on home. I'll catch up with both of you in a bit."

"Go ahead and bring the car right up to the doorway out front, Mrs. Edwards," the chief added. "I need to ask Ms. Lindstrom for her sandals."

When Roberta's gaze shot to Jenna's feet, Nicki quickly leaned over and whispered into her friend's ear. "Give him your flip-flops and just get out of here. I'll make sure Eddie's girlfriend keeps her opinions to herself."

Without saying a word, Jenna nodded, stood up, and stepped out of her flip-flops. Maxie got to her feet as well and took Jenna's arm before leading her away.

"Come with me, dear. You can wait on the walkway while I get the car. There's no sense in tramping across all that gravel in your bare feet."

Once they'd disappeared through the front door, Nicki pasted a frosty smile on her face and aimed it at Roberta.

"Ms. Horton," she began, borrowing from the chief's habit of using a formal address to get someone's full attention. Once Roberta had turned a hard brown-eyed gaze on her, Nicki continued. "It's a serious matter to throw around those kinds of accusations without any proof. I'd hate to have to follow after you and correct that false assumption with everyone you happen to talk to." Roberta opened her mouth, but Nicki continued before the belligerent waitress had a chance to say a word. "And Maxie wouldn't enjoy having to do such a thing either, though I have no doubt she would. Of course, she just might recommend an attorney to take care of the matter. I know she has several of them." Everyone in town knew how much weight Maxie's influence carried, and under the circumstances, Nicki had no problem shamelessly using her landlady's name. The kind of vicious gossip Roberta might start could do a lot of damage to Jenna, and to her business.

"Those kinds of rumors tend to get around fast," the chief agreed. "And it wouldn't make me very happy to hear about them. They'd be just as bad as a couple of townspeople seeing a close friend, or maybe a love interest, walked into the police station for questioning." He looked over at Roberta. "Can't stop that kind of thing from spreading like wildfire."

Roberta glared back at him. "Is that a threat, Chief Turnlow? Because it won't work. Me and Eddie broke up a couple of weeks ago."

The chief looked surprised. "Threat?" He glanced over at Danny. "Did you hear a threat, Deputy Findley?"

Danny shook his head. "Nope."

"I didn't either." Nicki smiled at Roberta.

The waitress's gaze slashed across the three of them before she shrugged. "Whatever. Since we aren't going to be open today, I'm going home."

The chief continued to hold her in place with his stare. "Not so fast, Ms. Horton. Who else was at the diner yesterday?"

Roberta glanced over at Nicki, who simply smiled at her, and then back at the chief. "The usual staff. The assistant manager and cook, Jake Garces, and me. But I left early. That high school kid, Tammi, came in the afternoon just as I was leaving. And Eddie was there all day." She paused for a long moment. "Oh yeah. And Gordon came in. At least for a few minutes anyway. Then there were the customers." She shrugged again. "I don't remember them all. I know those two stamp-collecting friends of his weren't here, so that was kind of weird. They usually come in every day." She frowned. "Maxie's husband was here yesterday, too."

"Chief Edwards?" Nicki blinked at that news. Maxie hadn't mentioned that myMason had been at the diner yesterday.

"Well he's not a chief anymore, is he?" Roberta's lips pulled back in a sneer.

"Do you remember what time *Chief* Edwards was here?" the current head of the police department calmly asked.

"Sometime in the morning." Roberta let out a loud snort. "He didn't even order anything. Just went back to the office with Eddie. He probably came to see if he could get a payment on that loan. Eddie was a nice enough guy, but he was tight with his money. Didn't like to spend a nickel unless he had to."

So the loan was common knowledge among the staff. Nicki pursed her lips and turned her back on Roberta. The nasty tone in the waitress's voice was setting her nerves on edge, and Nicki didn't want to give the woman the satisfaction of seeing how it was affecting her.

When the sound of the front door opening and closing echoed through the dining room, Nicki glanced over her shoulder and smiled.

"Oh great. Now the third one's here. That figures." Roberta heaved a big sigh and shot the chief a hard stare. "If you don't need me anymore, I want to go home." She pulled her mouth down at the corners. "This has been very upsetting for me."

"I can tell," Nicki muttered, then rolled her eyes when the chief sent her a warning look.

"That's fine. We'll be in touch." He nodded at Danny. "Deputy, why don't you walk Ms. Horton out to her car."

Roberta slid past the dark-haired woman who'd appeared near the doorway, a medical bag in her hand. As Danny followed the woman out, he smiled at the new arrival and tipped his head in greeting.

"Hi, Alex. I mean Dr. Kolman."

Alex's deep brown gaze followed the short woman and her

escort out the door before switching back to Nicki. "What was that about?"

Nicki grinned. "I don't think she likes you, Jenna, or me very much. What are you doing here? Did Maxie call you?"

Alex shook her head. Her sleek, dark-brown hair, cut short on one side and into a stylish and easy to maintain wedge on the other, gleamed in the sunshine coming in through the front windows. "No. The deputy called. Or rather he called the coroner's office." She did a quick look around. "Who's dead, and why are you here?"

"Eddie Parker's dead, and I'm here because Jenna found his body."

"What?" Alex's startled expression probably looked exactly the way Nicki's had when she had picked-up Jenna's call.

Chief Turnlow loudly cleared his throat. "If the two of you are through?" He shook his head when both women turned to stare at him. "Why are you here instead of Dr. Tom? Have you given up practicing emergency medicine at the hospital?"

Dr. Tom was the local nickname for the county coroner. He'd grown up in the valley and returned to take the coroner's position in his hometown after he'd finished medical school.

"Because he was in the middle of an autopsy and asked me to come. This part of forensic doctoring isn't hard. I just need to do a quick check of the body, take a few notes and a body temperature, and arrange to have it transported." She leaned toward Nicki and said in a loud stage whisper. "I'm still repaying Dr. Tom for that favor during the winemaker's case."

"I'm going to pretend I didn't hear that," the chief said.

Nicki's mouth formed into an "O" as Danny came back through the door.

"Want me to start calling the other staff members so they can come in for an interview, Chief?"

"That's a good idea." Chief Turnlow nodded at Alex. "I'm going to take Dr. Kolman to have a look at the body."

Nicki waited silently, finally smiling when Alex and Chief Turnlow headed for the kitchen. Since the chief didn't say she couldn't come along, Nicki fell into step behind Alex. She heard her friend mutter, "really?" and sigh when it became obvious that the chief was headed for the freezer in the back of the kitchen.

They all stopped just outside the door and Alex peeked inside. "Well, at least he's not in the rear of this icebox. I didn't bring my coat."

"Whoever dragged him in there didn't bother to go any further than he had to." Chief Turnlow shrugged out of his leather jacket. He handed it to Alex. "Here. This should work for a while, at least."

Alex took it but sent him a worried glance. "If you intend to come in with me, what are you going to wear?"

The big bear of a man smiled at the much more petite Alex. "I'll be okay. Just make it quick, Doc." He shook his head when Nicki took a step forward. "Not you, Sherlock. You stay out here. I don't need the doc distracted by having to treat you for frostbite. And don't worry. I'm sure your friend will talk her way through this loudly enough for you to hear."

"If you insist, Chief," Alex said with a perfectly straight face as she zipped up the very large borrowed jacket and stepped into the freezer.

The cold air slapped at Nicki, so she used the heavy door as a shield and peered around its edge, watching as the chief and her friend squatted on opposite sides of the body. Nicki did a quick scan of the interior. It wasn't a huge space. About nine feet by twelve feet, if she had to hazard a guess, and both sides were lined with shelves. Boxes of food, labeled with their contents, filled most of them. A gold jacket sporting red trim on the cuffs and neckline, was laid neatly on top of a box on the middle shelf closest to where Eddie lay. But aside from that, Nicki didn't see anything else unusual in the freezer. Well besides a dead body, of course.

"Okay," Alex began. "I don't see any marks or contusions other than the bump on the victim's head."

"Do you think that's what killed him?" Chief Turnlow asked.

Alex snorted. "I have no idea. Dr. Tom will have to determine that. But it was either the blow on the head, freezing, or from asphyxiation."

"Smothered?" Nicki called out. "You see something that makes you think he was smothered?"

"No," Alex said, raising her voice even louder. "From lack of oxygen due to the dry ice in here. Between that letting off carbon dioxide, and just his own breathing, the victim may have run out of air."

Nicki grimaced. Not a pleasant way to die. But then neither was freezing to death.

She stretched her neck out further. "Does it look like he tried to get out?"

"If you two are finished?" the chief cut in. "Keep quiet, Nicki, or I'll have Danny escort you out as well."

For several minutes there was nothing but the sound of Alex tapping away on her iPad. Nicki wondered how long the device would work in the cold as she listened for any more information Alex might throw out her way.

"All right," the doctor finally said. "I've got everything entered. The ambulance guys should be here any minute to take him back to the morgue."

The chief made a humming sound of agreement. "That's

fine. But let's go through his pockets first. There're evidence bags in my jacket pocket."

Nicki watched as Alex set her iPad aside and pulled out a handful of bags from the large side pocket in the leather jacket. "You mean these?" At the chief's nod, the doctor held one of the bags open. "I'll hold these, and you can go through his pockets."

The chief didn't answer. Since he'd already pulled on a pair of protective gloves, he reached across the body and into the pants pocket on the far side.

"Nothing there." He repeated the process on the pocket nearest to him. There was a jingling noise as he pulled out a small set of keys and dropped them into the bag Alex was holding.

She leaned in to take a closer look. "Okay. We have two keys on a round ring, and they're both labeled. One says, 'front door' and the other says, 'office door'."

"Thank you, Doctor." The chief's bone-dry tone said he knew exactly what Alex was up to.

He pulled out a few coins which he dropped into a second bag. "Two pennies, one dime and three quarters, in case you can't see this far, Ms. Connors."

Nicki wrinkled her nose. "Thank you, Chief."

"And here's a receipt from Starbucks, dated yesterday and stamped at twelve minutes past ten in the morning."

The Starbucks was located on the town square about a mile away.

Chief Turnlow carefully turned the body over to one side and patted down the rear pockets of the pants before he leaned back on his heels, holding a battered wallet in his hand. "Not much here," he said. "One five-dollar bill and two ones, a couple of credit cards, his license and some business cards." The chief took out several and thumbed through them. "Looks like vendors. One's for a meat delivery service, the other is for a bakery, and here's one for Green 'N Go." He looked over at Nicki. "Do you know what that is?"

"A pretty new chain of takeout food, kind of like Eddie's, except they only have salads," Nicki said. "Is there a cell phone?"

"Not on the victim."

Then no cell phone or apartment key. Nicki bit her lower lip. She hadn't seen them on top of the desk either and wondered if maybe Eddie had left them in one of the desk drawers and that's what the killer had been looking for.

The chief stood and held out a hand to help the doctor get to her feet as well. He shooed her out of the freezer. "That's about all the cold I can take for the moment." After the two of them had walked out, he herded both Alex and Nicki in front of him until they were all the way out of the diner and standing on the walkway in front of it.

He looked at Nicki as he put on the jacket that Alex had handed back to him. "The Doc and I will get the body ready for transport. You've seen and heard enough to answer any questions Jenna might have. Why don't you go on home now and take care of that?"

Realizing that was all she was going to get from the chief, Nicki reluctantly nodded her agreement. She turned and gave Alex a hug. "Give me a call later? Jenna's pretty shaken up."

"I'd have to agree with that," the chief said. "So she doesn't need any more shocks that come with a murder investigation." He gave Nicki a hard stare. "What that means, Ms. Connors, is that you need to stay away from this one."

CHAPTER FOUR

NICKI STOPPED JENNA'S LITTLE HONDA NEXT TO THE CURB bordering her friend's townhouse, and right in front of Maxie's Mercedes and Suzanne's red Buick. Since her own townhouse was right next door, Nicki didn't have far to walk as she did a quick-step to her front stoop. She was guessing that both her landlady and Jenna were inside with Suzanne, and hopefully relaxing over a warm cup of coffee. Still worried about how quiet Jenna had been when she'd left the diner, Nicki quietly opened the front door and stepped into the tiny foyer. She'd barely closed the door behind her when Suzanne came rushing down the hallway. She skidded to a stop, blocking Nicki's path to the kitchen.

"We have a problem," Suzanne said in a low whisper. She cast a quick glance back over her shoulder before returning her gaze to Nicki. "Maxie got a call from Chief Turnlow. He wants her to come to the station at what he called 'her earliest convenience'."

Nicki frowned. "Why? Did he tell her why he wanted her to come to the station?"

Suzanne shook her head. "No. And that upset her even more. And he said you were on your way home, and Maxie should wait and bring you along."

"He did?" Nicki bit her lip as she absorbed that news. Wondering what the chief was up to, she waited for Suzanne to move so she could get to the kitchen. She needed to check on Jenna and then collect Maxie for the ride back into town.

But Suzanne didn't budge. "So I called Fran back."

"You did?" Nicki sighed. She was sounding like a parrot.

The middle-aged woman bobbed her head up and down. "I did. And she said it had to do with myMason, but she wasn't sure why. And then Fran said that she was glad you'd be coming along, because she had something to tell you."

"Okay." Nicki pointed toward the kitchen. "I just need to check on Jenna and then we'll be on our way."

"That's our other problem. I'm worried about Jenna. I think you should call your doctor friend."

Suzanne's voice was so matter-of-fact that Nicki stared at her for a moment. "Alex?"

"Jenna hasn't said a word since she got here with Maxie," Suzanne went on in the same practical tone. "She needs to talk to someone. A professional someone. I volunteer at the battered women's shelter in Santa Rosa, and I've often seen this sort of emotional shut-down."

Nicki immediately nodded. She'd had her own experience with an emotional shock and the trauma that followed it. And if Jenna was going through that, Nicki was absolutely going to call Alex.

"This morning was hard on everyone, especially Jenna. Calling Alex is an excellent idea. But I need to talk to Jenna first." She sighed. "We have a pact to not go behind each other's backs and do something."

"Good friends make promises like that." A sadness crept into Suzanne's eyes.

Guessing she was thinking about her best friend, Catherine, whose murder had left a huge hole in Suzanne's life, Nicki gave her a sympathetic look. She couldn't imagine losing either of her best friends. But right now, she'd better get into the kitchen and see what was going on with one of them. Nicki sidled past Suzanne and continued along the hallway, not stopping until she was standing next to the tall stool where Jenna was perched.

The computer geek was hunched over, continually stirring a cup of coffee. She didn't even look around when Nicki walked up and leaned on the counter next to her.

"Jenna? What's going on?"

Her friend looked at her with a guarded expression. "Nothing. We're just waiting for you." She glanced over at Maxie. "Our landlady has to go downtown and pay the chief another visit."

Nicki shot Suzanne a telling look, and was surprised when her fellow society member got the message and briskly nodded. She wrapped a hand around Maxie's arm.

"C'mon, Maxie. Let's get your purse and sweater together while Nicki grabs a quick to-go cup of coffee."

Maxie looked between Nicki and Jenna before smiling. "Of course. Then we'll be all set to be on our way."

Suzanne winked at Nicki as she raised her voice. "You and Nicki will. I'm going to stay here to finish planning the first cooking class, and hope Jenna will be able to keep me company."

As the two made their exit, Nicki walked around the kitchen counter and headed for the cupboard where she kept a supply of to-go cups. "What's going on, Jenna?" Nicki repeated, frowning when her friend lifted her shoulders into a shrug. "You need to talk to me. I know this is a shock, but you weren't this quiet when mom was killed. So something is going on."

"I wasn't a suspect when your mom was killed." Jenna gave her coffee another hard stir.

"You aren't a suspect in Eddie Parker's murder either," Nicki pointed out, then hung onto her patience when her friend shrugged again.

Jenna looked over at the kitchen door that led into the hallway before lowering her voice to a whisper. "Then why did the chief want to see Maxie and not me? I think he wants to question her about anything I said when the two of us were sitting alone in the front of the diner."

"Oh." Nicki dropped her voice into the same whisper. "I think he wants to talk to her about her husband."

"What?" Jenna forgot she meant to whisper and gaped at Nicki. "That's completely random, Connors. Where do you come up with that stuff?"

Nicki grinned. "I didn't. Suzanne did. She called Fran to find out what the chief wanted. Fran didn't know exactly, but she said it had something to do with myMason."

"Why doesn't he just call myMason himself?" Jenna frowned.

"I don't know. Fran also said that she wants to talk to me."

Jenna's frown deepened. "Why does Fran want to talk to you?"

"I don't know." Nicki laughed and held up her hands when Jenna sent her an exasperated look.

"Well, I wish we knew something," Jenna declared. "This 'in-limbo' thing isn't working for me at all." She sighed and went back to stirring her coffee. "I can't get my mind off it. The diner, finding Eddie, thinking that I should have insisted we meet last night instead of this morning."

"Whoa! Wait just a minute." Nicki leaned across the counter and jabbed one finger into the white quartz top. "None of this is your fault, Jenna Lindstrom."

"I know. At least I keep telling myself that." She looked

over at Nicki with troubled eyes. "I wish there was something I could do. I'd feel better if there was something I could do."

Nicki straightened up and studied her friend for a long moment. She'd felt exactly the same way once. Maybe she had jumped into the winemaker's murder to help soothe an ache inside herself over feeling so helpless about her mom's murder. And then into Catherine Dunton's because Maxie was hurting, much in the same way Jenna was now. And there was no question that what she'd been willing to do for her landlady, she was certainly willing to do for Jenna. And so would Alex and her fiancé, Tyler. They could also count on Maxie, and Matt, the solid and very practical editor of the magazine she did her freelance articles for, and who was also friends with Jenna.

Nicki shook her head at herself. It seemed their little impromptu club was going to be meeting again after all.

"What was that head-shake thing for?" Jenna asked. "I really do wish I had done something for Eddie."

"Well, you couldn't have done anything to stop what happened to him," Nicki said decisively. She did not want Jenna to have any doubts about that. "But you can do something for him now."

"Such as?"

Nicki filled her to-go cup and grabbed her purse while Jenna's gaze followed her movements. "While Maxie and I are gone, you can set up the murder board."

"What?"

Nicki adjusted the long strap of her purse on her shoulder. "Get Suzanne to help you. It will keep her out of my kitchen, and she has excellent handwriting."

Jenna drew in a long audible breath. "I won't say that wouldn't help, because it would. But I can't ask you to get involved in another murder, Nicki."

"I'm going to whether you ask or not."

Her friend rubbed her hands together. "But what will Matt say? Forget that. What will the chief say?"

"You're the one who keeps calling us a club, and when Matt jumped in on Catherine's murder, he became a member. So he isn't going to object at all. He's going to help."

Nicki mentally crossed her fingers on that one. She was sure that Matt would have plenty to say, but that wasn't going to change a thing. They were going to help solve this murder to get that haunted look off of Jenna's face, and that was that.

Jenna crossed her arms and stared at Nicki. "And what about the chief?"

"He'd be disappointed if I didn't stick my nose into his investigation. I don't want to be responsible for disappointing the local police chief. Call Alex and see if she can come up this weekend. And bring her future husband if he isn't on duty at the firehouse. We may as well overwhelm the chief by the sheer number of us."

When Jenna burst out into laughter, Nicki knew butting into police business was the right thing to do. She smiled as she headed out the kitchen door.

FIFTEEN MINUTES LATER, she pulled her robin's-egg-blue, always-on-its-last-legs Toyota into one of the parking spaces next to the three reserved spots in front of the police station. No one in town parked in one of the bright orange reserved spots. Not unless they wanted their neighbors to think they were in hot water with the local law enforcement.

The station sat on one corner of the town square, with its neatly manicured lawn and gardens, thanks to Maxie's husband. At its center was a ten-foot-tall bronze statue of a bunch of grapes, because no one wanted a statue erected to the disgraced founding father.

On a trip back East almost one-hundred years ago, Grady Mucher had sold fake deeds to many of the already owned and occupied lots in the town named after him. While the founder had made off with his spoils, his former neighbors had had to deal with the parade of deed holders who'd shown up to claim their land. It hadn't taken long for the little town of Mucherville to become known as that "place that got sold off", and over the years, the name had stuck.

With the rising popularity of the wine industry, the whole area had prospered. While Soldoff hadn't grown as much as its more well-known neighbor, Sonoma, it had come to enjoy its own small place in the wine, arts and food festival world.

The town square was surrounded by eclectic and wildly different building styles, ranging from Southern colonial to a cement block, with a liberal sprinkling of the tiled and stucco Spanish adobes in between. Its overall look was so astonishing, that the square brought in a fair number of tourists each weekend who came to gape at it, and of course to spend time in the many tasting rooms tucked in all around the square.

Nicki had grown to love Soldoff and its quirkiness, as well as the beauty of the wine country in general. But right now, all that was lost on her as she led a worried-looking Maxie up the short walkway to the very compact police station. When she opened the door, Fran jumped out of her seat and rushed to the front counter, raising a finger to her lips.

The older woman turned a wrinkled cheek toward Nicki as she glanced at the opening to the back hallway.

"Shh. I need to talk to you before the chief finds out that you're here."

The low rasp in Fran's voice was more pronounced than usual, and Nicki knew why when Fran turned her gaze back to the women standing on the other side of the counter. The police clerk was definitely angry. Her faded blue eyes snapped behind the lenses of her wire-rimmed glasses.

"What?" Nicki mouthed, concerned about the older woman's heightened color.

"That Roberta Horton was in here not half an hour ago, waiting for the chief to come back from Eddie's diner. I couldn't believe the trash that woman was spouting." Fran's eyes narrowed even more. "She kept saying that Jenna was the one who found Eddie, and everyone knows what that means."

Maxie leaned forward. "Really?" She glanced over at Nicki. "Didn't you just tell me that you'd warned Roberta about indulging in that kind of gossip?"

Nicki nodded, her own temper spiking up to match Fran's.

"Apparently she didn't comprehend what you were saying, dear," Maxie said. "I might have to pay her a visit to explain it a bit more."

"You want to take my rifle?" Fran asked. "It makes a pretty good statement."

"No, she doesn't want to take your rifle," Nicki whispered. The last thing she needed in her life right now was to chase after a gun-waving Maxie. If her landlady didn't accidentally shoot someone, myMason just might shoot Fran for letting his wife have a gun in the first place.

The genealogist smiled and shook her head. "She's joking, dear. I doubt if Fran even has a rifle."

"Well, I could get one," Fran stated. "But I don't think you need to worry about her, Maxie. The chief made it clear that he'd lock her up for slander if he heard one peep about Jenna being a suspect. Because she isn't one." Fran rubbed her chin. "I need to write myself a reminder to tell that chairman of the city council to pass an ordinance to allow someone to be arrested for slander." She smiled at Nicki. "Wouldn't want the chief to get into trouble."

"Of course not," Nicki agreed. "Thanks for letting me know. I'll keep an eye, and an ear, out for Roberta."

Fran shook her head, her frizzy gray hair bouncing with the movement. "That's just part of it. The chief told her that she needed to meet him at Eddie's apartment at three this afternoon. She squawked some about being busy, but he told her she had no choice. The chief thinks she might be able to tell him if anything is missing or out of place."

"So he's going to meet Roberta at Eddie's apartment at three?" Nicki repeated slowly, thinking it over. "Has he been inside yet?"

"Nope. No key," Fran said. "There wasn't one on Eddie or in the diner that the chief could find. And the landlord lives in San Francisco. He can't get out here until two thirty, so the chief is going to meet him at the apartment then."

"Two thirty." Maxie nodded. "We've got it."

"If you're through whispering over there, I'd like to talk to Mrs. Edwards."

Three heads snapped up to look over at the chief, and Nicki hoped the other two didn't have as guilty an expression on their faces as she was sure she did. She felt the heat spreading in a rapid wave over her cheeks.

"I was just going to announce them, Chief," Fran said.

"I can see that." Chief Turnlow raised an eyebrow at his clerk. "Why don't you skip the announcing and send them back, Fran."

"I guess you can go right in, ladies." Smiling at the chief's loud snort, Fran winked at Nicki. "Good hunting."

Nicki returned her smile. "Is that another gun reference, Fran?"

The clerk's laughter followed them through the small gate at the end of the counter and down the short hallway. Nicki pulled Maxie into the closet-sized room that served as the police chief's office. There was barely enough space to scoot into the two visitor chairs placed in front of his desk. Once they were settled, the chief leaned back in his chair, ignoring its ominous creak of protest.

"I didn't suppose it would have done me any good to say I'd prefer to talk to Mrs. Edwards alone, so I thought I'd save us all an argument and just have you come in with her.

Maxie sat up straight, her back stiff and her mouth set in a line. "And I'm glad she's here for support if you're going to insist on calling me 'Mrs. Edwards' in that official tone of voice of yours. I know what that means. I'm married to the former chief, if you'll recall."

Chief Turnlow sighed and leaned forward, resting his forearms on his desk. "I'm sorry, Maxie. Force of habit."

"You do that whenever you're interviewing a witness or a suspect, Chief," Nicki pointed out.

Her landlady nodded. "That's right." Maxie directed an icy stare at the big man sitting calmly behind the small desk. "And which one would I be, Chief? A witness or a suspect?"

"Neither." He shrugged. "I've been trying to get hold of Chief Edwards, and he hasn't returned my calls. So I thought I'd ask you where he is?"

"Chief Edwards," Maxie said slowly. "Not Mason, but Chief Edwards? What do you consider my husband? A witness or a suspect?"

Nicki reached over and laid a gentle hand on Maxie's arm. "I'm sure he isn't either one, Maxie. But it seems to be common knowledge that Eddie owed your husband money." When Maxie stared at her, Nicki gave the older woman an encouraging smile. "Roberta mentioned it when we were in the diner." She returned her gaze to the chief. "I'm sure it's just something Chief Turnlow needs to verify."

"Nicki's right. I need to consider everything at this point." The chief smiled. "Where is Mason?"

"Fishing. He left early this morning."

The chief pursed his lips but kept his voice low and gentle. "Fishing? A trip he'd been planning for a while?"

"No. But he goes fishing all the time, and very often at the drop of a hat," Maxie insisted. "Or in this case, at the call of Charlie Freeman. That's all it took for him to be off to Charlie's boat."

Charlie Freeman was a local winemaker, mostly known for making the worst wine in the valley. He and Mason had been close friends for over thirty years, long before the quiet, serious Mason had married the outgoing genealogist from the city.

"So he's somewhere out on the ocean?" The chief frowned.

"Unless you know how to catch fish in a vineyard," Maxie returned. "And before you ask, he had a quick dinner with Charlie to plan out the last-minute details for their trip, and then he came right home. He was with me from eight o'clock until he left early this morning."

"Did he come straight home?"

Maxie drew in a deep breath and narrowed her gaze on the chief. "I don't know, but then I didn't ask, either. I don't make a habit of tracking my Mason's every move."

"What's this about, Chief?" Nicki asked. "You don't seriously consider Mason Edwards a suspect in Eddie's murder, do you?"

"Do I? No." The chief shook his head. "But there is information that needs to be explained and eliminated as part of the case."

"What information?" Maxie demanded.

"Now that will have to wait until Mason gets back and I can ask him. And when will that be, Maxie?"

"It's supposed to be a short trip, Chief. I'm expecting my husband back in two days or so." Maxie rose and inclined her

head, waiting with a stony expression as the chief stood as
well. "I'll let him know to stop by."

"Thank you." The chief glanced at Nicki. "And I'm
assuming I'll be seeing you later this afternoon?"

"Count on it," Nicki said before she followed a very
annoyed Maxie out the door.

CHAPTER FIVE

NICKI WALKED UP THE RICKETY IRON STAIRS, determination in the set of her jaw. Not only was Jenna upset, although Nicki had been glad to see that working on the murder board had certainly helped her friend's mood, but now Maxie was too. Her landlady was sure that her husband would be coming home only to be arrested on their doorstep. Nicki had done her best to first reason, and then sympathize, with Maxie's vocal concerns, but in the end, she'd been forced to turn her usually unflappable landlady over to Suzanne.

Nicki's opinion of the woman who'd been determined up until Catherine's murder, to mimic everything Nicki did, right down to her wardrobe, had undergone a drastic change in the last few hours. Suzanne's calm assessment of Jenna's shock, and the way she'd handled Maxie's fears, had been both jaw-dropping and very welcome, since Nicki certainly had her hands full with Jenna and a murder.

She hadn't heard back from Alex yet, had sent two calls from Matt to voice mail, and made an emergency run to Maxie's house for her landlady's special blend of tea. Nicki had badly needed help, and was grateful to Suzanne for stepping in so seamlessly and providing it. She made a mental promise to put more time into Suzanne's project of gourmet cooking classes.

Once the upset and confusion running rampant in her townhouse seemed at least somewhat under control, Nicki had been faced with the daunting task of keeping up with the murder investigation as best she could, without any of her usual help from her friends. The ignored calls from Matt popped into her mind. She really wished he was here now, but couldn't ask him to leave his business and fly out to the West Coast every time she came across a dead body. Which seemed to be often lately.

So she was climbing to the second floor of the worn-out apartment complex all by herself. Eddie Parker's place was just on the edge of town, and two blocks away from the diner. Nicki paused on the upper landing and looked around at the peeling and faded paint of the building he'd called home. It was a large rectangle, two stories tall, surrounded by an unpaved parking lot, and sitting in the middle of an overgrown field. Not seeing any kind of visual appeal to the place, Nicki turned to her left and walked the length of the building. Chief Turnlow was standing across from an open apartment door, leaning against the outside railing.

"Hi, Chief," Nicki said when she got close enough she didn't have to shout to be heard over the traffic whizzing by on the main highway that passed close to town. "I take it the landlord made the drive from San Francisco okay."

The chief straightened to his full height and stuck his hands in his jacket pockets. "He was early. He dropped the key off at the station along with a request that I let him know as soon as possible when it would be available for him to rent out again."

"Lovely," Nicki murmured under her breath before

managing a meager smile. "If you aren't waiting for the land-lord to show up, why are you standing out here?"

Chief Turnlow shrugged his broad shoulders. "Waiting for you. It was a sure bet that you'd be here, and I appreciate you being on time."

Nicki had the grace to blush but stood her ground. Just then her phone rang. She glanced at the screen before sighing and sending it to voice mail. At the chief's questioning glance, she turned her screen around so he could read the caller ID.

The big man made a face. "You aren't talking to your wannabe boyfriend?" He gave her a stern look. "Every time you decide not to talk to him, I get a complaint call."

"He's not my boyfriend, Chief. He's my editor." Nicki had told that to the chief, and to her friends, at least a dozen times, but none of them seemed inclined to believe her. "I have a boyfriend, Rob. Remember him? You met him the night we found Catherine dead in her dining room."

"Oh yeah. Him. The one who left you stranded on the porch." The chief produced a key from his pocket and turned toward the front door of the apartment.

Nicki blew out an exasperated breath. The police chief knew good and well that she'd told Rob to go on home that night, but she wasn't in the mood to argue with the man, especially since he had that "stern father" look on his face. At the moment she was far more curious to see the inside of Eddie's apartment. Chief Turnlow swung the door open and stepped over the threshold, stopping just inside the entrance.

"Great."

Even more curious than before, Nicki came around him, only to be brought up short by his long arm swinging out and blocking her from going any further. Her eyes opened wide as she slowly took in the room. The bookshelves on the far side of the small living area were bare. Their contents had been tossed across the floor, coffee table and sofa. Several pieces of what used to be a vase were shattered, and the entire contents of an ashtray had been dumped on the couch. It looked as if a small bomb had gone off in the room and thrown everything into the air, only to splatter out from wherever it had landed.

"Oh my," Nicki breathed. "Someone was pretty angry."

"Or looking for something," the chief said. "Stay to the edges and try not to step on anything. I want to see if the kitchen and bedroom are in the same shape."

Nicki followed the chief, tiptoeing close to the wall as she gingerly picked her way along toward the kitchen. It too had been ransacked, although not as badly as the living room. The chief gave it a quick look before heading to the bedroom. This was the worst of the three rooms. Dresser drawers had been upended and dumped on the floor, along with the contents of the closet. Large scrap books were scattered across the bed. A few of them had been left open, revealing rows of what looked like stamps, rather than photos.

"Wonder if he found what he was looking for?" The chief frowned as he studied the mess. He crossed his arms over his large chest and did another slow scan around the room.

Nicki did too. If there was anything missing, she had no idea how they would figure out what it was. She stared at the albums scattered across the bed and wondered if all of them were filled with stamps.

"Notice anything unusual about this place?" the chief asked, his eyes still moving over the room.

She tore her gaze away from the albums and glanced over at the far wall. "Besides the fact it's barely big enough for a bed and a nightstand? And that closet is so small it almost doesn't qualify as one?" At the chief's frown, she shrugged. "It's not nearly as neat as the trash job on his office at the diner."

"My thought, too." Chief Turnlow lowered his brow and

stuck his hands back into his jacket pockets. "Could mean he searched this place last and got frustrated when he still didn't find what he was looking for."

She nodded her agreement. "That certainly makes sense." Nicki looked around again. "Or maybe he knew whatever it was, wasn't in the diner, and that was just for show to throw us off."

"Us?"

Nicki cast a sideways glance at the chief. At least he wasn't frowning.

"This whole thing is wonky."

She smiled. "Wonky?"

The chief nodded, his eyes narrowed as he did another slow sweep of the room. "Why Eddie? And why the trash job?" At Nicki's puzzled frown, the chief shrugged. "The cash registers weren't opened and the safe didn't look as if it had been touched, and we found his wallet in his back pocket with cash still in it. So it wasn't a robbery. But it sure looks like the perp was searching for something." He shook his head. "Or maybe, like you said, the trash job was just a smoke screen."

"But a smoke screen for what?" Nicki voiced out loud, sure the chief was asking himself exactly the same question. "If it wasn't robbery, what does that mean?"

"I don't know." The chief ran a hand across the top of his head. "Could be any number of things. Eddie might have interrupted something, or the perp simply picked the wrong place. Could have been a personal argument gone bad."

"Did Eddie happen to have a cell phone?" Nicki asked. She glanced over at the top of the three-drawer dresser standing in the corner with all of its drawers hanging open.

"Haven't found one."

"Even Eddie wasn't quite this big a pig."

Nicki and the chief turned in tandem toward the

bedroom door at their backs. Roberta Horton stood there, her hands on her hips and what seemed like a perpetual sneer on her face.

"First time I've had a vacation day in years, and I get to spend it wading through a mess." She pursed her lips, the frizzy hair sprouting out from a ponytail dancing around as she shook her head. "How am I supposed to know if anything is missing when it's all on the floor? This is a total waste of my time." She turned around and started to walk away.

"Hang on, Ms. Horton."

The chief's quiet command had Roberta stopping in her tracks. She looked over her shoulder. "Why? I don't have any idea what's missing in this mess. And that's the reason I'm here, isn't it?"

"Since you walked through my crime scene, then you can answer a few questions."

Roberta turned around and stuck her chin out. "I don't have to answer anything. I watch all the TV shows. I have rights."

"Yes, you do." The chief's tone was even, and he kept a polite smile on his face. "You can voluntarily answer a few questions here, or you can come down to the station right now and we'll wait for your attorney to show up before you answer them there." His smile got a little wider. "It's entirely your choice, Ms. Horton."

The short stocky woman glared at the police chief for a brief moment before averting her eyes. "What questions?"

"Did Eddie have a cell phone?"

Roberta shifted from one foot to the other but nodded. "Yeah. Nothing fancy, but he had one."

"Did he usually carry it with him?"

She rolled her eyes. "What's the point of having one if you don't carry it with you?"

"Do you have a cell phone, Ms. Horton?"

Nicki wasn't surprised at the sudden wariness that leapt into Roberta's eyes, or the slow nod of her head.

"Mind if I take a look at it?"

"Why?" Roberta snapped out then clamped her mouth shut.

Chief Turnlow lifted one eyebrow as he kept his stare on her face. "Any reason why I can't?"

"Because you'd need a warrant or something to do that." Roberta's gaze dropped to the chief's empty hands. "Have you got one of those on you?"

Sure that the chief would most likely be getting one soon, Nicki decided it might be a good time to distract the woman and give her something else to think about besides tampering with whatever might be on her phone.

"Can you tell me what Eddie was like?" She tried for a friendly chatty tone, hoping it would defuse the confrontational tactic the chief was using.

"What do you mean?" Roberta snapped out, switching her angry gaze to Nicki.

"You mentioned that even he wasn't this messy. Was he not a very neat person?" Nicki smiled. "And there aren't many photographs around. I guess he wasn't much for family pictures?"

Roberta's shoulders relaxed, though her mouth was still thinned out into a straight line. "He wasn't particular about keeping everything in his place sparkly clean. He always said he had enough of that at the diner. But he kept it picked up."

"And why no family photos?" Nicki asked.

"You can't have photos of something you don't have. He had a nephew back East somewhere. That was about it. Left everything to him, is what he told me. That nephew he'd hardly ever seen, and to those stamp people."

Nicki caught the chief's sideways glance as she looked

over at the bed. "Stamp people? Was Eddie a stamp collector?"

"Why do I have to answer questions from her?" Roberta demanded, her glare back on the chief. "She's just some kind of writer, or a cook, or something like that. She's not a policeman."

"Ms. Connors is consulting on this case." Despite Nicki's double take, the chief didn't bat an eyelash at that statement. "Again, it's your choice. Here or at the station."

Roberta let out a loud snort, but slowly walked forward until she was standing next to the bed, looking down at the large albums. "He loved those stamps more than anything." Her shoulders scrunched over, and Nicki could see the tiny tremble run down her back.

"You'd think those stamps were made out of gold or something the way he pampered them. Spent his money on special holders and other shit like that." She swiveled around, her eyes glittering with unshed tears. "He was a cheap bastard. He didn't spend money on anything but those stamps. And they weren't worth much more than what you'd buy at the post office. Except for maybe that one he told me about, all they did was take up space."

"What one?" Nicki prompted.

The woman shrugged and backed away from the bed. "Some stamp he got at the post office that turned out to be worth a lot of money." She looked at Nicki with eyes that had cleared and the sneer back on her face. "I don't know. I never saw it. He told me it had some kind of airplane on it. Whenever he started talking about his friggin' stamps, I just tuned him out. He'd go on for hours about the stupid things."

She looked over at the chief who was calmly watching her. "Maybe that's what this is all about. That dumb stamp of his. You should be grilling those two friends of his that collect stamps instead of me." She gave a quick, sharp nod of her head. "It's the only thing Eddie owned that was worth anything. He'd sold his house and his car and took up to living in this dump."

Roberta held out one arm and swept it in a wide arc before pointing a finger at the bed. "Yeah. It's probably about that stamp. Go talk to his friends and leave me alone." Without another word she stomped out of the room. Nicki could hear her footsteps all the way across the living room and then the hard slam of the front door.

The chief sighed and shook his head. "I don't suppose you know anything about stamps?"

"Not a thing, Chief." Nicki stared at the albums scattered on the bed. Two of them were on the floor, lying open, face down.

Chief Turnlow followed her line of vision. "Stamps. Huh." He glanced over at Nicki. "Come on. I'll walk you out to your car before I tape this place off and call in the forensics team from Santa Rosa. Again. I don't think their chief will be too happy about having to send his guys out this way for a second time, especially since they just got finished in the diner."

Nicki followed the chief out the front door, being careful where she put her feet. It only took a couple of minutes before they were both standing next to Nicki's car. She opened the door before looking back over her shoulder.

"Are you going to get that warrant for Roberta's cell phone?"

"I'll think on it," the chief said. "Are you going to return your editor's phone calls and save me from having to deal with him?"

She gave him a cheeky smile. "I'll think on it."

He laughed. "Get in. I'll wait to be sure your car starts up."

Slightly embarrassed that everyone knew about her chronic car problems, Nicki got behind the wheel and inserted the key into the ignition. Saying a silent prayer, she let out a sigh of relief when the engine immediately turned over. The chief closed the door and leaned over to peer through the open window. Nicki usually forgot to roll it up or lock her car since there was a zero chance anyone would try to steal it.

"How's Jenna doing? And Maxie?"

"They could be better, Chief, but they're holding up okay. I'm heading home to check on them both."

He nodded and straightened up. "You do that. And call that wanna-be boyfriend of yours." He was back to his fatherly smile. "He worries about you. And then get a good night's sleep. It's been a hard day for everyone."

Nicki knew that was true and had a flash of guilt over putting off talking to her editor. While the chief headed for his cruiser, she dug out her cell phone. Her little guilt trip only got longer when she saw she'd missed another call from Matt. Deciding her life had suddenly gotten very complicated trying to keep all of her friends happy, Nicki punched in his private number and waited. After seven rings, which she'd silently counted off, Matt's voice mail clicked on. She left a message, apologizing for not getting back to him sooner, and that she'd run into a few distractions but would get to work on her latest assignment right away. After hanging up, she felt a little better that at least she'd tried, and a little disappointed that he hadn't answered his phone.

Refusing to dwell on what that meant, she put her car into gear and steered it carefully out of the overgrown parking lot toward the highway.

CHAPTER SIX

NICKI WALKED INTO HER TOWNHOUSE, LOOKING FORWARD to a shower after her morning run. The chief had been right about feeling better after a good night's sleep, and the exercise this morning had really helped to clear her head. She'd gotten a late start, so it was already midmorning and there was quite a bit she wanted to do today.

Including tracking down Matt. She'd tried calling him before her run, but once again had been sent straight to his voice mail.

She'd barely set foot inside her house when she heard voices coming from her office. Nicki set her house keys on the hallway table on her way to investigate, although she had a pretty good idea who'd invaded her home. She smiled when she saw the three women huddled in front of the murder board.

"Hi!" Nicki grinned when they all turned as if they were glued together.

Jenna pushed her glasses further up her nose and shook her head at her friend. "Hey! Hope you don't mind us just letting ourselves in. And I have a bone to pick with you."

"I talked to the bookkeeper last night," Maxie said at the same time. "And it wasn't great news. Did you find anything at the apartment?"

"We came up with the most marvelous idea! Wait until you hear it," Suzanne chimed in.

Nicki laughed and held up her hands. "Wait. I can't answer everyone at the same time, and I need a shower. Give me a half hour and we can all compare notes."

She sprinted off, taking the stairs two at a time as she headed for the bathroom. Fortunately, she'd never been one to fuss with her appearance, so it wasn't a problem for her to be showered and in clean clothes in record time.

Her hair was still slightly damp when she walked into her office a half hour later and pointed at Jenna.

"You start. What bone?"

Jenna crossed her arms and tapped her foot against the hardwood floor. "Did you call Alex and tell her she had to come out here with a straightjacket?"

"I did not," Nicki declared, but had to raise a hand to hide her smile. "I mean, I did call her, but I didn't say a word about bringing men in white coats. Is that what she said?"

"Not exactly," Jenna groused. "But she kept asking me these touchy-feely, how-are-you-doing, what-are-you-thinking kind of questions. So I figured you'd called her and told her I was taking a long walk off a short pier."

Nicki tilted her head to one side and studied the tall brunette. "Well if you were, you seem to have made a full recovery."

"We both have," Maxie declared. "It's because we're sure that we're going to solve this case." She smiled at Jenna. "Which will help Jenna put it behind her and prove my Mason is innocent."

Nicki laughed as she crossed the room and pulled out her desk chair. Taking a seat, she swiveled it around to face the murder board and the three women standing in front of it. She looked at Jenna.

"You were acting, well, wonky," Nicki said, borrowing a word from the chief. "And don't tell me that talking to Alex didn't help at all."

Jenna's forehead scrunched up. "It did. And so will seeing her. She'll be on her way here after her shift. Ty's coming with her and they'll be staying at my place, although I could hear him yelling in the background that he expected you to do all the cooking."

"Well, Nicki is a gourmet chef, and you only do takeout," Suzanne said.

Jenna laughed. "True words. And most of my takeout comes from Nicki's kitchen." She grinned at her friend. "It's the least you can do since you made the call in the first place."

Because she never minded spending time with any of her friends, and especially Alex and Jenna, Nicki didn't bother to put out even a token protest. "Nothing I love to do more than cook for an appreciative crowd."

"Especially when we're investigating a murder," Jenna said. "Which brings us to Maxie's news."

Nicki turned her attention to her landlady. "Is this about the elusive bookkeeper?"

"Gordon Twill," Maxie supplied, "A most unfortunate circumstance for a name."

Nicki silently agreed with her there. She searched her memory. But even though Soldoff was a small town, she couldn't recall ever meeting a Gordon Twill.

"Anyway," Maxie continued. "Gordon is a very nice man. He's lived in Soldoff almost his entire life. I believe his parents moved here when Gordon was eight or nine. He and Eddie had been friends from grade school. At least that's what he told me when I spoke with him last night. He has several clients here in town. We use him for our Ladies in Writing Society."

"Maxie," Nicki said patiently. "What did he tell you about Eddie?"

"Oh, yes. Of course, dear." Maxie walked over and settled onto the small two-person sofa across from Nicki's desk. "He said that the diner has been barely scraping by for the last six months. It seems Eddie was taking out a lot more cash than he usually did. And there are outstanding bills that still need to be paid, not to mention wages for the staff. Gordon said that if the diner isn't bringing in any income, there won't be enough cash in its bank account to cover everything." Maxie exhaled a long, drawn-out breath. "He doesn't think the diner can survive if it stays closed for long. And since it was mostly known for its hamburgers, which were made from a secret mix only Eddie had the recipe for, he doesn't know how the place can reopen again."

Jenna gave Maxie a sympathetic look. "Which means your husband will lose out on his loan, and me on being paid for the website."

Nicki felt a fissure of alarm when Maxie didn't agree with Jenna. Instead, her landlady turned a smile in the computer geek's direction. And when Nicki looked over at Suzanne, she was smiling too. *Uh oh. This can't be good.*

Knowing she'd probably regret asking, she gave Maxie a cautious look. "And I take it the three of you have a plan to get everyone properly paid?" Nicki sincerely hoped it didn't involve something like buying the diner and opening up a cooking school.

"Suzanne came up with it."

Maxie's enthusiasm didn't do a thing to reassure Nicki, who turned slowly toward the woman who was bouncing up and down on her toes, a wide smile still on her face.

"I don't know why the diner can't reopen," Suzanne

gushed. "Jake's been the assistant manager and cook there for years, so he could keep doing that. And I'm sure Roberta would stay on. But even if neither of them did, how hard can it be? Even I can flip a burger or write down a food order. And I already know how to work a cash register. You just tap in some numbers or swipe a card down the side."

"It won't be quite that easy," Jenna warned. "He's got an old-fashioned cash register, and one of those credit card machines."

"I can learn it," Suzanne stated, all confidence now.

"And what about this secret hamburger mixture that made an Eddie's Diner burger so special?" Nicki looked over at Jenna. "Isn't that why you liked them so much?"

"True," Jenna nodded. "But that can't be such a big deal."

"Not a big deal? The taste of the food is what any eating establishment is about. Otherwise, you would have gone to McDonalds. There's one just down the street from Eddie's."

Maxie shifted her position on the sofa and crossed her ankles, her sandals throwing off a sparkle from the rhinestones along the straps. "Of course we should help support our local economy. Which naturally includes the diner. I'm sure we can come close to replicating an Eddie's hamburger. That is, with your help, dear."

"My help?" Nicki echoed.

"I'm sure Eddie kept some of that mix stashed in his refrigerator. All you have to do is figure out how to duplicate it. With your skill that shouldn't be hard." Suzanne's eyes fairly glowed at the prospect.

"Uh huh." Nicki kept her voice neutral. She didn't know if she could or couldn't duplicate the meat mixture. She was inclined to think not, but didn't want to rain on everyone's parade. Not when they were so much more upbeat than they had been just hours before.

Jenna gave Suzanne a light friendly swat on the arm. "Nicki's burger mix is the ult. It would put Eddie's to shame."

"I'm sure the price of it would too," Nicki quickly spoke up. "If we can find a sample of Eddie's, I'll do my best to duplicate it. Provided," she hastily added, "I don't also have to do the cooking. I really don't have the time, between writing for Matt's magazine, keeping up with my own blog and trying to get the next Tyrone Blackstone novel done." She nodded at Suzanne. "Not to mention the cooking classes you want to do."

"And of course solving our latest case," Maxie said. "Which is a primary concern for all of us."

Suzanne waved a hand at the murder board. "You concentrate on this. I'll take care of everything with the diner and the cooking class. You won't have to put in hardly any time at all."

Nicki doubted that, but she was happy to get off the subject of hamburger mixtures and back to murder.

"Could we get Gordon Twill to meet us at the diner once the chief allows us back in there? And Jake, too? We'll start on that hamburger mix, and I'll ask Gordon if he knew who Eddie was supposed to meet that night at the diner." While Suzanne wrote "set up meeting with Gordon" under the To-Do section of the board, Nicki looked over at Jenna. "You did say the reason you had to meet with Eddie early in the morning was because he already had a meeting set up for the night he was killed?"

Jenna nodded. "That's right. And who would know the person Eddie was meeting with better than his accountant?"

"Bookkeeper, dear," Maxie corrected, looking up from the cell phone she was holding in one hand. "Accountants are much more expensive." She went back to tapping on her phone.

"Okay. Bookkeeper," Jenna repeated. "Jake might know

too, since he's worked with Eddie forever. We can talk to him at the same time." She inclined her head at Nicki. "Is there anyone else we should talk to?"

Nicki leaned back in her chair. "Do any of you know about a stamp collection Eddie had?"

"He didn't make any secret that he had a stamp collection, dear. Why do you ask?" Maxie set her phone on the sofa cushion and kept her questioning gaze on Nicki.

"It was something Roberta mentioned when I was at Eddie's apartment with Chief Turnlow.

"How'd that go?" Jenna pounced on Nicki's comment. "Did you find anything that could help identify the killer?"

"No, we didn't. But that would have been difficult to do since it had been trashed worse than his office was." Nicki nodded at the gasps from the three of them. "And Roberta said he had some kind of valuable stamp, and we should be talking to his two stamp-collecting friends."

"That would be Ben Caulkin and Sam Moore." Maxie tapped one perfectly manicured finger against her chin. "But I've never heard about a rare stamp." When her phone pinged, she picked it up and stared at the small screen. "Excellent."

Maxie looked up and beamed at Suzanne. "Fran checked with the chief, and he said he'd release the diner as a crime scene in two days. All we have to do is get everyone in there once it's released and get started."

Suzanne's head bobbed up and down, along with the rest of her body. "I'll just step into the living room and make a few calls. See who I can get to come in."

Nicki smiled and shook her head as the short blond bounced her way out of the room. "She certainly seems excited about keeping the diner open."

"I think she's excited about finding a life for herself instead of imitating yours, or following along after Catherine," Maxie commented before her smile deflated. "My Mason will be home in two days. I don't know how I'm going to explain this to him."

Nicki rose and went to join her landlady on the small sofa. She put an arm around Maxie's shoulders and gave them a comforting squeeze. "I wish you wouldn't worry. No one within fifty miles of here would think Chief Edwards had anything to do with a murder, and certainly not Eddie's." She glanced over to Jenna for support.

"That really is a ridiculous idea," her friend instantly chimed in. "I think this whole stamp thing is a great lead. I mean, his office is trashed and then his apartment? Or who knows, it might have been the other way around. Someone couldn't find the stamp in Eddie's apartment and then went looking for it in his office, and Eddie surprised him." She nodded. "Sounds like the perfect scenario to me."

Maxie's whole expression brightened. "It does, doesn't it? Why, anyone could have known about that stamp. I'll be sure to have my Mason mention that to Chief Turnlow."

Since Jenna's theory had obviously made Maxie feel better about the current chief of police wanting to question her husband, Nicki didn't bother to remind either of them that the chief had been standing right there beside her when Roberta mentioned this unknown, and as yet not seen or verified, stamp.

With a last gentle pat on Maxie's back, Nicki stood and walked over to look at the murder board. "We have quite a few people we need to talk to. And I still have to write something for my blog today, and finish an article for Matt."

"Right." Jenna stretched her arms over her head. "And I need to get some work done for my newest client. Trident Industries will more than make up for any loss I take from Eddie's account."

"And money is only money." Maxie nodded, getting into

the spirit of the discussion. "Not having that loan paid back isn't going to affect us in the long run. Losing a friend is the much bigger issue. Which reminds me. I don't know if Eddie has any family who will be making final arrangements for him."

Nicki frowned. "According to Roberta, he only has a nephew, whom he hasn't seen in a long time."

"Then it's up to his friends to be sure he is properly laid to rest," Maxie declared. "I'll be on hand to talk to Gordon and find out if he knows about any wishes Eddie might have left, and of course make sure everything is taken care of."

Nicki smiled her approval. It did feel good to be doing something instead of sitting around wallowing in an ocean of unanswered questions. When the doorbell rang, she looked at her watch. She hadn't expected Alex this early, but maybe the emergency room hadn't been busy today and the doctor didn't have to work her full shift after all. When Suzanne's voice rang out with a cheery, "I'll get it", Nicki went back to studying the murder board.

A few seconds later, Suzanne appeared in the doorway to the office. "Um, Nicki? You have a visitor."

Not bothering to turn around, Nicki waved a hand out to one side. "Just have Ty drop your bags anywhere, Alex."

"I'll be happy to convey that message when he gets here."

Nicki froze for a long second before she caught Jenna's grin from the corner of her eye. Slowly turning around, she stared at her visitor. Her mouth opened, but no sound came out. Not even the mental groan that was echoing in her head.

"Oh." Maxie stopped and cleared her throat. "I'm sorry, dear. Did I forget to mention that Matt called last night and told me that he was on his way here? He asked if he could stay with us, and of course I'm happy to have him as our guest for as long as he would like to stay."

Nicki closed her eyes. "Of course you are."

CHAPTER SEVEN

"HI, NICKI." MATT'S SIX-FOOT FRAME TOOK UP MOST OF the doorway's height, and the intense gaze behind his glasses with their thick black frame was glued to Nicki.

Nicki raised her eyebrows in a silent question, fighting not to smile when her editor adjusted his glasses and shoved an unruly lock of dark hair out of his eyes. It was such a Matt thing to do. A dimple in his cheek peeked through when he did a perfect imitation of raising an eyebrow of his own.

"What are you doing here, Matt?"

"I wanted to ask you why you haven't returned any of my calls." He paused and adjusted his glasses again, a sure sign he was either irritated or embarrassed. Nicki wondered which one it was, but had a feeling she wouldn't have to wait long to find out.

"Well?"

Nicki blinked at him. "Well what?"

Jenna coughed loudly from behind her. "As absorbing as this conversation is, I have things I need to do in the kitchen."

"I'll help you, dear." Maxie pushed herself off the sofa and crossed over to the doorway, sliding past Matt before latching onto Suzanne's arm and pulling her out of sight.

Jenna was close to Matt's height, so she just stood nose-to-nose with him until he moved aside. Nicki's good friend turned her head and winked before also vanishing down the hallway.

Nicki put her hands on her hips and shook her head. "You didn't even say hello to Jenna or Maxie. That was rude, Matt."

"So is not answering my calls."

"I'm sorry. Did you have an urgent assignment for me that you failed to mention in your voice mails?"

"No."

Nicki shrugged. "Then there isn't any reason for my editor to be so impatient."

Matt's eyes narrowed. "How about being rude to a friend?"

"Now that I *am* sorry about." Nicki smiled and held out her hand. "But you should have told me you were coming. I have voice mail, too, you know. Truce?"

"It depends." Matt's eyes shifted to the large whiteboard on the opposite wall. "What's that?"

"Oh, that?" Nicki waved a negligent hand and bought herself a little time by walking back to her desk and getting settled into her chair. When Matt continued to stare at her in silence, she knew the jig was up and she might as well get the lecture she was sure would be coming, over with. "The strangest thing happened yesterday."

Matt's arms crossed over his chest. "How strange?"

"Jenna had an early morning meeting at Eddie's Diner yesterday. I think you had a hamburger or two from there when you came to the world famous 'Art & Wine Sell Off Festival' here last month."

"It's been over three months, Nicki, and keep talking. I haven't heard anything strange yet." He pinned her with a hard look. "And I'm hoping it doesn't involve any dead bodies."

"No, it doesn't involve dead bodies."

Matt's shoulders started to relax. "Then what does it involve?"

Nicki cleared her throat and squirmed in her chair for a moment. Her editor, and friend, was definitely not going to like this.

"There was only one dead body."

"One dead...." Matt ran a hand through his thick dark hair, leaving several strands of it standing on end. "A dead body. Tell me you're joking."

Nicki bit her lower lip and shook her head, wincing when Matt carefully unbuttoned his jacket and tossed it onto the sofa.

"When had you planned on telling me about this dead body?"

"When I had something concrete to talk to you about." She nodded her head emphatically at his skeptical look. "Really."

"How about a name? Is that concrete enough?"

Nicki sighed. Matt rarely got angry, but it was plain enough he was rapidly working his way in that direction. "Eddie Parker."

That brought her editor up short. "Not *the* Eddie? As in the owner of the diner?"

"Eddie Parker, the Eddie of Eddie's Burger Diner," Nicki clarified. "And before you ask, I'm not the one who found him. Jenna did. He was one of her clients."

"Well that's something, at least."

"Matt!" Nicki's eyes narrowed and she leaned forward in her chair. "That's not funny. It was horrible for Jenna, and she's still upset about it. So is Maxie for that matter."

Matt pushed his hair off his forehead, sending two more

tufts into an upright position. "I realize it isn't funny. And I wouldn't wish that on anyone. I haven't seen you for almost four months, but we're talking every day so it's going fine. And then suddenly we aren't talking, and I knew. I just knew it had something to do with a murder." He suddenly stopped the tirade he was building up steam on and frowned. "Wait a minute. Why is Maxie upset? Was she there too?"

"No. But Chief Turnlow wants to question myMason about where he was the night of the murder."

The tall lanky editor's jaw dropped to his chest. "What? Mason? He wants to question Mason? We are talking about the former chief of police, aren't we? Mason Edwards?"

"He's the only husband Maxie has, as far as I know." Nicki's dry response was followed by several long moments of silence.

"That is ridiculous."

Nicki smiled. "Which is what Jenna said, and what I've been telling Maxie."

"Great." Matt sat on the sofa and threw one arm along its back. "What did Mason have to say to Chief Turnlow?"

"Um. Nothing yet." She shrugged when Matt tipped his head to one side. "He went fishing."

"Who? Mason or Chief Turnlow?" When Nicki didn't bother to answer his feeble attempt at humor, he smiled. "Sorry. Okay. When did Mason leave for this trip?"

"The morning after the murder."

"And how long had he been planning for this trip?"

Nicki wrinkled her nose. "Maybe a day or so."

Matt was looking grimmer with each answer. "And when will he be back?"

"Tomorrow, or maybe the day after. Maxie isn't sure."

He groaned. "So he left on a sudden and not really pre-planned trip, the morning the body was found, and no one is sure when he'll be back?"

"Coincidence," Nicki stated firmly.

"Obviously. But one that needs explaining." He rolled his eyes to the ceiling before glancing over at the murder board. "Why don't you catch me up?"

Two days later Matt was sitting at the counter of Eddie's Burger Diner, his head in his hands. Jenna was sitting next to him, slightly hunched over and holding her midriff. Both of them looked a little pale.

Nicki glanced at them through the pass-through into the kitchen where she was standing next to the stove along with Jake, the assistant manager. She turned her head so neither of them would see her smile. It seemed they'd finally had their fill of hamburgers, and then some.

"We'll have a couple more for you to try in a minute or two," she called out, holding in her laughter at the clear sound of a double groan. She grinned at Alex who was sitting at the large prep table in back of her. "I think Matt is going to throw up."

Alex looked over at the two miserable individuals sitting at the counter and squinted as she studied their faces. "No. I think he's going to do the gentlemanly thing and let Jenna go first."

"Too bad. He's been working me into the ground on magazine business while we waited for the chief to let us back into the diner."

Alex lowered her voice. "Has myMason come home yet?"

"Maxie's expecting him tonight," Nicki whispered. Alex nodded and went back to reading her magazine.

"It won't be a big deal. Chief Edwards didn't do anything to Eddie." Jake Garces, the assistant manager, was standing in front of the stove, keeping a close eye on the sizzling burgers.

His dark eyes lit up with humor when he looked over at Nicki. "I think your two friends are in luck. These are cooking just the right way." He flashed a smile that showed a set of brilliant white teeth. "I think you did it, Chef Connors."

"I'm not a chef, Jake. You're the chef here."

The short dark-haired man ducked his head. "Not me. I'm only a line cook. You're the one who went to that fancy culinary school in New York."

Since she had indeed attended a very fancy culinary school in New York, one of the best in the world, Nicki inclined her head at the compliment. "But I only cook for friends and family now, Jake. So I'm not really a chef anymore."

"But you will be," he insisted. "Mrs. Suzanne told me that you're going to be giving cooking classes soon. I wish I could come. I'd like to learn some of that fancy cooking." He flipped over one burger, and then the other two next to it. "But I'll need to be looking for a job first." He nodded. "I appreciate you and Maxie wanting to keep this place open for a while. It will help us all out. But you can't do that forever."

Unfortunately, that was true enough. Nicki wished she could help out more than the few weeks it might take for Chief Turnlow to track down the next of kin and get him here. That is if Roberta was correct about Eddie having a nephew. But at least there was one little thing she could do for the friendly assistant manager.

"You come to the classes, Jake. There won't be any charge." She shook her head at his instant protest. "It means a lot to my friends to keep the diner going for a while, and it couldn't have been done without your help in figuring out what Eddie put into his burger mix."

Jake beamed at her. "Thank you. I was happy to help. And to watch how you did all those different mixtures of meat and spices until you got it just right." He pointed his spatula at the stove. "And those are just right. I know it."

Nicki leaned closer and dropped her voice. "I hope so. I think our two taste testers are about to keel over."

Jake laughed and slid the burgers onto buns. He held out the two plates to Alex. "These are ready."

Alex grinned as she juggled the plates. "They could taste like dog food and those two would swear they're exactly like Eddie's to get out of eating any more hamburgers." Her grin grew even wider. "This should cure Jenna of her hamburger habit."

Even though she doubted that very much, Nicki nodded anyway, and watched as the doctor triumphantly swept out the kitchen door, a plate with a huge hamburger on top in either hand. While Alex delivered the next offering to their long-suffering test subjects, Nicki stood quietly and watched Jake scrape his spatula back and forth over the large flat-topped grill. Her gaze wandered over to the freezer, its door closed, its smooth metal surface giving no sign of being the scene of a murder. But it did remind her of something

"Jake, did Eddie have a cell phone?"

The assistant manager glanced over his shoulder. "Yeah. He kept everything on there. All his phone numbers, his bank passwords and anything else he didn't want to memorize. But he was always forgetting to put it back into his pocket after he'd used it to call someone or look something up, so he was always forgetting to bring it with him here, or leaving it here when he went home."

"Do you remember if he'd left it at home the day he was murdered?"

The cook at Eddie's Diner for more than a decade closed his eyes for a long moment. "I think he did. He made a crack about not knowing if his appointment after work would cancel or not, because he'd left his cell at home. Why?"

"We didn't find one here." Or at the apartment as far as she knew. She'd have to remember to ask Chief Turnlow about that. "Jake, do you remember ever seeing a jacket that was a gold-ish color with red trim around the neck and sleeves?"

He grinned at her. "A gold jacket with red trim? Why do you ask?"

"It was hanging in the freezer, and I was wondering who it belonged to. I know that isn't much to go on, but I thought you might remember it."

"Not much to go on?" Jake laughed until he was almost bent over double.

"What's the joke?" Matt walked into the kitchen, holding his sides. He gave Nicki a weak smile. "We decided that last one was a perfect match to an Eddie's burger."

"Did you?" Nicki glanced toward the pass-through. "Where's Jenna?"

Matt plopped onto the stool Alex had vacated and propped his head up with one hand. "She had to go to the ladies' room."

"Okay," Nicki said cheerfully. Poor Matt was gradually turning a lovely shade of green.

"So what's the joke?" Matt repeated. He gritted his teeth and barely managed to stifle a moan.

Jake's eyes fairly danced with suppressed laughter. "Nicki wants to know if I've ever seen a jacket that was gold with red trim."

Even despite what must have been the continual protest of his stomach, Matt managed a grin. "Did it happen to have anything on it?"

"Like what?" Nicki frowned at both of them.

"Like a football," Jake said while Matt nodded. "Those are the colors of San Francisco's football team."

"The 49ers," Matt put in. "Ever heard of them?"

"Kind of." Nicki rolled her eyes at Matt before returning her gaze to Jake. "I'm from New York, and I don't like football.

Jake's horrified look was met by a nod from Matt. "She really doesn't. You'll have to overlook that. She has a lot of other great qualities."

Ignoring them both, along with the whole subject of football, Nicki kept her stare on Jake. "Do you know who owns that jacket?"

"It was Eddie's. He wore it all the time. He was a big fan. Even bought tickets to go to one of their games occasionally."

"But not often?" Nicki asked.

Jake shrugged. "They were expensive. Eddie didn't like to spend money."

So I've heard. Nicki pondered the jacket for a minute. "Did he always keep it in the freezer?"

Jake's eyes flew open. "He never kept it in there. He always hung it on a hook in his office." He glanced from Nicki to Matt and back again. "Why are you asking me this?"

"Just something else that's curious about this whole thing."

Alex walked in, holding a plastic trashcan in one hand. "Maxie wanted to let you know that those two stamp collectors have pulled into the parking lot."

Nicki pointed to her hand. "What are you doing with that?"

"I'm going to escort your very macho editor to the bathroom, and this," she held the trashcan up, "this is to be sure he doesn't make a mess along the way."

Matt gingerly slid off his stool, one hand splayed out across his stomach. "Don't do any interrogating until I get back."

Nicki gave him a jaunty salute as he hobbled out the door, leaning on Alex.

CHAPTER EIGHT

Nicki was still drying her hands on a dishtowel when two men strolled through the front door. She set the damp towel on the counter and smiled a greeting. Sam and Ben had the same medium height, the same slender builds and nearly identical light-brown hair and brown eyes, and both looked to be on the far side of middle-aged. At a quick glance, they could have been twins, or at least brothers.

"I'm Sam. Sam Moore. And you must be Nicki?"

The man in the red cardigan sweater crossed the room with his hand held out. Nicki took it for a brief, friendly handshake.

"I am. Nicki Connors, Mr. Moore, and it's a pleasure to meet you."

The man's slightly crooked front teeth only added to the charm of his smile. "Please, call me Sam, since I have every intention of calling you Nicki. Small town residents never stand on ceremony." He turned and clamped a hand on the shoulder of the man standing behind him, pulling him forward. "And this shy fellow is Ben Caulkin. He always gets tongue-tied around beautiful women."

Nicki laughed at the compliment and held her hand out to Ben. He also wore a sweater, only his was a much more conservative, dark-green pullover, and his eyes were a pinch deeper shade of brown than his friend Sam's. He shook Nicki's hand for a full five seconds, keeping his gaze on the ground the whole time. Not wanting to make him any more uncomfortable than he already seemed to be, Nicki turned back to Sam.

"I'm glad you could meet us here at Eddie's today."

Sam's smile widened. "No one in the entire county would dare ignore a request from Maxie Edwards." He winked at her. "Or should I say a command?"

"Sam, be polite. Maxie's a good friend," Ben protested. He raised his eyes and looked at his fellow companion. "And so was Eddie." He nodded at Nicki. "We're happy to help any way that we can."

Sam added his nod then shifted his gaze to somewhere over Nicki's shoulder. "Well, hello? Who is this?"

Nicki looked around at Matt, who was slowly walking toward them. While he was missing the usual spring in his step, she was happy to see that his face no longer showed any tint of green.

"Feeling better?" she asked when he came to a stop beside her.

"I may never eat another hamburger again. I'm supposed to tell you that Alex took Jenna outside for some fresh air." Matt glanced over at the two men and held out his hand. "Hi. I'm Matt Dillon."

"Ah." Sam shook Matt's hand as he looked between the tall editor and Nicki. "As in the TV character from *Gunsmoke?*"

"My mom was a big fan."

Sam laughed and nudged Ben in the side. "So, which one is he? The always absent boyfriend or the better choice one?"

Nicki leaned her head back and closed her eyes. She refused to meet the annoyed stare she was sure Matt was sending her way.

"I'm the editor for *Food & Wine Online.*"

Matt didn't sound offended, so Nicki opened her eyes to find him grinning at her.

"And the better choice," he added with a wink.

"So everyone says." Sam crossed his arms and gave Matt a quizzical look. "What's your holdup in making it clear to the absentee one that his attentions are no longer needed?"

"Sam, you're embarrassing her."

Nicki certainly welcomed Ben's defense, especially since her face was radiating enough heat to tell her it was probably a fire-engine red. She gave Matt a jab with her elbow.

"Behave, or I'll have to send you home." She narrowed her eyes. "To Kansas City." She looked at Sam. "Where he lives. We did have a reason for asking you to meet us here. Are you able to answer a few questions about Eddie?"

"Of course," Sam said as Ben added his nod. "Maxie told us you'd jumped in to help find his killer, and we're both happy to help. Isn't that right, Ben?"

"Yes, we certainly are. What can we tell you?"

Nicki pursed her lips and considered where to start, settling on the subject they'd know the most about. "I saw his stamp collection in his apartment. Did he ever show it to you?"

Sam waved a hand back and forth. "Oh certainly. Ben and I are collectors as well, and we met with Eddie regularly to discuss stamps and show off our most prized ones."

Ben's face fell into sober lines. "There're only two things Eddie loved. Good wine and stamps. And he enjoyed trying his hand at both, although he always said he could only afford one of those hobbies."

Sam nodded his agreement. "And it wasn't because he was

some modern-day Scrooge, like Roberta is so fond of saying. Eddie was simply careful with his money. Especially if he had something big he wanted to do."

"Or buy?" Nicki asked. At their blank looks, she tried for something more direct. "Such as a very expensive wine? Or stamp?"

"He depended on his wine club to keep him supplied in wine, and I very much doubt that he ever bought anything outside the usual offerings," Sam said. "At least he never mentioned it to me."

"He belonged to the club at Holland Winery," Ben offered. His eyes suddenly widened. "Do you think this has something to do with Holland Winery? Their winemaker was murdered just last year. I believe he was poisoned?" He turned his whole body toward Sam. "Remember that distasteful little man we met once? With the French name and the very bad French accent?"

"Lanciere," Matt supplied. "He went by George Lanciere."

"Does this have anything to do with his murder? Maybe Eddie was sent one of those poisoned bottles of wine by mistake?" Ben's hand flew to cover his mouth.

Nicki had to admit, the man certainly had a good imagination. "No. I'm sure Eddie's murder had nothing to do with what happened at Holland Winery. So if Eddie didn't spend his money on expensive wine, how about expensive stamps?"

Sam shrugged. "He never bought anything at an auction that a high-end collector would get excited about."

"Or through a private sale as far as we know," Ben added.

"Oh." Nicki deflated. It seemed to be another dead end. "Roberta said he had a very valuable stamp, with an old airplane on it?"

"Trust Roberta not to get something so important to Eddie right." Sam rolled his eyes. "That wasn't a stamp. It was a sheet of stamps of an uninverted Jenny."

"A sheet?" Nicki exchanged a triumphant look with Matt.

"If the plane was uninverted, that means it was flying right-side up?" Matt asked. "Why did that make this sheet so valuable?"

"Because there were only fifty sheets made by the US postal service," Ben said.

"It was supposed to commemorate the mistake the post office made back near the end of World War I. It was a stamp issued to mark the start of airmail service in 1918. Back then they used a two-seat biplane that had the second seat removed to make room for the mail, and was nicknamed 'the Jenny'. But when the stamp was issued, at least one sheet had the plane's image mistakenly printed upside down." Ben became more animated as he warmed up to the subject. "Naturally over the years those stamps have become quite valuable. So to spark a wider interest in stamps, the postal service decided to print over a million of those same inverted Jennys in 2013. But they also deliberately printed fifty sheets of stamps with the corrected version of the Jennys. Those sheets had the plane flying right-side up."

Matt took his glasses off and wiped the lenses with the bottom of his shirt. "I get it. By only printing fifty sheets, they automatically created a rare stamp. Only this time it was an upright airplane instead of an upside down one."

"That's right," Ben enthused. "They sent thirty of the sheets to the top-selling postal markets in the country, and randomly distributed the other twenty throughout the U.S."

"And guess where one of those sheets ended up? And then who happened to hit the jackpot in stamp collecting by purchasing it at the one-man post office a block from the square?" Sam grinned. "Eddie goes into that little one-man place to buy just regular stamps, and old Grover, who's still the postmaster there, pulled out this sheet and asks Eddie if he'd like the one that had just come in with an old airplane on it. Grover didn't know why he'd only been sent one sheet, but he knew Eddie collected stamps and thought he might like to have it."

Ben gave a long dramatic sigh. "Grover had no idea what that sheet was, or what it was worth. To him it was just another decorative stamp, like the ones he sold every Christmas."

"But Eddie knew what they were?" Nicki waited for the two nods. "What did he do?"

"Of course he snatched them right up. And like any good collector, he ordered a special sleeve and a case, so they'd stay in absolutely perfect condition. Since he didn't have a safe deposit box, he simply kept them well hidden, and he rarely showed them." Sam looked over at Ben. "I think we've only seen them maybe once a year since he'd had them."

"And he got them in 2013?" Nicki asked. When Ben gave a confirming nod, she wrinkled her nose, visualizing all the albums scattered across Eddie's bed rather than simply thrown on the floor. Someone could easily have been looking for those stamps. And when they weren't in any of the albums, ransacked the rest of the apartment searching for them. "Did he keep the sheet of stamps somewhere in his apartment?"

Sam laughed. "Oh heavens, no. He always said anyone could pop his lock with the edge of a credit card. He kept them here at the diner."

Nicki's heart sank. He might have kept them in a box in the freezer, but then he'd run the risk of any one of his employees stumbling across them. Which only left one place. "They were in his office safe, then?"

Both men held their hands up, palms facing outward. "No, no," they chanted in unison.

"He would never do such an ordinary thing. He kept them in his wine cellar, of course," Sam said.

Nicki's eyebrows flew up several inches. "Wine cellar?" She took a quick look around. "Here?"

The collector shrugged. "Not many people knew about it, and he never told anyone where he kept the key. So if you want to see those stamps, you'll have to break into his basement." He paused and blinked several times. "Oh dear. Unless it's already been broken into?"

"I don't know," Nicki said. "I had no idea there *was* a wine cellar here."

"We can show you," Ben offered. "We've been there several times. Whenever it was Eddie's turn to host a meeting with the three of us, we'd always go have a glass of wine, burgers and fries in his wine cellar. He'd set up a card table and chairs in the center." He tugged on the hem of his pullover sweater. "It was fun, sitting in that secret cellar, drinking wine and talking about stamps. I'm going to miss that."

Sam put a hand on his friend's shoulder. "Me too."

"How much is it worth?" Matt asked. "Do you know what that sheet of stamps is worth?"

"Well, let's see. Not millions, if that's what you're thinking, or Eddie would have sold it long ago." Sam's forehead wrinkled. "I believe one sheet sold for fifty thousand dollars three or four years ago."

"Fifty thousand..." Nicki trailed off as she looked at Matt.

Without breaking away from her gaze, Matt reached into his back pocket and pulled out his cell phone. "I'm calling Chief Turnlow."

She nodded her agreement and looked back at the two men standing silently, shoulder-to-shoulder. "When the chief gets here, can you show us where this cellar is?"

"Of course." Sam said.

"That's good," Matt hit the disconnect button and lowered his phone. "Because he'll be here in ten minutes."

CHAPTER NINE

"Is THIS EVERYBODY?" CHIEF TURNLOW SLOWLY LOOKED down the line of people in front of him. He was in his usual stance, with his hands in the pockets of his leather jacket. His expression was blank, giving no clue to what he was thinking.

When the two stamp collectors and the assistant manager shuffled their feet, Nicki had to work at stifling a smile. It seemed they weren't used to what she privately called the chief's "deadly detective stare". He'd undoubtedly perfected it during his twenty years with the Los Angeles Police Department.

The chief looked over at Nicki. "I saw the doctor pulling out of the parking lot. Is she headed home?"

"Yes," Nicki glanced at the group around her. "And this seems to be everyone."

The chief and former LAPD detective nodded and shifted his attention to Sam. "I understand you're claiming that you've seen this expensive stamp that Eddie Parker owned?"

Sam nodded. "That's right. Ben and I have both seen it. And it isn't a stamp, Chief Turnlow. It's a whole sheet of stamps. One hundred to be exact. And worth at least fifty thousand."

"One hundred stamps worth fifty thousand dollars," the chief repeated before he swung his gaze over to Jake. "Have you seen these stamps?"

"No, Sir."

Nicki felt a pang of sympathy for the usually cheerful assistant manager. He looked terrified, as if he expected to be hauled off to jail at any moment.

"I haven't seen them either," Nicki spoke up, mostly to take the chief's stare off of poor Jake.

"Me either," Matt and Jenna said at the same time.

The chief gave all three of them an exasperated look. "I didn't ask if you had." He turned his attention back to Jake who was frozen in place. "I assume you knew your boss had a wine cellar in the basement?"

Jake gave a stiff nod, his eyes staring straight-ahead.

"But you didn't mention it the other day when I was asking you about Eddie?"

"Why would I mention it?" Jake's voice squeaked out the question. "Eddie was found in the freezer, not the basement."

The chief showed no reaction to that statement but continued on in the same low authoritative voice. "How do you get into this wine cellar?"

Jake pointed at the double doors leading into the kitchen and back hallway. "Through the storage room. There's a door at the far end."

"And it's always locked according to what Eddie said." Sam looked to Ben who nodded his agreement.

"Who else knew about the cellar? Did Eddie usually talk about it?"

Sam shook his head. "I never heard him talk about it, so I have no idea if anyone else knew about it."

"But all the staff at the diner knew about it, didn't they?" Nicki asked, directing her question to Jake.

"Yes. But except for me, no one who works here has ever been in it," Jake stated. "Not even Roberta. Eddie never trusted her enough to show it to her. He told me that."

Nicki wouldn't have argued with Eddie on that point. From her two encounters with Eddie's girlfriend, she wouldn't have trusted Roberta very far either.

"You don't say." Chief Turnlow frowned for a moment before his shoulders relaxed and so did his stance, making Nicki believe he'd decided the grilling was finished.

"Sam, Ben. Did either of you ever hear Eddie say that he'd hidden this sheet of stamps in the wine cellar?" the chief asked.

"No," Sam admitted. "But that's the only place we ever saw it, so I've always assumed he kept the sheet down there somewhere."

"Has anyone else ever seen these stamps anywhere besides in the wine cellar?"

The two stamp collectors shook their head.

Jake did the same before adding, "I've never seen the stamps. Eddie described them to me once. Said there was an airplane on them. But I've never seen even one of them."

Sam chuckled. "The sheet is still intact, Jake. If you'd seen one, you would have seen them all."

"All right," the chief interrupted. "I guess I'd better take a look."

Not without me. Nicki fell in behind him.

"Chief, we might need to break the lock since no one knows where the key is." She casually included the word "we".

"We could take the door off its hinges," Matt put in, following Nicki's lead by also assuming there would be more than just the chief going along to search the cellar.

The chief sighed and ran a hand over the thinning hair on

top of his head. "I could declare the basement as a crime scene, but it's pretty obvious Eddie was struck in his office and dragged into the freezer. I didn't find any other blood trails when I did my walk-through of the place. And as far as the key goes..." He reached into his pocket and withdrew a clear plastic evidence bag. He walked over and held the bag out so Ben and Sam could see its contents. "Do any of these look like the key to the wine cellar?"

Ben shook his head. "It was a big heavy key. Very old-fashioned."

Sam squinted at the bag. "I agree with Ben. None of those are the key to the basement door."

The chief walked over and held the bag up in front of Jake, who agreed with what Sam and Ben had said. "Not the key, Chief Turnlow."

"The deputy and I searched the office and didn't find any keys, but it wouldn't hurt to go through it again." He glanced at Nicki. "Why don't you come along and help, Sherlock." He raised a hand to stop Matt when the editor stepped forward. "You stay here and make sure no one leaves."

Not looking very happy, Matt reluctantly nodded

Nicki didn't need a second invitation. She immediately headed toward the double doors and down the back hallway. Since the door to Eddie's office was wide open, she gave the chief a questioning look and received his nod before proceeding into the room.

The chief stepped in beside her and slowly looked around. "He could have kept the key in his apartment, and the killer has already made a trip to the cellar."

"If the killer had already found the key in the apartment, why search the office?" Nicki glanced over at the safe sitting in the corner. "Unless he thought there was a lot of money in the safe?"

"Then he'd be disappointed. The safe was empty."

Startled, Nicki's mouth dropped open. "There wasn't anything at all in the safe?"

"Nope. The vic might have had that key on a separate ring, and the thief took it after he was surprised in the middle of a robbery." The chief shrugged. "You can come up with a million theories on how the killer could have gotten his hands on it. But..." He looked around again.

"But?" Nicki prompted.

"He probably kept it here. If it was one of those large old-fashioned keys, he wasn't likely to be lugging it around in his pocket all the time. And his wine and that pricey stamp were here, so why would he want to run back to his apartment to get the key whenever he wanted to get into that basement?" He glanced over at Nicki. "Unless you have another idea?"

She quickly shook her head. "No other ideas here, Chief."

"Excuse me." Jake stood in the doorway, his hands clasped in front of him.

"Your boyfriend said I should come right back." Jake ducked his head and cast a sideways glance at the Chief of Police.

"And why did Nicki's boyfriend say that?"

Nicki bristled at the laughter in the chief's voice and sent him a glare. Everyone, even the assistant manager of Eddie's Burger Diner, seemed determined to see Matt as her boyfriend.

"He said I should tell you what I heard."

"Heard?" Nicki echoed. "Did you overhear Eddie say something about where the key is? Or about the stamp?"

"What did you hear, Jake?" the chief asked quietly.

"There was this one time when Eddie said he'd just realized it was our tenth anniversary of working together. And he wanted to celebrate with a glass of wine. So when the diner closed, we came back here." Jake raised a hand and swept it in front of him. "He told me to wait in this hallway, and he went inside and closed the door. When he came out again, he had the key in his hand."

Nicki frowned. "So he did keep the basement key in his office?"

"Yes," Jake confirmed. "But the office door wasn't closed all the way. I couldn't see him, but I heard a drawer open."

The chief glanced over at the desk. "He opened a desk drawer?"

"No, no. Not in the desk." Eddie pointed toward the filing cabinet. "One of those. It clanged when he shut it, like those do."

Turning to the filing cabinet, Nicki stood in front of the tall five-drawer piece of furniture and looked it over. She tilted her head to one side as she studied it.

"Is that a fact?" The chief nodded at the assistant manager. "Thank you, Jake. You can go back to Nicki's boyfriend. We'll be out there in a few minutes."

Once the short dark-haired man had disappeared back down the hallway, the chief walked over and stood next to Nicki. "Want to split it? You take one half of the drawers and I'll take the other."

Nicki didn't answer but pulled open the top drawer, reached over to read the last file at the very back and then closed the drawer. The chief gave her a puzzled look.

"Not much of a search, Ms. Connors. Got one of those hunches of yours?"

Keeping her thoughts to herself, Nicki opened the second drawer and started to finger walk her way through the tops of the file folders. "Hansen's Paper Products, Hickory Meats... Ah, here it is." She pulled out a folder that was too heavy to be just holding papers. She grinned at the chief as she reached into the folder and pulled out a large old-fashioned key. "Eddie belonged to the wine club out at Holland Winery."

The chief bowed his head. "Nice deduction there, Sherlock." He held out his hand and Nicki dropped the key into it. "I'll go give this a try if you want to bring along Sam and Ben. And your boyfriend of course." He chuckled at Nicki's annoyed frown. "And tell Jake and Jenna they can go on home. I'm betting the basement isn't that big, so we'll just bring along the two who have actually seen that stamp."

Nicki quickly did as she was told and was back standing in front of the open door at the far end of the storeroom in no time at all. She peered down the wooden steps that looked as if they hadn't been repainted in a decade or two.

A small lightbulb in the ceiling at the bottom of the stairs gave off a dim light that barely lit up the narrow passageway and a ring of cement at the bottom. She carefully set one foot on the top step, and when it didn't give way, repeated the process for the next step, and then the next, until she finally reached the bottom. She looked around the small completely enclosed space, surrounded by floor-to-ceiling wine racks on three sides. In the center of the room was a sagging card table and four chairs. Matt stepped around her and stood for a moment studying the tall racks holding dozens of wine bottles.

"Huh. No wonder he kept the stamp down here." He pointed to the humidifier in one corner. "Temperature controlled." He walked over to the nearest wine rack and started pulling out bottles and reading their labels before pushing them back into place.

Skirting past him so Ben and Sam had room to join them, Nicki sidestepped around the card table and went to stand next to the chief. He motioned for the two stamp collectors to descend the last few steps and join them in the cramped space.

"This is where you two and Eddie would come and have a drink and talk about stamps?" The chief gave them a skeptical look. "Not as inviting as the corner bar."

"But so much more secretive and mysterious." Sam's eyes crinkled at the corners. "And we got a free meal."

"Best burgers in town." Ben walked forward and leaned a hand against the back of one of the metal chairs. "The sheet of stamps was always out and in the center of the table whenever he felt like showing it to us. We never saw where it came from."

"Not a lot of places to hide something down here," the chief said.

They all looked around the cramped room. Except for Matt. He was still busy pulling out bottles and then shoving them back into place.

"What are you looking for, Matt?" Nicki craned her neck to watch what he was doing.

"I'm not sure," Matt threw out over his shoulder. "I'll let you know if I find it."

Only the sound of bottles sliding in and out of the wine racks bounced around the walls of the basement as they all stood and waited, while Matt slowly made his way around the room.

About halfway through all the wine racks, he pulled one bottle out and held it in his hands, staring down at the label. He set it on the floor and pulled out a second bottle that was nestled in a spot next to the first one. He looked at the label and nodded, then pulled out a third and a fourth. Nicki walked over and picked up one of them then glanced at Matt and smiled.

"Bottled in 2013. The same year the Jenny stamp was issued."

Matt nodded. "It's the only 2013 wine I've found. The rest are only a year or two old." He glanced over at the chief.

"Like you said, there aren't a lot of places to hide anything in here, except behind the wine."

When he had nine bottles lined up on the cement floor, he took a small step back. "Okay. That's it. All the other bottles around these are more recent." He bent over and peered into the empty niches with Nicki leaning over his shoulder. "A flashlight would be helpful." He reached into his back pocket and grabbed his cell phone. After tapping out a few keys, a light came out of its back. He handed it to Nicki. "Point this in here."

Nicki aimed the flashlight where he'd indicated and held it steady as Matt took a good long look before he reached an arm in and pulled out the wooden pieces separating the niche.

"These have been cut through, and there's something tucked in the back."

Everyone leaned forward as he tugged a square object through the now enlarged opening. He carried his prize over to the card table and placed it in the center, face up. It was a plain, square case, with four prongs mounted on the inside.

"It's empty." Sam's statement fell flat into the silent room as they all stared at the case with the glass front. "We just saw the stamps. They were here last week."

"Is that a fact? I don't recall you mentioning that until just now, Sam." The chief raised a questioning eyebrow at the stamp collector.

"I didn't think it was important. I wouldn't believe in a million years that anyone besides the three of us knew those stamps were even in this room, much less be able to find them," Sam said.

"I saw them last week, too," Ben volunteered. "And I agree with Sam. It never crossed my mind. I mean, who would think to look behind the wine bottles? Who would have known what wine bottles to even look behind?"

The chief pointed at Matt. "He did. So someone else could have figured it out too." He looked at the empty case. "Or the killer may have gotten Eddie to tell him."

Ben gasped. "Are you saying that poor Eddie was tortured, and once he told what he knew, he was killed?"

Nicki leaned closer to Matt's ear. "Ben has a very vivid imagination," she whispered.

Matt grinned. "I can tell."

"Don't jump to conclusions, Ben," Chief Turnlow said. "I didn't see any signs that Eddie had been tortured. We'll have to wait for the coroner's report before we know for sure, but I doubt it." He heaved a deep sigh. "I've seen that before."

The chief looked grim as he gestured toward the staircase. "Let's go."

They trooped back up to the main dining room and then, at the chief's insistence, out the front door. Once they were in the open air again, Nicki took a deep breath. Eddie may have liked his little wine cellar, but she certainly wouldn't want to spend a lot of time down there.

"I'd appreciate it if you two," the chief paused and pointed at Sam and Ben, "would follow me down to the station so we can chat for a while longer?" He looked over at Nicki and Matt. "And you two should go home. Find something else to do besides talk about murder. It isn't healthy."

He nodded at them and put his hands into his jacket pockets before turning on his heel and walking toward his cruiser.

Nicki looked up at Matt. "Nice work, Dr. Watson."

Matt laughed. "Elementary, Sherlock. Although I think that's usually Sherlock's line." He gazed after the chief. "So what would you like to do? Something healthy?"

She followed his gaze and watched Chief Turnlow climb into his cruiser. "I'd like to go back home and update the murder board."

"Something unhealthy then. Okay, Sherlock. Let's go talk murder."

CHAPTER TEN

"How did you know that was Sherlock's line?"

Nicki slid half of the thickly sliced and grilled sandwich onto the plate in front of Matt, and the other half onto her own. He took in a deep appreciative sniff before grinning at her.

"That looks and smells amazing, what's in it?"

She leaned her elbows on the counter and rested her chin on her raised hands. "Bread, cheese, turkey and apple butter. Do you want me to write out the recipe for you?"

Matt picked it up and admired the cheese dripping over the sides of the thick slices of bread before taking a big bite. Closing his eyes, he chewed slowly, making a humming noise in the back of his throat. "If the kitchen renovation Maxie did helped you to cook like this, I might pay for another one." He looked around. "What else do you need?"

"Nothing," Nicki laughed. "And for your information, Mathew Dillon, I cooked like this before Maxie had the kitchen redone. Now I'm just doing it in the new surroundings."

"A happy cook is a better cook." Matt took another huge bite of his sandwich.

Nicki eyed the last bit of her creation that he still held in his hand, amazed he'd managed to down the whole thing in a couple of bites. Especially after he'd nearly burst at the seams from eating hamburgers all morning. Shaking her head at how much food Matt could consume, she silently switched her plate for his. He looked at it and sighed.

"You need to eat that. You hardly eat much anyway, and haven't had anything since breakfast. And that probably was one bite of a muffin and a cup of coffee." He glanced at her coffee maker. "Although you do make really superior coffee."

She smiled at the sincerity in his voice. "I make really superior everything and paid a lot of money to be sure I could. Culinary school wasn't cheap." She leaned forward again on the counter. "And I did have something to eat at the diner. I tried that last hamburger that you and Jenna declared the winner."

Matt grinned. "Actually, Jenna said it was better than Eddie's, but close enough to get by. I didn't have any idea if it was close or not. I just thought it was good."

"And you couldn't eat another bite," Nicki laughed. "You'd both turned green."

"Well, I had a lot more bites than the single one that you bothered to take." He shoved the plate with the half sandwich toward Nicki.

She pushed it right back. "Think of it as a bribe."

Matt eyed her suspiciously. "Bribe for what? And if you're using a food bride, it's probably something I'm not going to like."

"I only want you to answer the question."

"What question?"

Nicki's mouth twitched at the corners. Matt was clearly

stalling. "How did you know that 'elementary' was more Sherlock's line than Watson's?

A faint red stain crept up the editor's cheeks. "That? Everybody knows that."

"Not unless they've read the books, or at least seen one of the Sherlock Holmes movies, which you told me you hadn't." Nicki's eyes sparkled with amusement as the red on Matt's cheeks got deeper. "Did you do something incredibly sweet by reading a book that I told you about?"

"I read a lot," Matt mumbled. When Nicki continued to smile at him, he sighed. "Okay. I did pick up one or two."

"And which one or two would that have been?" Nicki asked sweetly, enjoying how adorable he looked when he was clearly embarrassed to be caught in something so innocent as reading a Sherlock Holmes novel.

"*A Study in Scarle*t and *The Sign of the Four*." Matt shrugged. "I thought I'd try them in order."

"It's a good thought." Nicki pointed to the sandwich. "I'd say you earned that." When he shook his head, she reached over to her knife block and pulled out one of the smaller ones. She cut the remaining sandwich in half, picked up one piece and pushed the plate back to Matt. "Here, we'll compromise."

He looked at the quarter sandwich and then back up at her. "Compromise in a relationship is always a good thing."

Nicki blinked. *Relationship? As in friends?* But the tone in his voice and the look in his eyes wasn't saying "friends".

The sound of her front door opening echoed down the short hallway to the kitchen.

"Hey? Saw your car out front. Where are you two?"

"Brace yourself," Nicki warned in a whisper before raising her voice. "We're in the kitchen, Jenna."

In the next second the door slammed shut, rattling on its

hinges, and was followed by the slap of flip-flops hitting the floorboards. Jenna appeared in the doorway, dressed in her usual attire of tight jeans and a baggy sweatshirt. Her long kinky hair was pulled into an unruly ponytail at the nape of her neck.

"Why didn't you call when you got here?" She spied the sandwich and gaped at Matt. "You have got to be kidding me?"

Matt grinned. "I'm a growing boy."

"Who apparently can eat his weight in food every twenty-four hours," Jenna shook her head before switching her gaze to Nicki.

"Well? Did you find the stamp?"

"No. Unfortunately we didn't."

"Yoo hoo? Nicki, dear, are you here? Your door's wide open."

"Now all we're missing is Alex and Ty," Matt observed. He picked up the quarter sandwich and downed it in one bite.

Nicki rolled her eyes at Jenna then walked around the large island, intending to intercept Maxie and make a detour into her office. "We're coming your way, Maxie. We were about to start updating the murder board."

"Splendid. I'll meet you in your office."

"Okay." Nicki looked back over her shoulder. "Are you two coming, or do you need more to eat?"

Jenna made an abrupt about-face and followed Nicki while Matt stepped into line behind her. By the time they'd reached the office, Maxie was there with one hand holding a black marker poised over the large whiteboard.

Making her way to her desk, Nicki took the office chair and swiveled around to face Maxie, while Jenna settled herself on the small sofa. Matt chose to lean against the edge of the desk, next to Nicki.

Maxie beamed at the two of them and then looked over

to smile at Jenna. "So? How did the hamburger mix experiment go this morning?"

"Great," Jenna said. "We have a winner. Suzanne is going to order the meat we need, and whatever else was on Jake's list, and we should be ready to open tomorrow."

"That's wonderful!" Maxie exclaimed. "My Mason called an hour ago. He'll be home the day after tomorrow. They went further up the coast than they'd originally planned. I told him Paul wanted to talk to him, and he wasn't concerned at all about it. He said he'd call the chief and let him know about the delay. My Mason even said that talking to Paul would give him a chance to find out the inside scoop about what was going on."

Nicki smiled. Maxie calling the Soldoff Chief of Police by his given name of "Paul", was a good sign that myMason had managed to rid his wife of her anxieties. And with Jenna back to slamming doors and throwing good-natured digs at Matt, everything was returning to normal. Well. Except for the dead diner owner, the missing stamps, and a murder that was making less and less sense to her.

"So, do we have anything new?" Despite the depressing topic on the board, Maxie's voice held a decidedly cheerful note.

"They didn't find the stamp," Jenna said.

Maxie's face fell. "Oh, that's too bad. I'd hate to think Eddie was murdered for money."

"What do you think he should have been murdered for? Hey!" Matt rubbed the spot on his arm where Nicki had delivered a solid poke with her fingernail.

"Ignore him, Maxie. He's on food overload." Nicki pointed at the board. "The missing stamps should go under motive. Whoever took it was very neat, and knew something about valuable stamps. The stamps, and the special sleeve they were in, were removed from their case which was put back into place behind the wine bottles."

Matt raised a hand and rubbed it across his chin. "That's true. Most thieves would have left the case out after grabbing the stamps and the sleeve." He frowned. "And they knew the stamps were valuable. I didn't. I had to check it out online while we were waiting for the chief and Nicki to find the key to the wine cellar."

"Where was it, by the way?" Jenna asked as Maxie wrote on the board.

"In the file cabinet, under Holland Wine Club." Nicki nodded at her friend. "Jake was waiting in the hallway once for Eddie to get the key, and he heard the file drawer open and close. Which was very strange."

"Why is that, dear?"

Nicki shrugged. "Because the rest of the office was sort of trashed, but the file cabinet didn't look as if it had been touched."

"So the killer must have known where the key was," Jenna said triumphantly. "Who knew that?"

"Jake knew about the wine cellar and generally where the key was, but he didn't know much about the stamps," Matt said. "Eddie never told him about them, other than saying they had a plane on them."

"Or so he says," Jenna declared.

"Yes, that's true. But Roberta knew about the cellar and the stamps, but not where they were, or where the key was hidden," Nicki added so Maxie could note it all on the board. "And she called it 'a stamp'. She didn't know it was a whole sheet, so I'm guessing she's never seen them. She also thought Eddie kept the stamp and the key hidden in the apartment."

"But Ben and Sam knew about the cellar and that the stamps were there, but not exactly where they were hidden, or where to find the basement key." Matt dropped his hand

and looked over at Nicki. "But they did know the value of that sheet of stamps."

"And the bookkeeper might have known, but we haven't had the chance to talk to him yet. He told Maxie that he was too busy to meet with us until tomorrow. Which is also very strange," Nicki said.

"Why is *that* strange?" Jenna asked.

"He can't be delayed because of his business," Maxie chimed in from her place in front of the board. "He doesn't have many clients. At least not in Soldoff." She shrugged at Nicki's questioning look. "He's a nice mild man, but has never had much energy for building his business. He prefers to sit on his porch or stroll around the square. It wouldn't surprise me if Eddie was his biggest client."

"Then he's not showing much interest in what happened to his biggest client," Nicki pointed out. "That's why he's going on the list."

Maxie turned around and started writing, although Nicki smiled when her landlady put the "nice and mild" Gordon Twill at the bottom. Even below Sam and Ben, who Nicki knew Maxie liked very much.

"So what we've learned is that no one knew all the pieces to be able to steal the stamps." Matt smiled at Nicki. "Is there anything else, Sherlock?"

"Indeed there is, Watson."

Jenna groaned. "Maybe we could cut down on the cuteness and get on with listing out the clues?"

Nicki laughed. "Certainly. So murders are either about money or relationships or simply for the thrill of it." She smiled at Maxie's stare. "I've gleaned that much from reading mysteries all my life."

"I don't think this was a thrill killing," Jenna said slowly. "At least I hope it wasn't."

"It wasn't," Nicki assured her. "Otherwise the apartment

wouldn't have been torn apart along with the office." She glanced over at the board. "What we know is that Eddie was either attacked or killed in his office and then put into the freezer. And that the killer took his apartment key and his cell phone." Nicki started ticking off points on her fingers. "His office was neatly searched, and his apartment was very violently ransacked. Eddie didn't like to spend money, but he did have a valuable sheet of stamps. The stamps are missing, and the wine cellar wasn't broken into, or look as if it had been searched. Eddie also had an oddly distant relationship with his long-standing girlfriend. At least he didn't seem to tell her much. And according to her, they'd recently broken up."

Nicki raised another finger. "He had a bookkeeper he'd known most of his life who doesn't act interested in his murder, and two fellow stamp collectors that he let in on a lot of the secrets he'd never told either his girlfriend or his assistant manager. Even though that assistant manager has worked in the diner for more than a decade. And not one of these people had all the answers on how to find the stamps and the key to the wine cellar."

Matt nodded as he listened and studied the board. "Which means the only relationship he had that might be worth murdering someone about, was with his girlfriend. And with everyone else, or maybe someone we haven't heard about yet, it would be about those stamps and money. Or maybe one of them is named in the will?" He looked around the room at all the shrugs that followed his question.

"We think a nephew back East is the beneficiary. The chief is checking it out, but as far as I know, he hasn't found the actual will yet," Nicki said.

Matt blew out a breath. "I don't think the diner is worth much. I say we follow the real money. And that means the stamps."

"And how do you propose we do that, Watson?" Jenna asked. "The stamp is gone, and we can't go snooping into people's bank accounts." Jenna grinned. "Well I could give it a try, but that would be totally illegal."

"The chief can get bank records," Maxie declared. "We just need to give him a reason to go looking at someone in particular."

"Oh gosh, is that all?" Nicki muttered under her breath. She'd laid her cell phone on her desk, and when it rang, she looked over at the caller ID. "It's Alex," she announced to the room as she picked it up and tapped the answer icon. "Hey, Alex. I have you on speaker and everyone's here. Did you make it home okay?"

"Yes, I did. But I dropped by Dr. Tom's office before I came home. I thought I'd left my coat there."

Nicki grinned. "Oh really? Did you find it?"

"No," Alex's voice breezed along. "But Dr. Tom did mention that he'd sent his preliminary autopsy results on the Eddie Parker murder to Chief Turnlow. I guess it was very air-sucking, on top of being a chilling report."

"That's interesting." Nicki paused for a brief moment. "Did the coroner happen to have any other descriptive observations about his report?"

"No, there was nothing else. Just those," Alex said. "Apparently the report was a knock-out blow. First it was breathless and then chilling to read. But it would be quick. You'd be done around nine, give or take an hour."

"I'll have to drop by the police department and see if he'll share it with me," Nicki said.

"You do that. I have to go, I'm due at the hospital in a couple of hours, but I'll call you again later tonight. Will you be home?"

Wondering what else Alex had to tell her that she didn't want to say in front of the whole group, Nicki assured her friend she'd be home and to call any time. Alex said she'd do that before she clicked off.

Matt chuckled. "Not much of a code, Connors. I take it that the blow to his head knocked Eddie out and then he..." His words trailed off when Nicki shot a very obvious sideways glance at Jenna.

The computer nerd had gone pale, and her arms were wrapped around her middle. She licked her lips as she stared at the floor. "And then he froze to death." She raised her gaze to meet Matt's. "That's what you were going to say, wasn't it? That he froze to death?"

"It's supposed to be a painless way to die." Matt clamped his mouth shut when he realized he wasn't helping matters much. A sheen of moisture had appeared in Jenna's eyes.

"Then you don't know much about freezing to death, Matt. It's a horrible way to die." Jenna's voice trembled. "I grew up in Nebraska. I know what happens when you freeze to death."

Matt ran a hand through his hair, leaving the usual strands sticking straight up. "It isn't your fault, Jenna. You couldn't have found him in time to save him."

"You can't know that." Her gaze returned to the floor. "Neither can I."

"But I do." Nicki got up and walked over to sit beside Jenna. "You know how precise Alex is. She listed the causes of death in order, which was breath-sucking and chilling."

Jenna's brows beetled together. "So it was too cold to breathe, and Eddie froze to death."

"No," Nicki corrected laying a hand over the two Jenna had clasped in her lap. "Eddie's freezer was old and didn't keep as cold as it needed to be. So he used a lot more dry ice than most commercial freezers usually have."

"Oh. That's why Alex said breathless. Makes sense." Matt nodded. When Jenna shook her head and lifted her shoulders, he added, "dry ice gives off a lot of carbon dioxide. If you're around dry ice too long in a small sealed room, you could suffocate to death."

"Which is what Alex was saying," Nicki confirmed. "Eddie died before he froze. And long before you arrived the next morning. Alex said about nine that night, give or take an hour."

"Oh." Jenna looked up. She was silent a long moment before she slowly nodded. "Then I guess the best I can do for him is to help get him justice."

Nicki smiled and gave Jenna's arm a gentle pat while she exchanged a long look with Matt. He nodded his understanding.

Finding justice for Eddie would be a lot easier said than done.

CHAPTER ELEVEN

AN HOUR LATER, NICKI WALKED BACK INTO THE townhouse and shut the door behind her. She'd just left Jenna, who was going to settle into her own mini home office and dive into a web design, when Alex had called. The conversation had been brief and to the point, leaving Nicki feeling daunted with the task in front of her.

On the short walk from Jenna's, she'd decided a good glass of wine might be the perfect thing to help her think it through, so she headed straight back to the kitchen. And stopped dead in her tracks when she saw Matt sitting on a tall stool and leaning back against his elbows, which were planted on top of the island's counter.

"I thought you'd left with Maxie." Nicki smiled when Matt picked up a half-full wine glass and held it out to her.

"Nope. I wanted to stick around and hear what Alex didn't want to talk about in front of everyone."

Nicki sighed. She should have known Matt would pick up on that. Not much got by him. "She just wanted to let me know that Jenna is counting on this whole 'justice for Eddie' thing more than she's letting on. Finding his body has really shaken her up."

Matt nodded. "I'd have to agree with that. I'm sorry I upset her by tossing out there how he died."

"It's okay. You wouldn't be able to tell how on edge this has made her. She puts on a good front."

"This whole 'justice for Eddie' thing puts a lot on you." Matt's eyes were troubled. "What if the killer isn't found? What happens then?"

"It doesn't matter because it isn't going to happen." Nicki looked over at the far wall. A picture of her mother standing with Nicki on the day she'd graduated from culinary school hung in the center, and was flanked by Nicki's diploma. "Jenna and Alex helped me through the worst period in my life. I'd never let either of them down."

"But some things can't be done, Nicki," Matt said quietly. "And that shouldn't be on you."

She knew that. Whoever had killed her mom had never been caught. But that was New York City, and this was Soldoff. She'd figure it out, or help the chief so he could figure it out. Either way it would be justice for Eddie and peace for Jenna. That was her first priority.

"Fine." Matt nodded as if she'd spoken out loud. "We'll just have to find this guy. And toward that end, in all the excitement of searching the basement-turned-into-a-wine-cellar, I forgot to mention something Ben and Sam said."

Nicki perched herself on the stool next to Matt's and took a sip of her wine. "What was that?"

"Well, apparently the last time they were in that cellar and saw those stamps, there was a fourth person there."

Her eyes widened. "What? Who?"

"Sam mentioned that his friend from Maryland had been visiting and was lucky enough to get an invitation to join them in the wine cellar the night before he flew home. Eddie had the stamps out to show him, since this friend is a pretty prominent stamp collector."

"When did this happen?"

Matt grinned. "I asked Sam that very same thing, and he said about two weeks before Eddie was murdered."

And Sam has never said a word? She could not believe it. "Did he tell Chief Turnlow about this friend of his?"

"I asked him that too, and he said, 'No. Should I?' I assured him he should, so I imagine the chief heard about it when he talked with both of them at the station."

"That leaves us two more people to talk to tomorrow, after we meet Mr. Gordon Twill at the diner." Nicki made a mental note to call Maxie later and ask her how to find Sam and Ben during the day.

"The accountant?" Matt asked.

"Bookkeeper," Nicki corrected. "Maxie says an accountant costs a lot more. According to Roberta, he was at the diner the day of the murder. Jenna said Eddie had an appointment that evening, and I'm hoping Mr. Twill will know who it was that Eddie was supposed to meet with."

"Sounds good. Unless this bookkeeper is the killer. In which case, you definitely should not be alone with the guy."

"I'll make sure I tell him that a dozen people know I am meeting with him."

Matt nodded. "That's good. And I'll make sure he knows that I'm sitting in the corner, drinking coffee and watching him."

Nicki barely stopped herself from rolling her eyes. "It won't do any good if he has a gun. He'll just shoot both of us."

"Oh, yeah. Let's put that mental image out there. You alone in a diner with a man who has a gun. That makes me feel much better." Matt looked over at the counter as Nicki's phone went off, playing the tune of *She's So Far Away*.

Nicki let it ring several times before picking it up. Giving Matt an apologetic look, she tapped the answer button. She was surprised when Matt didn't get up and leave the room the way he always did whenever Rob called. Usually when the ringtone she'd assigned to her boyfriend sounded, Matt was out the door before the second bar of the song. But this time he stayed firmly planted on the stool and crossed his arms over his chest.

"Hi, Rob."

"Nicki? I'm glad I caught you." Rob's smooth voice came through the speaker. "Listen babe. I'm sorry to disappoint you, and me too, but I won't be able to make our dinner date at the end of the week. This business trip has..."

Since Rob barely made half their dinner dates due to his extensive travel as the assistant wine buyer for the Catalan House chain of restaurants, Nicki automatically tuned him out. She made an occasional sound of agreement as he went into a long explanation for why he had to break their date.

"How's everything going with you? I haven't heard from you in a couple of days. Is everything all right?"

It took a moment for Rob's question to register. "Everything's fine, Rob. I've just been busy planning out those cooking classes we've talked about, and trying to keep up with my other work."

"Okay, babe. We're good then? I'll give you a call in a day or so, when I have a better handle on my schedule."

Nicki smiled. "That's fine, Rob. I'll wait to hear from you. Bye." She clicked off before he could say anything more, and raised an eyebrow at a grinning Matt.

"What's so funny, Dillon?"

"Oh nothing. I just wondered if you thought dead bodies and murder were simply another part of your other work?"

Nicki reached over and grabbed a napkin from the holder on the counter. She wadded it up in one hand and threw it at

Matt's chest. "It's rude to listen in on other people's telephone conversations."

"It's rude to answer the phone when you're talking to someone else," Matt countered.

She wrinkled her nose and considered that for a moment. "Very true. I apologize."

Matt shook his head. "I guess Rob broke another date?"

"Yes, he did." Nicki made a small pathetic noise to go along with her dramatic sigh. "And to think I not only had to apologize to you, but I'm out a dinner as well."

He smiled. "Maybe you could fix that last part by making dinner here?"

He sounded so hopeful that Nicki had to laugh. "Fine. But I can't believe you're hungry after all you've had to eat today."

"Me neither, but I am." Matt looked over toward the refrigerator. "And I'll be happy to eat anything you want to make."

She hopped off her stool. "Okay. But be careful with that kind of statement. You never know just what a chef might have in her fridge." She gave him a sunny smile. "I think I have a package of white ant eggs in the freezer, if you'd please get it out and put it in a bowl of water."

Matt made a strange gagging noise. "You're kidding?"

Nicki grinned at him. "I am. But I could make something with them, if I actually had the ants." She put her hands on her hips and gave him an exaggerated blink of her eyes. "And I just might serve the soup up first, and tell you what was in it later, if you keep eavesdropping on my phone calls."

He ignored that threat and gave her a fascinated look. "I have a food magazine and I've never heard of ant egg soup. Is that a real thing?"

"It certainly is. Very popular in Thailand. We'll have to go there and try it sometime." Nicki flashed a smile before turning around and opening her refrigerator.

"That sounds like a good plan," Matt said softly.

CHAPTER TWELVE

THE NEXT MORNING, MATT WAS BACK ON HER DOORSTEP bright and early. Nicki greeted him with a cheerful smile and a heavenly smelling cup of coffee.

"My prayers have been answered." Matt grabbed the to-go cup and waved it under his nose. He closed his eyes as he inhaled the rich scent. "I thought we'd have to stop at Starbucks."

Nicki made a sour face. "Starbucks? Why? Do you want some kind of caramel substitute in your coffee?"

Matt shook his head. "No. But after bullying you into making dinner last night, I wasn't about to demand coffee this morning."

She smiled. It was just like Matt to think his request for dinner, accompanied by those adorable "puppy eyes" that had been magnified behind the lenses of his glasses, qualified as "bullying". She doubted if the man had any idea how to go about something like that.

"It wasn't a problem. I was going to make a meal for myself anyway. Despite what you think, Mr. Dillon, I do eat on a regular basis." She frowned when he headed for his rental car. "We can take my car."

He laughed. "Nicki, no one wants to ride in your car. Not if they want a better than fifty-fifty chance of getting to where they want to go." He opened the passenger side door and waited for her. "And no matter what the weather, both the heater and the air conditioner in this car works."

Thinking that really was a plus since it was promising to be a very typically warm California day, Nicki murmured "thanks" and climbed in, settling herself into the plush seat of the high-end SUV that Matt typically rented.

"Speaking of your car," Matt started.

Nicki cut him off with a wave of her hand. "We aren't speaking of my car. And no, you aren't going to give me a huge advance so I can buy a new one."

"I wasn't talking about an advance." Matt didn't look at her but kept his eyes straight-ahead as he maneuvered the SUV around the cul-de-sac before heading out the long driveway toward the road. "Since you always refuse to take one."

"That's good. Because I already have a plan to look for a new car next spring." At least she hoped so. As long as the sales for her spy novels held up, and her blog continued to grow, she should stay on track to be out looking at cars at about the same time new vines would be planted all over Sonoma Valley.

"Another used car?"

Matt didn't sound happy, but since that's what she could afford, he'd just have to learn to live with it.

"Maxie didn't want to come with us to talk with Gordon?" Nicki changed the subject to something that wouldn't lead to an argument. It was too nice a morning for one, with the sun already shining brightly overhead, painting the sky a brilliant blue.

"She had genealogy work she needed to get done and thought you'd do fine on the interviews without her." He shrugged. "Provided I behaved."

"Which is good advice," Nicki said as the bright yellow diner came into view.

"Uh huh. What time is this Twill person supposed to be at the diner?" Matt turned into the parking lot where the only other vehicle was the battered pickup truck that Jake drove.

Nicki glanced at her watch. "In about ten minutes." She unsnapped her seat belt and hopped out of the car before Matt could get to her side to open the door. Their old-fashioned manners were something he and Rob had in common, although she doubted if Matt would welcome any kind of comparison with the Catalan House wine buyer. *And it's probably the only way that they are alike*, Nicki admitted to herself.

They walked into the diner together. Nicki scanned the room but didn't see any sign of Jake. And if the assistant manager was in the kitchen, he was in a spot that wasn't visible from the pass-through window. But she could definitely see that the door to the walk-in freezer was wide open. A tremor of nerves mixed with fear raced down her back and arms.

"Hello?" Matt called out. "Are you around somewhere, Jake?"

Relief flooded through Nicki when Jake's head appeared around the edge of the freezer door.

"Hey! I was just getting out some hamburger buns." He stepped out into the kitchen, a large plastic bag in one hand, and closed the freezer door. "We'll have to use our emergency stash since we aren't getting a bread delivery for another two days. I had to call most of our vendors to get us put back on their schedules."

Nicki walked over to the long counter and set her purse

down. She smiled at Jake when he came through the double doors. "How did the diner get off the delivery schedules?"

"I guess they got a call from Gordon, since he pays the bills."

Matt frowned. "That was fast for a guy who hasn't shown up here since his client was murdered."

Jake winced and hunched his shoulders. "Didn't surprise me any. Eddie always said Gordon was the most organized person he knew. And like you said, he hasn't been around, so he didn't know we were planning to reopen." He looked past Matt and nodded. "Well, I guess he can hear all about it now. He just pulled up."

Nicki turned around and walked closer to the front window as Gordon Twill exited his small, very practical compact car. Short and lean, the bookkeeper had jet black hair and narrow shoulders. He carefully locked his car before walking toward the front door, carrying a thick book that Nicki thought was an old-school day planner. She stepped back quickly to stand next to Matt, who grinned at her.

"Nothing like grilled meat for breakfast."

She shook her head at Jake's snort of laughter and pressed a quick elbow into Matt's side. "Remember what Maxie told you and behave."

"No promises," Matt whispered back just as the door opened and Gordon Twill stepped inside.

The short man, dressed in a pair of khaki pants that had clearly been pressed, and a neat tan shirt with a collar, stopped short at the sight of three people staring at him.

He rubbed his free hand against the side of his pant leg before politely inclining his head at Nicki. "Ms. Connors?"

Nicki stepped forward, her hand out in the traditional greeting of an offered handshake. "Mr. Twill. And please call me Nicki."

"Gordon," came the automatic response as the bookkeeper's gaze jumped to Matt.

"This is Matt Dillon. He's the editor of an on-line magazine and a good friend."

Matt stepped forward and held out his hand. "A very good friend."

As Gordon reluctantly shook hands, Nicki made a mental note to talk to Matt about sounding as if he were her protector. She appreciated his concern, but she didn't need one, and was getting a little exasperated that he clearly thought she did.

Deciding to take charge of the interview before Gordon flew off in fear from Matt's unblinking stare, she pointed to the nearest table. "Shall we sit and be comfortable while we talk?" She smiled at Matt. "Maybe Jake could show you how to make coffee in the machine over on the counter?"

Her editor rolled his eyes at her blatant hint for a little privacy with the bookkeeper, but nodded anyway. "What do you take in your coffee, Gordon?"

"Just a teaspoon of sugar and a dollop of cream. Thank you."

"Sure."

Matt strolled off and Nicki could almost hear him asking himself what in the world a "dollop" was.

Deciding to start with her newest piece of information, Nicki gave Gordon a friendly smile. "I'm glad to finally meet you, Gordon. Maxie told me you've been Eddie Parker's bookkeeper since he opened his diner."

The slightly built man sat ramrod straight in his seat across the table from her. "That's right. Jake and I both have been with the diner from the very start."

Thinking all that was missing to complete the picture Gordon Twill made with his rigid posture and straight-ahead stare, was the glare from a low-hanging overhead light and a pair of handcuffs, Nicki tried to keep her voice and smile as casual as she could manage.

"Speaking of Jake, he just told us you'd canceled the scheduled deliveries from the vendors?"

Gordon nodded. "That's right. No use in getting more food that will never be used. Those expenses can add up very fast, and there won't be any more money coming in. Until the assets are sold, of course."

"Of course," Nicki agreed. The bookkeeper wasn't acting too upset over his longtime client's demise.

"Well, it may have been a little premature since we're opening the diner again."

Gordon's head jerked back. "Who made that decision?"

"Maxie did, for the most part. But quite a few of her friends are helping out. And Jake says the whole staff will be back too."

"The whole staff? Including Roberta?"

Nicki tilted her head to one side. "You sound surprised?"

He cleared his throat and leaned back in his chair. "Well... that is, I would have thought as his girlfriend and his long-time employee, she'd be too upset to return to work this soon."

As his longtime bookkeeper and someone who's known Eddie most of his life, I would have said the same about you, Nicki thought, but she kept that to herself.

The bookkeeper cleared his throat again and glanced around the room. "There are other problems with keeping the diner open." At Nicki's questioning look, he slanted his head toward the kitchen. "Only Eddie knew what went into that hamburger mix of his that made it so special."

"Nicki's managed to duplicate it," Matt said, setting a cup of coffee in front of Gordon. He didn't stay around for a response but headed back to the counter while Gordon stared into the black cup of coffee in front of him.

"You duplicated the mix?" he repeated slowly.

"Yes, I did. Or at least close to it." Nicki smiled. "It's difficult to exactly match something that good. Eddie certainly made an exceptional hamburger."

Gordon ignored her and looked around the room again. "It isn't just the hamburger mixture, but it's also the inspections."

"What inspections?"

He was back to sitting on the edge of his chair with his back stiff and his chin tilted upward. "The fire inspection is in a couple of days, and Eddie's the only one who's ever done that walk-through with the county inspector. There's also a health department and a building inspection. They aren't due for several months, but given what happened here, I wouldn't be surprised if there wasn't an unscheduled visit from either one very soon." His head bobbed up and down. "I mean, there was a dead body in the freezer."

"I emptied the freezer and scrubbed every inch of it," Jake called out from the seat he'd taken at the counter. "I called the county health inspector and asked him what I should do, and then did exactly what he said."

Matt was back at their table and carrying a bowl of sugar and a basket filled with small plastic cups of creamer. "I wasn't sure what a dollop was." He set them both in front of the bookkeeper before retreating again to take a seat next to Jake at the counter.

"I'm sure it will be fine," Nicki said before abruptly switching gears. "Roberta told us that you were here at the dinner the day Eddie was killed."

She pretended not to notice that Gordon's hand resting on the table jerked in response.

"Roberta said that?"

Nodding, Nicki kept her gaze on his face. "Was she wrong?"

"No. No. I was here." He sighed and ran a hand through his neatly combed hair and then immediately patted it back into place. "The chief already asked me all about that."

"Oh, good." Nicki added additional wattage to her smile and leaned slightly forward. "Then it shouldn't be any trouble to tell me what you told the chief."

"Why should I do that?"

She smiled. "Because the chief said I was a consultant on this case." She reached for her cell phone and held it up. "I can call the chief and you can talk to him about it, if you'd like?"

Gordon stared at her hand as if she was holding a deadly snake rather than a phone. "No. No. I'm sure it's fine." He picked up a cup of the creamer and peeled back the lid. "What was your question?"

Nicki had been certain the bookkeeper wouldn't like talking to the chief. She set her phone on the table and folded her hands in front of her. "You were at the diner the day your client was killed?"

"Just for a short while. I stopped by in the early afternoon to drop off a few checks for Eddie to sign." He peered down his nose at Nicki. "I believe one of them was for that friend of yours? To do the completely unnecessary website for the diner."

"I'll let Jenna know she can expect a check soon," Nicki said, sidestepping his comment about the website. She didn't want to get into a debate with the man. "Did you stay and have a hamburger?"

"No." Gordon looked horrified. "I don't eat that way. I was only here fifteen minutes or so. I had an engagement that evening."

She nodded her understanding. "Running your own business does call for a lot of late hours, doesn't it?"

He cleared his throat, which seemed to be an odd habit of

his. "Yes, it can. But as it happens, my engagement that evening was social, not professional."

"You had a date?"

His back stiffened even more. "It is the common way for single people to interact with each other, and yes, I had a date. We had dinner at Mario's. I arrived back at my house around ten p.m. Is that a thorough enough explanation for you?"

Not put off in the least by Gordon's stiffly delivered response, Nicki filed the information away and moved on. "Did you know Eddie had an appointment that evening?"

"No. Since it obviously didn't involve me, why should I?"

"Did you have any other appointments with Eddie?"

Gordon made a show of opening the book he'd brought with him. Even from across the table Nicki could see it was indeed a day planner. She could also see that most of the pages Gordon flipped through were empty.

"No," the bookkeeper finally said. "No other appointments." He carefully closed the book and looked up. "But then we rarely made appointments. I had a standing meeting with Eddie once a month, to go over his accounts. Other than that, I usually stopped by for a few minutes whenever I had something which needed his signature."

"Like the checks?"

"Yes. Like the checks."

Nicki thought it over for a moment. "Did you pay all of Eddie's bills?"

"Yes. I paid the bills, kept track of the expenses, prepared the paperwork for his taxes," Gordon said. "The standard duties for a bookkeeper."

"His personal bills and taxes too?"

"Yes, those too. And there was nothing unusual about any of it, Ms. Connors. No large expenses, no unexplained income or payments. Nothing out of the ordinary at all. Not for this year, or last year, or the year before that. And I won't divulge anything else about his personal finances."

Hoping to catch him by surprise, she jumped to another topic. "Do you know who will inherit the diner?"

Gordon frowned. "His nephew, I guess. But Eddie told me that a long time ago." He took a sip of his coffee then set the cup down and reached for the sugar bowl. "I'm not the executor, which wouldn't be proper since I would be paying the bills and probably much of the final settlements. And I've never actually seen a copy of his will. I told the chief that I thought he must have kept it in his safe in the office, or maybe somewhere in his apartment. He never told me where it was. All I know is that he mentioned his nephew, although I've certainly never met the man. And I have no idea whether or not Eddie'd even seen him in the last decade or two."

"Did you know that Eddie collected stamps?" Nicki asked, trying for another dramatic switch in topics.

"Yes. You couldn't be around him for more than an hour without him telling you all about it. And I know he had a valuable stamp of some sort." He started to rise. "If there's nothing else?"

"That valuable stamp is missing, "Nicki said quietly, sticking to referring to the sheet as a single stamp, the way Gordon had.

"You're jumping to conclusions," the bookkeeper said. He was now standing next to the table, his appointment book clutched to his chest. "The chief told me it hadn't yet been found in the apartment. But from what Roberta said, the place was a complete mess. So it may turn up soon."

Nicki stood as well. "One more question, Gordon." She smiled when he hesitated before nodding at her. "Did you know about Eddie's wine cellar?"

"You mean his basement with wine racks around the walls?" Gordon lifted his thin shoulders up and down. "I know that's why he bought this building. He wanted a base-ment where he could store wine. I was also down there once." He shuddered slightly. "It was dark and very dusty. Now, I really do have other business I need to see to."

She held out her hand again. "Thank you for your time, Gordon. I'm sorry we met under such horrible circumstances."

Gordon slowly reached out and gave her hand one quick shake. "Yes. Well. Be sure to tell Ms. Lindstrom that I'll have her check in the mail in just a few days. I know the two of you are friends."

Matt walked over to stand by Nicki as the bookkeeper made his way out the door.

"Eddie's bookkeeper has a couple of serious issues."

Nicki tipped her head back and looked up at him. "Most numbers guys aren't very good with people." She grinned. "Kind of like engineers."

"Former engineer. And there's always an exception. No, I was talking about him having the hots for Roberta."

Startled, Nicki had a sudden coughing fit. "Why do you say that?"

Matt shrugged. "Just going by the look on his face when you mentioned her name." He rubbed the side of his jaw. "Didn't the murder board say Roberta left work early that day because she had a date?"

Nicki certainly hadn't connected those dots, but she could see how the very logical, ex-engineer Matt would. "That would be simple enough to check. How do you feel about having lunch at Mario's?"

He glanced at his watch. "It's a little early, but I could eat something."

"I meant after we paid a visit to Sam. His shop should be open by now. Maxie said he opens at eleven."

"Nice hours if you can get them," Matt said. "Okay, Sherlock, let's go."

Nicki turned and waved at Jake. "We have another stop to make. Will you be okay here by yourself?"

"I've been here by myself a lot of times, so don't you worry. Mrs. Suzanne is going to be by soon, and we're going to go over her checklist to be sure everything is ready to open the doors for business again."

Nicki smiled at his enthusiasm. It was clear that Jake cared a lot about the diner. "Call me if you need anything at all."

Jake nodded and waved them out the door. Matt also raised his hand in farewell before following Nicki outside. She was standing still, with her face turned up to the sunshine.

"It feels good." She glanced over only to find his intense stare on her face. "What? Is something wrong?"

He shook his head. "Not a thing."

CHAPTER THIRTEEN

LESS THAN TEN MINUTES LATER MATT MANEUVERED THE
SUV into a parking spot along the main square. He rested his
hands on the wheel and turned sideways to look at his
passenger.

"You're quiet."

"Just thinking about what to ask Sam."

"Uh huh. You got quite a bit out of Gordon Twill."

Nicki pursed her lips together. "What did you mean when
you said Gordon had a couple of social issues? You mentioned
his crush on Roberta. What was the other one?"

"I don't think he could tell a lie if he was tortured into it."
At Nicki's exasperated look, Matt shrugged. "A guy should
know that he can tell a little white lie when it's necessary. But
Gordon didn't seem to get that gene."

She had to agree. The bookkeeper could definitely use a
lesson or two on how to be friendly, but he didn't strike Nicki
as a liar. She wondered what Chief Turnlow thought about
the interview he'd conducted with the man. She'd have to
remember to ask him.

"Now I want to know something. Where did you learn to bluff like that?"

Matt's question brought Nicki right out of her own thoughts. "Bluff? What bluff?"

He laughed. "When you told Gordon that the chief had made you a consultant on this case. That bluff."

Nicki lifted her nose up a little higher and gave a loud sniff. "I didn't lie, Mr. Dillon. The chief did say that. When he and I were walking through Eddie's apartment." She gave up the pretense of being offended and grinned. "He really did. You can call and ask him if you don't believe me."

"Oh, I believe you, Connors." He opened the car door and put one foot on the ground. "You don't lie very well either."

"And I suppose you do?" Nicki hopped out of her side of the car and threw the question over the roof of the SUV.

Matt didn't say a word as he walked around the car and grabbed her hand to tuck it into the crook of his arm. "That will keep you from jabbing me with one of your fingernails. And to answer your question, yeah. I'm sure I'm a much better liar than you are. But..." he hastily added when her free hand came up and she pointed a slender finger with a well-manicured nail at his chest. "I've never seen the point to it, so I don't bother."

Nicki lowered her hand. "Good answer, Mr. Dillon."

"Thank you. Now which way is this gift shop that Sam owns?"

"Around the corner and off one of the shop alleyways." Nicki and Matt walked companionably side by side. "I've been in Tasteful & Tacky several times. It's a wonderfully cute shop."

"So is that name." Matt's dry tone had Nicki laughing.

It only took two minutes to reach the shop, tucked into the bend of one of the fashionable "alleys" that ran off of the town square. Its most notable features were a snow-white awning and a door painted in a vivid eye-catching orange. A bell over the entrance tinkled softly when they entered the shop that was lined with shelves featuring unique and whimsical table toppers, along with small display items to meet every decorating taste. Sam looked up and smiled from his seat behind a wide counter that spanned the entire back of the shop.

"I was expecting you two. Maxie called and informed me that I'm to tell you everything I told the chief, and anything I forgot to tell him."

Nicki grinned. "That was thorough of her."

"Yes it was, wasn't it? But I'd expect nothing less from a world-renown genealogist." He pointed to a curtain in back of him. "Let's go into my office and be more comfortable. I'll hear the bell if someone comes in."

He held the curtain aside for them, then let it fall back into place as he made a straight line over to a chair in front of a desk that was more of an antique writing desk than something that fit the sleek laptop sitting on its highly polished surface. Matt and Nicki sat together on the small sofa that took up one wall of the cozy room.

"So. What can I tell you? I was at home, and quite alone, the night of the murder. Which means I have absolutely no alibi. But then again, I had no reason to kill Eddie either. We were friends."

"You also both collected stamps. What about the right-side-up sheet of the Jenny? Fifty thousand dollars is enough to kill someone for," Matt pointed out.

Sam leaned back and touched his fingertips together in front of his chest. "Yes. There is that. But I had no idea where he hid his stamps. Or where he kept the key to his improvised wine cellar either. And, of course, there's the biggest reason of all that I didn't kill him."

"What's that, Sam?" Nicki asked.

Eddie's longtime friend smiled at her. "I don't have the sheet of stamps." His smile grew wider. "But you'll have to take my word for that. Or you're free to tag along if the chief decides to search my home or shop."

He glanced between the two people on the sofa staring back at him.

"Look. I wouldn't kill for a stamp, or even a sheet of stamps. Much less kill a friend for them. Especially a friend who was as happy as Eddie was the last time I spoke with him. It's a serious challenge to your karma to destroy any kind of happiness in the world."

Nicki laid a hand on Matt's knee as a signal for him to keep quiet. She wanted to let Sam talk. "When was that?"

"Two days before he was murdered." Sam drew in a deep breath. "He was very excited about a trip he was planning on making the following week." He looked at the floor. "Or rather he would have been making this week. He wouldn't tell me anything about it except that it was his dream come true." Sam stopped. His breathing became more ragged as he visibly tried to hold back his emotions. "If I had known he'd be gone two days later, I would have spent every minute camped out at that run-down diner of his."

He lifted his gaze, eyes glittering with unshed tears. "He was so proud of that place. It didn't take much to make Eddie happy. He'd already sold his house and his car, and a lot of his furnishings, and chosen to live in a simple apartment so he could walk to work. He never promised anyone anything he couldn't give, and he never hurt anyone. He was careful with his money, but so are a lot of people. Why would someone hurt a man like that? He didn't have any enemies. This should never have happened."

"No one should be murdered, Sam," Nicki said softly. "What were Eddie's dreams?"

The shop owner took several breaths before he managed

to pull himself together. "I don't know. I thought it was the diner." He looked over at her. "But my friend might know. He and Eddie had quite a conversation about that sheet of stamps, as well as a lot of other stuff according to Drew." Sam shrugged. "Sometimes you're more comfortable talking to a stranger than a friend."

"Drew?"

"My friend who came out to visit." He nodded at Matt. "The one I told you about, who Eddie invited to his wine cellar to show him the stamps?"

The editor nodded but kept his silence. Nicki smiled. Matt Dillon made a great sidekick.

"His name is Drew?"

Sam turned around and grabbed a pen. He did a quick scribble on a piece of paper before getting up from his chair and walking across the room. He handed the scrap of paper to Nicki. "This is his number. We admired those stamps through two bottles of wine, as I recall. Drew is a serious collector, and he expressed a keen interest in buying the stamps. But Eddie said he wouldn't sell them to Drew, which was no surprise to either Ben or me."

"Do you remember the exact date you all gathered in that basement?" Nicki asked.

"Two weeks to the day before Eddie was murdered. We always met on a Monday because it was one of the days that the diner closed early."

The bell from the front room let out its cheerful tinkle. Taking that as their cue of sorts, the three of them stood at once.

Nicki stepped up and gave Sam a hug. "Thank you for talking with us." She smiled when Sam hugged her back.

"I hope you find whoever did this to my friend, so I'll say thank you as well." He stepped back and reached over to shake Matt's hand. He wiggled his eyebrows up and down at the tall editor with the large glasses and barely controlled mop of dark hair. "She's a keeper."

Matt put a hand in the middle of Nicki's back and gave her a gentle nudge. "Yes, she is."

Once they were standing in the alleyway in front of the shop, Matt made a show of looking at his watch.

"Lunch? I think I was promised a stop at Mario's."

"So you were." Nicki slipped her arm through his again and guided him back through the little alleyway lined with shops. "As a thank you for letting me do most of the talking in Sam's shop, I'll buy lunch."

"I only did what a good Watson would do, and no, you aren't."

She glanced up at him. "Why not? This isn't the 1950s, Matt. It's perfectly acceptable for a woman friend to buy you lunch."

"And I'm fine with that," Matt countered. "But I'd rather you put the money into your car fund."

Nicki sighed. When it came to her car, Matt was like a dog with a bone. He just wouldn't let it go.

MARIO'S WAS ONLY a short ten-minute walk around to the opposite side of the square, and five minutes if you took the walk along the flower-lined path directly through the square. Knowing Matt, and his stomach, Nicki headed toward the path, passing by the town's signature ten-foot-tall bronze statue of grapes as she spoke to Tyler, Alex's fiancé, on her phone. Once she'd made the arrangements to meet him at the diner for the fire inspection, she put away her cell and smiled at Matt, who was busy taking in the entire square.

"This town really does have everything you need, doesn't it?" Matt asked as they neared the end of the path. "A neighborly feel during the week, and the big-city bustle of tourists and festivals on the weekends, a coffee place, restaurants, plenty of places to taste wine, and of course the police department, all right here in one convenient location." He grinned at her. "Not to mention the truly wonderful decorative art on public display."

"Ha, ha, Mr. Dillon." Nicki took a quick glance around the square. "Actually, this is a great place to live. And just because you maligned my little town, we'll split the lunch bill." She smiled up at him. "A compromise to keep your masculine ego intact."

"My ego is just fine, thank you very much. It's your car that I take issue with."

"And here's Mario's," Nicki announced in a loud, overly cheerful voice. She wished she knew what subject would distract Matt as easily as she could Rob. *Maybe that's the problem with Rob?* Nicki blinked at the inner voice that had come into her head out of nowhere.

Blinking again, she shook the thought off. She absently nodded her thanks when Matt held open the door to the quaint Italian *ristorante*, with pictures of iconic scenes in Italy on every wall, and named after its owner.

This afternoon Mario was nowhere in sight, but his daughter Lisa was. She greeted Nicki politely and beamed at Matt before leading them to a table next to the front window. She took a few seconds longer than necessary to hand a menu to Matt, but Nicki was used to the hostess flirting with every man she'd ever brought to the restaurant. Lisa practically drooled every time Rob walked through the doors.

The young woman looked disappointed when Matt looked up with a faint smile and said a quick thank you before returning his attention to Nicki, who gave Lisa a sympathetic smile. It wasn't easy to be so totally ignored by the opposite sex. She'd have to talk to the oblivious Matt about that.

"What did you think?"

Nicki yanked her attention away from inadvertently crushing a young woman's self-esteem to focusing on Matt. "Think about what?"

"Sam. And his mysterious friend who saw the stamps just before they disappeared."

"I don't know." She unfolded her napkin and smoothed it out over her lap. "I'll definitely be calling him since I'm sure he's already been forewarned about it. Otherwise Sam wouldn't have given up his number so easily."

"Okay. If that needs time to percolate with you, then how about we discuss Rob?"

Nicki gave her head a slight shake. She couldn't have heard him correctly. "Did you say Rob?" When he nodded, she frowned. "I don't suppose you know another one besides my boyfriend?"

Matt folded his hands in front of him and started tapping his thumbs together. "Nope. He's it." Matt met her wary look with a steady calm in his gaze. "Why doesn't he ever make an appearance whenever you're involved with murder?"

She laughed. "He did. He was there when we both discovered Catherine's body a few months ago. Remember?"

"I remember that he left you standing on her porch to find your own way home, and then got out of town as fast as he could." Matt's jawline hardened. "Not very boyfriend-like behavior."

Wondering what Matt would consider as "boyfriend-like behavior", Nicki gave him a puzzled look. "That's not exactly fair, Matt. I told him to go home. And he has a hectic schedule which I don't think I should interrupt every time I run across a little problem."

"Murder isn't a 'little problem', Nicki."

"Murders in Soldoff also aren't Rob's problem," she pointed out patiently. "And I'm aware of how busy you are too. I don't like interrupting your schedule either."

Matt leaned back in his chair. His hand wrapped around the empty water glass next to the silverware. "You aren't an interruption, Nicki, and that's my point. It shouldn't be an interruption to your boyfriend either."

"Rob and I understand each other, and our relationship, very well." Nicki put a sharp firmness into her voice and hoped that Matt would get the message that this topic was closed.

He adjusted his glasses but kept his gaze on her. "Well, I wish you'd explain it to me."

Nicki sighed. "Rob has always been honest with me, and I've always been the same with him. That's really all I'm going to say on the subject, Matt."

"Fine." Matt clamped his mouth shut as Joe, the friendly waiter who'd served them the last time he and Nicki had been in Mario's, stopped by the table.

He smiled at Nicki. "So, second time here with this guy, and you're already bickering." He shifted his smile to Matt. "Are you two a thing now?"

"Define 'thing'," Matt muttered before settling on a non-committal shrug.

"Seems to be a lot of new couples in town," Joe went on cheerfully. He poured water into their glasses before setting the crystal pitcher on the table and taking out his iPad. "The Marleys have separated, and he's already stepping out with a woman who lives over in Sonoma. And then Roberta and Gordon came in last week. And Lisa might be interested in that young deputy. Maxie was in having lunch with him and made a big point of introducing him to Lisa. What's his name? Bobby?"

"Danny," Nicki supplied. "You said Roberta was in here

with Gordon? Would that be Gordon Twill?" When Joe nodded, she and Matt exchanged a quick look

"Do you remember what day that was?" Matt asked.

"More like early evening, although Gordon was late getting here. Roberta sat by herself for over half an hour. When he finally got here, I heard him making excuses about his car. But it didn't seem to matter much to Roberta. They stayed right here at this table until we closed at nine. And I won't ever forget the day. It was the same day Eddie Parker was killed. I heard about it the next afternoon when I came in for my shift. So it was a week ago, on Monday. I think Mario's is the only sit-down restaurant in town that's open on a Monday. Unless there's a festival going on, of course." He winked at Nicki. "No one wants to miss out on those tourist tips."

"What time were they here?" Nicki asked.

Joe frowned. "Early. But then we close earlier on Mondays than our usual eleven p.m. time. I'm sure Roberta got here about six thirty or so, and Gordon showed up maybe thirty or forty minutes later." He raised his iPad. "So, what can I get for you?"

Once the friendly waiter had retreated with their order, and Matt had done his usual head-shaking at Nicki's choice of soup and a dinner salad over his steak sandwich, he leaned across the table and grinned at her. "I told you Gordon had a thing for Roberta."

"Define 'thing'," Nicki said, echoing Matt's question to their waiter.

"Not the same kind of 'thing' we have."

Nicki rolled her eyes. "Forget about the 'thing' for a moment. Don't you find it odd that the two of them, Eddie's longtime bookkeeper and his longtime girlfriend, had a date on the night he was murdered?"

"If they wanted to go out on a date, they were entitled to.

Didn't the murder board list Roberta and Eddie as having broken up? And if either one of them were worried about Eddie being upset for their date, then wouldn't the best time to go out be when her boyfriend and his client were otherwise engaged? Like in meeting someone else at his diner."

Matt's eyes narrowed. "Maybe it wasn't a business meeting at all. Maybe Eddie was meeting another woman at a place where Roberta wouldn't see them after hours, while she was doing the same with Gordon?"

"Maybe," Nicki conceded. She hadn't considered that the meeting might have been for something besides business.

"Besides," Matt continued. "It sounds like they were sitting right here when Eddie was murdered. Alex did say that occurred around nine p.m."

Nicki sighed and glanced out the window with its clear view of the police department, the square and all the shops surrounding it. Who knows how many of the town's residents were taking a stroll that night and saw Gordon and Roberta through the big window?

Matt reached across the table and tapped a long lean finger against the back of her hand. "Hey. Stop obsessing about Gordon's very limited social life. We still have to talk to Ben today, and Mason will be home tonight. That means a trip to see Chief Turnlow tomorrow." He bit into his sandwich, then set it down and sighed.

"I never thought a steak smothered in peppers and onions wouldn't taste as good as a grilled cheese with turkey."

CHAPTER FOURTEEN

NICKI AND MATT WALKED INTO THE SMALL SHOP RIGHT ON the square, directly across from the police department. Glass cases lined both walls going down its full length, and wooden racks, holding dozens of pairs of earrings as well as necklaces and bracelets, were scattered across the tiled floor. More racks hung from the wall, and a large "earring tree" that was as tall as Nicki stood just inside the entrance.

When no one appeared after a chime had announced their presence, Nicki called out loud enough for her voice to carry into the back room. "Hello? Ben? It's Nicki Connors and Matt Dillon."

Matt walked over to the cash register on the end of one counter and picked up a sign left propped in the middle of a cleared-off spot next to it. He held it up for Nicki to see.

"It says he'll be back in five minutes." He looked around at the crowded space, with every inch taken up by various pieces of jewelry. "Do you think he makes this stuff himself?"

"He has a lot of very nice pieces." Nicki picked up a pair of earrings with tiny red beads woven along a curved piece of silver.

"There's just too much of it," Matt observed. "Hey, where are you going?"

"Into the back, and stop shouting," Nicki said. "Be a good Watson and keep a look out." She walked through the curtain separating the main floor from the back room before Matt could get a word out.

The space was even more cluttered with stacks of boxes alongside a wide table. Small open bins of beads, crystals and other decorative items were lined up across the back of the table. Nicki gave it a quick glance. *This must be where Ben makes his jewelry.*

Turning toward the opposite wall, she stepped up to the desk and carefully scanned its top. The card immediately caught her eye. Stopping to listen for any sounds from the other side of the cloth, she smiled to herself at the silence. She could just imagine Matt, standing stiff as a board, waiting at the entrance of the shop.

Since all seemed well, she picked up the card and stared at the gold embossed logo of the most prestigious auction house in San Francisco. Not the kind of place Ben would be selling the jewelry he made with beads and wire. But maybe a valuable stamp? She froze when the chime sounded.

"Oh. Hello. I didn't see you come in. I was just next door visiting with Wanda." Ben's voice floated through the closed curtain. "She owns the crystal and amulet shop."

Nicki held her breath when there was a brief silence.

"Did you come alone? When Maxie called, I was told it would be Nicki paying me a visit."

"Yes. That is... what I mean is that Nicki's here too. She just had to step out for a moment."

Nicki almost giggled at Matt stumbling along. So much for his talents at lying. She quietly opened the rear door, leading from the office to a narrow passageway in back of the shop. After easing the door shut, she raced along the tight opening, only slowing when she reached the sidewalk at the end of the block. Quickly covering the distance from the corner back to the front door of Ben's establishment, she stopped just short of the window and drew in several slow breaths before casually strolling back through the front door.

"Oh, hi Ben!" She put on a wide smile and stepped around Ben and took up a position next to Matt. "I thought maybe you were next door, so I popped in there for a moment."

Ben pulled on one ear lobe. "But I *was* next door, visiting with Wanda."

"Oh no," Nicki laughed. "I went into the shop on the other side."

The jewelry maker looked even more puzzled. "The tobacco shop? But I don't smoke."

"Oh, really? That's good to know," Nicki said brightly, moving closer to Matt so she could press an elbow into his side.

Matt wrapped a long arm around her shoulders, pulling her even closer and effectively trapping her arm between their bodies. "Nicki had a few questions, Ben, if you can spare the time right now?"

"Certainly." He walked forward and leaned against the counter next to them. "What can I help you with?"

"Aside from those silver earrings with the red beads?" Nicki pointed to the pair in the case that she'd admired earlier. "I was wondering about Drew, the friend from back East? Was he your good friend or Sam's?"

Ben shrugged. "Both, I guess. We all met at the same time. At a lecture on stamps at the University of Maryland. Sam and I were attending, and Drew was giving the lecture. He's actually Dr. Drew Weston. He's an English professor at the university." He lowered his voice as if he'd suddenly entered a church. "Drew Weston is also a serious collector."

From his hushed tone and the clear admiration in his

voice, Nicki guessed that being called a "serious collector" was a high compliment in Ben's mind.

"Sam said he was interested in buying Eddie's sheet of stamps. Did you get that impression too?" Matt asked.

"I did indeed. But then it wasn't just an impression. Drew asked Eddie outright if he could buy them. Of course Eddie said 'no'. He always said 'no'." Ben paused and looked at a point beyond the two people standing in front of him. "The night went as they usually did. Eddie let us into the diner and we all headed downstairs to his wine cellar. Drew made a polite compliment about it, but his eyes were on the sheet of stamps that Eddie had already placed in the center of the table. We admired it, just like we always do, had a few glasses of wine and talked about stamps for an hour or so. Then we were sent upstairs while Eddie put the stamps away and locked up the cellar. He made hamburgers and fries, and after we were done eating, Sam, Drew and I left, and I assume after Eddie cleaned up, he went home too."

"It doesn't sound as if anything was out of the ordinary," Nicki said. "Except for Drew being there."

Ben laughed. "I wouldn't say Drew being there was as unusual as Eddie inviting him to see the sheet of stamps. As far as I know, except for Sam and me, Eddie hadn't shown it to anyone."

Nicki thought that over. So why show them to Drew? She looked up at Matt who shook his head. Apparently her side-kick had no idea either.

"I can get you Drew's number, if you'd like to talk to him. He might remember something I don't recall." A gleam of mischief came into Ben's eyes. "Aren't you going to ask me where I was at the time of the murder? Don't all detectives ask that? Or has the chief already told you?"

"No, I haven't talked to Chief Turnlow, so I guess I'll have to ask you myself." Nicki put on a serious expression, although she couldn't quite keep the corners of her mouth from twitching upward. "Where were you the night of the murder?"

"In the city with friends," Ben said in an artificially high, squeaky voice. He shook his head and grinned, his voice lowering to its normal pitch. "The chief has already contacted them to verify that I was there. So I guess I'm in the clear." He added a laugh to his smile. "Sorry. I know it's been hard coming up with suspects. If it was indeed a random stranger attack, I have no idea how the chief will ever solve this."

"Unless someone comes forward as a witness, those kinds of crimes are tough," Matt agreed smoothly. "Did you know what Eddie's big dream was? Sam mentioned that Eddie felt like a trip he was planning to take was going to make a dream come true for him."

Nicki's shoulders relaxed under Matt's arm. When Ben had mentioned that Eddie might have been attacked by a stranger, her mind had instantly leaped to her mom's murder, so she was grateful for the quick change in subject to something she'd almost forgotten she'd wanted to ask Ben about.

"He never told me." Ben closed his eyes. "The only future plan that I ever heard Eddie talk about, was wanting to franchise." He opened his eyes and chuckled quietly. "Whenever he said that, I always got a mental picture of burger diners, all painted in that god-awful yellow with a striped awning over the front, popping up all over the countryside. Kind of like the Starbucks of burger joints."

"That would have been a shock," Nicki laughed. "But it certainly would have made Jenna happy." She took a step away from Matt, so he dropped his arm back to his side. "It would have made Matt happy, too."

Her Dr. Watson laughed. "I'm not so sure. I'm developing a taste for grilled feta cheese sandwiches with sliced turkey."

Ben wagged a finger at him. "You're making me hungry and I have work to get done. If there's nothing else?"

"No, I think we asked everything we need to." Nicki started to hold out her hand.

"Not a problem at all," Ben said, stepping around the end of the display case and slipping in behind it. He plucked a card out of a small holder on top of the glass counter and held it out to her. "If you need to ask anything else, just call. Or come around any time."

Nicki took the card with a smile. "I'll do that. And you save those earrings for me."

Ben gave her a jaunty salute as she and Matt headed out the door, where they almost plowed right into Jim Holland. The big man did a quick sidestep, one arm coming out to fend them off.

"Whoa there." His frown turned up at the corners when he saw Nicki. "Hello, Nicki. You and your friend seem to be in a hurry."

Nicki's hand stayed clutched onto Matt's arm where she'd grabbed it to steady herself. She pushed a lock of her honey-blond hair out of her eyes before smiling at the winery owner. They'd become casual friends after she'd stumbled across the body of his head winemaker and uncovered his killer.

"Hi, Jim." She tilted her head at Matt. "I'm sure you've already met Matt Dillon, the owner and editor of *Food & Wine Online*?"

Jim Holland held out a large beefy hand. "Good to see you again, Matt."

Matt shook the offered hand. "You too, Jim. How'd the crush go this year?"

Jim shook his head, a sad glint in his eyes. "We didn't lose any vines to the fire, but it was close. Came right up to our outer fence line. Luckily our grapes were already in, so they weren't affected by the smoke. Wish I could say the same for

our suppliers nearer the coast and just north of Santa Rosa."
He gave Nicki a sympathetic smile. "I understand you liked
that little winery, Bon Vin? It burned to the ground. That was
one nasty fire. Lost some of the wineries up there, and in
Napa, along with big pieces of the towns."

Nicki immediately sobered. She and Jenna had also had
to evacuate. She'd grabbed her mother's jewelry and the
family cookbook, while Jenna had toted both of their
laptops under one arm, and a small box of backup CDs
under the other. Maxie had met them at the gate leading to
the main road, and they'd caravanned south toward San
Francisco. Nicki had worried about Alex, who'd stayed to
help evacuate patients from the hospital that had been
rapidly filling with smoke. And she'd been terrified for Alex's
fiancé, Tyler, who was a fireman with the Santa Rosa fire
department.

Nicki had been fourteen years old and living in New York
when the twin towers had been attacked and then collapsed
in a plume of smoke and fire, and now she'd been in the wildfires in the Northern California wine country. She sincerely
hoped that was the last disaster she would ever be in.

Beside her Matt visibly tensed, and the arm beneath her
hand went rock hard. "Those fires were terrifying for everyone. I couldn't get hold of Nicki or Maxie, or anyone, for
twenty-four hours. I almost got on a plane to come looking
for them." He frowned at Nicki. "Especially since I knew
firsthand how unreliable your getaway vehicle was."

Nicki gave him an exasperated look. "Would you please
forget about my car?".

Matt ignored her to glance over at Jim Holland. "Have
you seen her car?"

The winery owner smiled. "I've seen it. I wouldn't let
Gloria drive around in that, but then she's my wife." He
winked at Nicki who glared back at him.

"If that's what it takes," Matt said under his breath, running a hand through his hair.

Now it was Nicki's turn to ignore *him*. Matt could say the oddest things whenever he got agitated. She decided to get him calmed down before he had every hair on his head standing on end.

"I assume you've heard about Eddie Parker?"

Jim nodded. "Heard about it *and* got a call from the chief." He nodded again at Nicki's questioning look. "He wanted me to search through my records and see if Eddie had ever purchased any of our high-priced wines. I got back to him and told the chief that I didn't see Eddie purchasing anything outside the regular wine club shipments. Sent the last one a few months ago — two bottles of white, one red and one blush."

Nicki thought that made sense. The chief was obviously looking for anything else expensive, besides the sheet of stamps, that Eddie might have had in that cellar.

"I didn't know Eddie well. We exchanged small talk whenever he came to the winery, or I went into his diner for a burger. Nothing much beyond that. If Eddie had an expensive bottle of wine stashed in that wine cellar the chief mentioned, it wasn't from my winery." Jim glanced toward the corner. "I have a couple of friends waiting for me at the coffee place, so I'd better get going." He smiled at Nicki. "It's nice seeing you." He nodded to Matt. "Bring her by to taste this year's blends if you can tear her away from her latest murder."

"I'll do that." Matt looked at Nicki as Jim strolled away. "Any chance I can tear you away from murder for a while?"

"Maybe. What did you want to do? Work on a few articles for the magazine?"

Matt shook his head. "I was thinking more of a nice dinner where we didn't discuss investigating anything or interrogating anyone." He gave her a direct look. "And that I pay for."

Nicki considered it for a moment. "Well, we can stop at the store and get whatever you want, and I'll show you the best way to make it." She grinned at his frown. "And you can pay for the food."

Matt pushed his glasses further up his nose and looked adorably hesitant at her suggestion. "I'd like that. But you shouldn't have to cook all the time, Nicki."

"I like to cook. And really don't get to indulge in it as often as you'd think since I live alone."

"With one of your best friends right next door, who's always happy to mooch a meal from you," Matt grinned.

"Who prefers fast food and chocolate, if given a choice."

He laughed. "Okay. The grocery store it is, and I pay."

She held out her hand. "It's a deal."

CHAPTER FIFTEEN

NICKI HAD JUST WALKED INTO THE KITCHEN OF HER townhouse, with Matt and his armful of groceries trailing behind her, when her cell rang. She glanced at the caller ID before pressing the "answer" button and setting her phone on the small stand in the middle of the island.

"Hi, Maxie. Matt's here with me."

"Well isn't that wonderful, dear?"

Nicki shook her head at the sound of absolute delight in her landlady's voice.

"I was wondering where he'd gotten himself off to. I'm so glad you were able to spend the day together."

Maxie paused and spoke to someone behind her. Nicki laughed when she heard a muffled "I am not interfering", before Maxie's voice came through loud and clear again.

"My Mason just arrived home, and he was hoping he could talk to you before he had to make an appearance at the police station."

"I'm not going to see the chief to turn myself in." Mason's exasperated voice floated through the speakers.

Matt chuckled as he began to unload the grocery bags.

Nicki put a finger to her lips which had him quieting down, but his grin stayed in place.

"I'd be happy to talk to my...." Nicki quickly coughed to cover up her automatic use of the former chief's nickname. "Um... Mason. I'd be happy to talk to Mason." She eyed the huge pile of food Matt had accumulated on the counter and wondered what she was supposed to do with all of it, since most of what he'd insisted on buying had nothing to do with the meal she had planned. "I'm about to make southern-style stuffed peppers. You and Mason are welcome to join us. We certainly have plenty to go around."

"Really, dear? What makes them southern style?"

"Besides the usual ground beef mixture, it also involves ham and baby shrimp."

Maxie laughed. "My Mason is already halfway out the door. We'll be there shortly, dear. And thank you for the invitation."

"See you soon." Nicki clicked off the phone and looked over at Matt. "Would you mind if I ran next door and checked on Jenna?"

Matt stepped in front of the last grocery bag and started pulling items out. "She's not home."

"How do you know that?"

He stuck his hand further into the bag and pulled out a package of ground beef. "I sent her a text while you were looking over the peppers for any invisible flaws, to invite her to join us."

Nicki's eyes widened. "You did?"

"I didn't see any reason why she should eat alone when we had a ton of food right next door." Matt frowned at the loaded counter and started moving things around.

"Which you insisted on buying," Nicki reminded him. She curled her lips under to keep from laughing as the former engineer shifted all the groceries into their respective food groups, with the canned goods stacked together and the meat lined up side by side.

"Maybe we should have picked up another vegetable."

"Matt, the peppers are a vegetable," Nicki said patiently. "And where is Jenna? Did she say?"

"With a client. Someone she called her 'giant client'." Matt glanced over at her. "Maybe we should have bought something for dessert?"

"There's half a pie sitting in the refrigerator."

He frowned. "Will that be enough?"

It is for most people. Nicki wondered just how big Matt's monthly food bill was. "There're cookies if you're still hungry after the pie." She laughed when his expression immediately brightened.

Nicki started sorting through Matt's piles, separating out what was needed for their meal and putting away the rest that Matt had tossed into the cart with a "just in case" comment.

She held up a package of steaks in one hand and pork chops in the other. "You weren't trying to keep me in groceries for a month or so, were you?"

"That would last you a month?" Matt shook his head. "I don't think so."

"I don't think Sherlock could have afforded to feed Watson if he ate the way you do," Nicki said.

"I don't think Sherlock eats enough."

"I think Watson wants Sherlock to get fat."

"What in the world are you two talking about?" Maxie stood in the kitchen doorway with her husband peering over her shoulder.

"Matt's idea of the proper amount of food consumption." Nicki walked around the counter and gave the older woman a hug. She repeated it with Mason Edwards, who put a friendly arm around her shoulders as the two of them joined Maxie near the large island.

The former police chief, with his closely trimmed hair and deep tan, looked fit and healthy as he smiled at Matt. "They don't eat much, son. And what they do eat has a lot of green in it. You'll learn to accept that and hold your ground when it comes to meat on the plate too."

"I'm beginning to realize that." Matt gave a long soulful sigh then grinned when Nicki rolled her eyes.

She picked up the bag of peppers and walked over to the sink, looking at Matt as she pointed at the small refrigerator tucked under the far end of the counter. "If your moaning over my eating habits is done, could you please open a nice pinot gris for everyone to enjoy while I get our dinner ready and put into the oven."

"Sure thing." Matt headed for the wine refrigerator while Nicki quickly washed and prepped the vegetables before placing a skillet on the stove. Within minutes the kitchen was filled with the enticing aroma of onions, celery, garlic and spices sizzling together in a bed of hot oil.

Mason and Matt were sniffing the air when Maxie reached out her hands and latched onto both their arms. "Let's go take a look at the murder board before you both end up collapsing from hunger just from the smell of Nicki's food."

"This won't take long." Nicki added the ground beef to the skillet. "I'll be there in a few minutes."

Good to her word, she walked into her home office ten minutes later. Maxie, Mason and Matt were all standing in front of the big whiteboard, studying it in silence. Nicki walked over and leaned against the edge of her desk. Maxie smiled at her and picked up the black marker.

"Oh good. Now that you're here we can update the board with the new information that you and Matt gathered today." She raised an eyebrow at the two men standing next to her. "You can both go find a seat now."

Matt moved away to stand next to Nicki and lean against

her desk, but Mason ignored his wife's command and continued to study the board. He glanced over his shoulder at Nicki.

"Why don't you give me the short version of all of this?"

Nicki's gaze slowly went across and down the board. "It's a lot of pieces that don't seem to fit together."

Mason nodded. "They usually don't until you find that missing piece. But what do you have so far? It looks like you've concentrated on five people here."

"Six if you throw in Dr. Drew Weston." Matt said. "He's the mysterious guest who also saw Eddie's stamps. And wanted to buy them."

"We haven't had a chance to call him yet," Nicki added. "I'll do that tomorrow."

Maxie immediately wrote "Call Drew" under the to-do section on the board.

"If you're making a list of things to do tomorrow, you can add 'pay a visit to Chief Turnlow'." Mason turned around and walked to the sofa. He sat as Maxie scribbled onto the board. "All of us might as well go. It will save time since I'd just have to report back on every word that was said anyway. And..." he gave Nicki a calm stare. "We're going to tell the chief everything we've found out, so he may as well hear it firsthand."

Nodding her agreement, Nicki went back to reading the board. "What we have right now are a lot of people who each know something that the murderer needed to know, but not everything. And some missing stamps."

"That are worth fifty thousand dollars," Matt added.

"Something to consider." Mason crossed his arms over his chest. "Who needs the fifty thousand the most?"

"Roberta." Matt shrugged when everyone looked at him. "She's a waitress and cashier at a diner, so she's probably living paycheck to paycheck, and now she's out of a job. Or will be once the nephew gets here."

"Gordon." Maxie nodded. "He's never built up much of a clientele and has lived on a shoestring forever. Maybe he got tired of it and decided to take the stamps."

"Either of the two stamp collectors looks good." Mason's eyes narrowed as he stared at the board. "They both knew about the cellar and that the stamps were kept there. Doesn't look like the girlfriend or the bookkeeper knew much about the stamps themselves, though."

"Sheet of stamps," Nicki said. "And you're right. Both Ben and Sam referred to Eddie's prize possession as a 'sheet', while Roberta and Gordon called it a 'stamp'. I don't think either of them ever saw it, so even if they had gone looking for it, they wouldn't have known what they were looking for."

Matt ran a hand through his hair. "Or where to look. Neither of them knew the stamps were in the cellar."

Mason inclined his head at the board. "And only the assistant manager had any idea where the key to the cellar was." His gaze shifted to Nicki. "What's his alibi for that night?"

Nicki blinked. "I've never asked him."

"No matter." Mason smiled at her. "We'll find out from the chief tomorrow. You can bet he asked Jake where he was when Eddie was killed."

"Well, Roberta and Gordon were at dinner at Mario's, as strange as that seems considering how long Roberta had been Eddie's girlfriend." Maxie shook her head. "Even if they'd broken up, she certainly didn't waste any time in taking up with one of Eddie's friends."

"And I was out running errands and then spent the evening with my wife." Mason smiled at Maxie's snort.

"I am not adding your name to this board," she declared. "You are not a suspect, and that's all there is to that. I intend to remind the chief of that tomorrow if necessary."

Her husband chuckled. "Okay. Then it's back to the rest

of the suspects. Gordon and Roberta have an alibi. What about the stamp collectors?"

"Ben was in the city with friends, and Sam was home alone." Nicki gave Maxie an apologetic smile. She knew how fond her landlady was of Sam. "At least we can keep Jim Holland off the list this time."

"What on earth does Jim have to do with all of this?" Maxie demanded.

"Nothing," Matt quickly put in which had Maxie back to smiling. "We ran into him, almost literally, outside of Ben's shop. The chief asked him to check if Eddie had bought any expensive wine, which he hadn't. At least not from Holland Winery."

"Then what we have left here is Sam and possibly Jake who have no alibis. With this Weston person as an unknown in the whole equation." Mason pursed his lips. "Or a complete stranger, which doesn't seem likely. And whoever Eddie had that evening appointment with."

"Why not?" his wife demanded. "Someone could have walked in on Eddie when he was alone in the diner."

"I don't think so either." Nicki rose and walked over to the board. "A stranger wouldn't have known where Eddie lived, and his apartment was searched as well as his office. I'm voting for whoever it was that Eddie had that appointment with."

"Why?" Matt adjusted his glasses and gave her a curious look. "The person could have met Eddie before he was attacked, or could have canceled at the last minute."

"Maybe, if he's from out of town and still isn't aware that Eddie was murdered," Nicki conceded. "Otherwise that person would have come forward by now. But I think he killed Eddie and took his cell phone to cover his tracks."

Matt rubbed his chin. "The cell phone *is* still missing."

"With Eddie's calendar, and any calls he made," Nicki said.

"Finding that cell phone is important." Mason took another long look at the board. "Well, we won't know much more until we talk to the chief. But unless some outside person shows up on his radar, it looks like Sam, Jake and Drew Weston are the best suspects."

"How long until dinner?" Matt asked, smiling at Nicki's incredulous look.

She glanced at her watch and calculated the time. "About half an hour."

Maxie set the marker on the tray at the bottom of the board. "Well, we should let this rest for a while and enjoy another glass of this excellent wine before dinner."

Mason stood. "I'll second that, honey. A man likes to have a final drink and a good meal before he's thrown into prison."

"Don't talk like that," Maxie scolded as she walked over to her husband and took his arm. "Pour me a glass of wine and we'll see if you still remember how to get me slightly tipsy."

The former police chief wiggled his eyebrows at his wife. "I would never forget something like that."

Nicki smiled at the sound of Maxie's laughter as the couple strolled out of the office, arm in arm.

"Think I could learn how to get *you* a little tipsy?" Matt's voice was close to her ear.

She turned to face him and smiled at her grinning editor with tufts of dark hair standing straight up from his forehead. "Not likely. I learned to hold my own in some of the most notorious bars in New York City." She followed the chief's lead and gave him a wink. "But you're welcome to try."

Matt laughed as he held out his arm. "Okay, Sherlock, warning taken. Let's go eat."

CHAPTER SIXTEEN

NICKI TURNED HER LITTLE TOYOTA ONTO THE MAIN ROAD leading into town, and right past Eddie's diner. She'd already sent Matt and Maxie a text, letting them know that she'd meet them later at the police station. Matt had replied that the chief had asked Mason to come in about one that afternoon, so they were going to have lunch in Soldoff and then walk to the station. If anything changed, he'd let her know. She agreed to meet them at the station since she intended to go home for lunch and check on Jenna. But first she had to do the walk-through with the fire inspector, Jake and Tyler.

It was a beautiful day. Clear and bright, with just a puff or two of clouds in the sky, it promised to be a great day to wander about outdoors, or to do a little wine tasting on a shaded patio. Since tomorrow was the start of the weekend, and the forecast promised the same perfect weather for the next five days, Nicki expected the town would be packed. Which was perfect timing for reopening the diner. Provided, of course, it passed the fire inspector's keen eye. With the still very recent disaster of the wildfires all around the wine country, Nicki was sure the inspector would be even more diligent than before.

She arrived at the diner a few minutes later and parked her car near the front door. There weren't any other cars in the front lot, but she spotted Jake's battered truck near the side entrance. Nicki turned off her car and waited the usual five seconds before the engine finally shut off with a last sputter. Hoping she really would be able to afford a new car in the spring, Nicki pushed open the door and stepped out, stretching her back and shoulders as she took a moment to enjoy the warmth of the sun. *Sure beats New York in March.* She smiled at the thought. It was hard to believe that spring wasn't too far away.

Mentally going over her to-do list for the day, Nicki made her way to the front door. It was unlocked, and a pile of mail was scattered across the floor. Scooping it up, she casually flipped through it. She set aside the one from the energy company with its "go solar and save" stamp on the front, and the plain brown envelope from the local bank with its notice of "Loan Information" printed next to the diner's address. The third envelope looked more interesting. Its return address said "NSDA" with "National Stamp Dealers' Association" printed in small letters beneath that.

Nicki set the other two, along with several advertisements, on the counter for Gordon to deal with, and turned the NSDA letter over. There wasn't any marking on the backside of the envelope, so she flipped it over again and held it up to the light. That didn't get her anywhere either. Frowning, she thought about it several moments, then decided she'd just take it along to Chief Turnlow and let him open it. She doubted if he'd get arrested for tampering with the US Mail.

She looked around at the sound of the front door opening and closing, surprised when Gordon Twill walked into the diner. He pulled up short when he saw her. She smiled at him and pointed to the small stack of mail on the counter. "I put the bills right over there."

He stared at her hand. "What's that one?"

She held up the white envelope. "Doesn't look like a bill. It's from the NSDA, the stamp association for dealers. I thought I'd take it to Chief Turnlow since I'm going over there after I run back to my house for lunch." She smiled. "Unless you'd like to open it?"

Gordon shook his head. "No. No. You can take that to the police. I don't think Eddie would be getting a bill from them." He looked around before his gaze returned to Nicki. "I came to meet the fire inspector. Why are you here?"

"Oh. You didn't mention you were going to take care of that. Actually, I'm here for the same reason," Nicki said cheerfully. "I've also asked Tyler Johnson to meet us here. He's the fiancé of a close friend of mine, and a fireman. I thought he could help."

"That's a good idea." Gordon took a seat at the nearest table and set his day planner down in front of him. He opened it up and stared at the page.

Okay. He didn't want to talk. But there was a small detail or two Nicki wanted to discuss with him, so she pretended not to notice that he was deliberately ignoring her and walked over to take a seat across from him.

"I'm still consulting on this case concerning Eddie's murder." She smiled when he reluctantly raised his head and his eyes met hers. "I'm glad you're here, there are a couple of things I wanted to ask you."

"I don't know what else I can tell you." Gordon turned another blank page in his appointment book and stared at it.

"I was wondering why you were late for your dinner date with Roberta?"

The bookkeeper's head snapped up. "What?"

"Your dinner date with Roberta the night Eddie was

killed?" Nicki kept to her chatty conversational voice. "That is who your date was with, wasn't it?"

Gordon stared at her before slowly nodding. "We had dinner at Mario's."

"But you were late?" Nicki prompted.

"I had car trouble." Gordon went back to looking at his day planner. "It happens."

"I'm surprised Roberta waited over thirty minutes for you to get there. She doesn't seem like she'd be willing to do that."

His cheeks flushed and he shifted in his chair, but he never looked away from the blank page of his planner. "I sent her a text message that I'd be late. She said it was okay."

"That was thoughtful of you," Nicki's bright voice bounced around the empty diner. "I've dated men who wouldn't have bothered."

For a brief moment Gordon's face twisted into a nasty sneer before falling back into its usual bland expression. "I doubt that." He looked at his watch. "I have to make a few phone calls." Without offering any other word of apology for his abrupt departure, Gordon stood and walked out the front door.

Apparently he wants to be sure his calls are private, Nicki mused. He'd looked pretty uncomfortable over a couple of simple questions, but she couldn't really fault him for that. After all, he'd been out on a dinner date with a client's girlfriend at the same time his client had been murdered in his own diner. Since Gordon's story matched what the waiter at Mario's had said, she decided to wander back to the kitchen and keep Jake company while they waited for the fire inspector and Tyler.

~

AN HOUR later she was on her way back home. Happily

humming to herself, she couldn't wait to tell Jenna that Alex had surprised her by coming along with Ty. The whole walk-through had gone well, and Tyler was finishing up a few last notes with the fire inspector before he and Alex would be on their way to meet her at the townhouse. Gordon hadn't stayed one extra minute more than necessary, and was already gone by the time she'd left a smiling Jake to finish the prepa-rations for the reopening and climbed into her car.

It was still a little early for tourists, so the country road, dotted with wild flowers on both sides, was deserted as she zipped along. Another five minutes and she'd be home. Nicki glanced into her rearview mirror and frowned at the pickup rapidly coming up behind her. She wrinkled her nose in annoyance. People loved to speed along these two-lane back roads. Resigned to having the big truck zoom right by her, she pulled as far over to the right as she could, to let it pass. Instead, it kept coming up closer to her small Toyota, until her entire rearview mirror was filled with the image of a white hood on top of a wide silver grille.

Pressing the gas pedal down to put more distance between them, Nicki looked over at her side view mirror as she stuck her arm out the window and waved for the truck to go by. She caught a glimpse of tinted windows and a foggy image of a driver. He had a large hat pulled down over his forehead, and a bandanna covering his lower face.

Before that fact fully registered, the truck hit her small car's back bumper, sending it flying a few feet down the road. Nicki lurched forward as the tires hit solid ground again. She'd barely caught another breath before there was another, even harder, jolt from behind. This time the car spun side-ways, heading right for the large open ditch running alongside the road. When the front of the compact Toyota hit the side of the solid dirt wall, it crumpled into an accordion. The jarring impact had Nicki slamming violently back against her seat and then lurching forward. Her head and chest smacked hard against the steering wheel. She slumped over, fighting for breath when her vision went black.

IT WAS the pounding in her head that got her attention first, and somewhere behind it was a vaguely heard voice, asking her if she was all right. She groaned as she lifted her head, taking in a quick breath at the sharp jab of pain. She moaned softly and slumped back against the steering wheel.

"I've called for help. You just hold on there young lady. And don't move. I gave your door a good yank, but it's stuck. Now don't you worry. I don't think the car's going to explode or anything."

That's good to know, she thought, keeping her eyes closed against the noise of the voice. It sounded female, and a bit older, but that's all her muddled brain could comprehend.

"Here's some more people, come to help. Nice big man, too. I'm sure he can get you out of there."

"Nicki? Hang on!"

Nicki heard the frantic voice and managed the tiniest of smiles. It sounded like Alex. That would be nice since her friend was a doctor and all. Nicki took a shallow breath and let herself drift off again, only to be rudely awakened by a series of quick light slaps on her cheek.

"Nicki? Can you hear me?"

"Stop hitting me, Alex," Nicki mumbled. She tried lifting herself up again, but this time a firm but gentle hand on her back kept her where she was.

Alex's voice was close to her ear. "Don't move. Just stay where you are. An ambulance is on its way. Can you tell me if it hurts when you breathe?"

Nicki took in a very slow breath, drawing air into her

lungs by inches. At about the halfway point, her chest threw out a warning signal. "It hurts," she whispered, slowly exhaling what air she'd managed to take in, and keeping her breaths shallow.

Nicki didn't remember much of the next thirty minutes. She'd heard the sirens drawing closer until they felt as if they were blaring directly into her head. She remembered the first gentle slide of her legs out of the car, then being carried out of the ditch and lifted onto a stretcher. But everything after that was a complete blank, until she was being wheeled into the emergency door of a hospital. She opened one eye, expecting to see Alex bending over her. Instead it was an older man in blue scrubs, with a stethoscope around his neck.

"Hi there. I'm Dr. Fedlan, and you're in the emergency room at Sonoma hospital. Can you tell me your name?"

She squinted against the bright light in the room. "Nicki. Nicki Connors," she croaked out. "What happened?"

"Now everyone is hoping you can tell us that, but right now we need to get you into x-ray. You've got a nasty bump on your head that we need to watch, and likely some pretty extensive bruising on you ribs. Do you understand what I'm saying, Nicki?"

"Yes." Nicki closed her eyes against the light. "Need an x-ray."

"That's right. A nurse is here, and she's going to help you. After the x-rays, we'll get you out of those clothes and into a more comfortable bed. Okay? Don't nod, I know it hurts. I'll see you after you're done in x-ray." The sounds of his footsteps faded away and was replaced with several other voices.

For the next hour Nicki was put through the usual just-in-an-accident procedures, and by the time she was finally in a fresh hospital gown and transferred to a bed in a private room, she was exhausted. And she wanted badly to see a familiar face. So when the door to her room opened and it was Alex who popped in, tears started to trickle down her cheeks.

"What's wrong? Are you hurting somewhere?"

"I'm fine." Nicki grabbed a tissue from the small tray next to her bed and dabbed at her eyes. "I'm just glad to see you. This hasn't been much fun, and I need a hug from a friend."

Alex quickly stepped over to the bed and leaned over to wrap her arms around Nicki. "I'm so glad to see you too. I almost had a heart attack when we came up on that accident on the way to your place and realized it was your car." With her eyes misting over, she gave Nicki a watery smile. "Ty was wonderful. He wouldn't let anyone else lift you out of the car. He carried you out of that ditch and up to the gurney the paramedics had ready."

Nicki squeezed her friend's hand. "I'm fine, so stop worrying. And Tyler will have the dinner of his choice the minute I'm out of here." She sighed. "So. How am I doing?"

"Dr. Fedlan wants to keep you overnight for observation, but your images came back fine. Your ribs are probably bruised, and I'm sure your chest is too, from hitting that steering wheel. But other than that, everything looked good. You should be released in the morning."

"I'm sorry to put you through all this."

"Don't be silly." Alex's eyes suddenly cleared, and an amused smile appeared out of nowhere. "Oh, if you are handing out sympathy, I'd save it for Chief Turnlow."

"Why is that?"

"He's the one who had to tell Matt about your accident." Her smile blossomed into a full grin. "He pulled up just as I was climbing into the ambulance to ride with you. Tyler told me that he called Jenna and then punched in Matt's number and handed the phone to the chief. My big brave hunky fireman said that there was no way he was going to tell Matt that you'd been in an accident and were on your way to the hospital." Alex put her hands on her hips. "I convinced the whole gang to let me come in and check on you first, but they're all down the hall just waiting to descend on you. And guess who will be in front of the pack?"

Pulling her covers up to her chin, Nicki slid lower into the bed. In her head she could already hear the long stern lecture she'd be getting from her editor. Her eyes peeked over the edge of the blanket at Alex. "Suddenly I don't feel so well. Maybe you should only let a couple of them in. Like Jenna and Maxie?"

Alex shook her head. "Not a chance, pal. He needs to see you. He looks like he might explode at any minute. Oh, and the chief is here too. He looks almost as grim as Matt."

The doctor winked at her. "Almost, but not quite."

CHAPTER SEVENTEEN

"GREAT," NICKI GRUMBLED AS ALEX LEFT THE ROOM.

Her friend didn't go far. Just out into the hallway where she waved her hand, which was immediately followed by the sound of a herd of footsteps.

Just as Alex had predicted, Matt was the first through the door. Nicki had a glimpse of everyone else stopping just outside before Matt leaned over the bed, bracing his hands on either side of her pillow.

"Are you alright?"

His face was only inches from hers.

"I'm fine. And it hardly hurts at all as long as I don't move around too much."

Matt drew in a deep breath. "That'll work."

Before Nicki could blink, he'd lowered his head and was giving her a heart-stopping and thorough kiss.

"How long do we have to stand out here?"

Jenna's voice was heavy with laughter, and her question had the rest of the group overcome with sudden coughing fits. Matt took his time breaking off the kiss and raising his head.

"You're sure you're okay?"

"Yes," Nicki whispered back. She closed her eyes when he gently touched his forehead to hers.

"That's good." He stood up and took one of her hands in his before turning and gesturing to the five faces peering in from the doorway. "Come on in."

The rush began, with Jenna leading the way. She skidded to a halt at the bedside opposite from where Matt had taken up a permanent spot, and leaned over to give Nicki a long hug.

"You scared us. I mean really, really scared us."

"I know." Nicki ignored the pain and returned the fierce hug with her free arm. "I'm sorry."

"Don't be sorry, just get better."

Jenna smiled and stepped aside, and her place was claimed by Maxie. Nicki was overwhelmed by the love she felt. She considered every single person in the room to be part of her family. She even extended that thought to the big man who removed his hat as he walked into the room

"Hi, Chief." Nicki looked up at Matt when the editor closer to the bed.

"Chief, I don't know if she's up for this yet." Matt took a tighter hold on her hand as she glanced between him and the chief.

Nicki pushed herself up on her pillows. "I'm fine. Have you seen my car?"

"We saw it," Tyler said. He glanced at Matt and then over at Nicki. "It's toast."

"Great." She sighed. It seemed spring would be getting here a bit early this year.

"Don't worry about it." Matt gave her hand a light squeeze.

"Can you tell me what happened, Nicki?" The chief held up his hand before she could say anything. "I'd like to hear from her without any side comments." He smiled when Jenna put her hands on her hips and huffed out a breath.

Tyler held his muscular arms straight out and began herding everyone out of the room. "Let's go. We can get something to drink and then come right back." He nodded at the chief. "That should give you a good quarter hour or so to get the details."

Chief Turnlow returned the nod. "I appreciate it."

"And I'm staying," Matt declared, not budging one inch from his spot by Nicki's bed.

"I wish someone would ask for *my* opinion," Nicki said as she watched the last of her friends disappear from view.

The chief stepped to the end of her bed and folded his arms across his broad chest. "Okay. I'll ask you something. What happened?"

Both men stared at her. Nicki braced herself. "Well, it wasn't an accident." She waited for their reaction to that statement and was surprised when the chief only nodded.

"So Mary Swenson thought, but she wasn't sure."

"Who?" Nicki asked.

"Mary Swenson. She was the first person on the scene and saw that truck speeding up behind you. Next thing she knew, you were spinning into the ditch." The chief's eyes narrowed. "Is that what happened, or did him coming up on you so fast make you lose control of your car?"

Nicki looked up at Matt, whose expression had gone grim. Now she gave *his* hand a reassuring squeeze. "I'm afraid Mary Swenson was right. The truck hit me. Twice. It was the second time that sent me into the ditch."

"Bastard," Matt muttered and then fell silent again.

"I managed to give your car a good once-over before it was towed off. It looked like it was hit from behind. The trunk is smashed in. Judging by the position of the dent, it must have been a fairly big truck." The chief ran a hand through his thinning hair.

Matt's arm grew more rigid with every word the chief said. Nicki finally reached over and ran a soothing hand up and down his forearm.

"It was a white pickup with a big silver grille on the front. And it was jacked up on some big tires."

The chief nodded. "Fits the damage I saw. You didn't happen to get a look at the driver, did you?"

Nicki bit her lower lip. If Matt was tense now, he really wasn't going to like this. "No. The windows had a tint on them, so I didn't see him very clearly. He did have on a cowboy hat." She took in a deep breath and let it out slowly. "And a cloth or bandanna around the lower part of his face."

The room went so silent Nicki could almost hear herself blink. And she was pretty sure she was the only one who was doing any blinking.

Finally the chief broke the silence. "Is that a fact?"

She gave a slight nod. "It is. I saw that much in my side mirror when I was waving for him to go around me. He was too close for me to see his license plate."

"Mrs. Swenson said it looked like the truck was chasing you, and then deliberately caused you to go into that ditch."

"I'd say Mrs. Swenson was right again." Nicki thought back to that first voice she heard. "Is she a little older? She called me 'young lady', I think. And told me that it didn't look like my car was going to blow up." She smiled up at Matt. "It was nice of her to stop and help."

He didn't say anything but managed a brief smile.

"She is a bit older," the chief confirmed. After a long pointed look at Matt, he turned a smile on Nicki. "She's somewhere around eighty, if I had to guess. I promised to give her a call and let her know that you're all right."

"I'd like to thank her too." Nicki was grateful to Mrs.

Swenson. She was sure the older woman was the one who'd called 911 and climbed into that ditch to try to help her.

"That's good. Because making phone calls from your bed is all you'll be doing for a while," Matt said.

"Maybe just a day or so. Alex said I can go home tomorrow."

"We're going to have to talk about that, Nicki."

"Okay." She smiled. "Talk away. But I'm still going home tomorrow and getting back to work. I'm going to have to buy another car,"

"I don't suppose I could persuade you to leave town for a few days?" The chief raised an eyebrow at her. "Just until I figure out who tried to run you off the road?"

Matt nodded. "We can go to Kansas City. I can keep an eye on her there."

"Or..." Nicki interrupted. "You could take me to my own home right here in Soldoff, and you go back to Kansas City and catch up on your own work."

"Not a chance, Nicki," Matt shot back.

The chief loudly cleared his throat. "You two can have that discussion later." He looked directly at Matt. "But whatever the outcome, I doubt if she's going to let Eddie Parker's murder go, so now she's your responsibility." He put his hat back on. "Whatever you two decide, I don't want to get daily calls every time Ms. Connors doesn't return a text message."

"I'm responsible for myself, Chief," Nicki called to his retreating back.

He waved his arm in Matt's general direction. "Talk to him about it."

Matt ran a hand through his thick hair, leaving the usual number of dark strands sticking straight up. "I know you're a capable person and not a child, and that you grew up in New York City and can look after yourself." He glanced at her.

"Did I leave anything out?" Nicki folded her arms and looked up at him. "We'll see. Go on."

The corners of Matt's mouth tugged upward. "Okay. Someone deliberately tried to run you off the road. And unless there's a lunatic reader out there who really has an issue with your novels or your blog, the odds are it has to do with the investigation into Eddie Parker's murder."

She nodded. "I think the same thing. So the sooner it's solved, the better." She gave him a suspicious look. "And I can't solve it from Kansas City."

"I won't argue with that. But you need help, and I need peace of mind. Which means it would be best if we stick together, so I can watch your back and you can use my rental car." He looked at the ceiling. "You did say you needed a car, didn't you?"

He had her there. If she didn't have a car, she'd be stuck either borrowing Jenna's, which she didn't want to do, especially if there was some nutty person cruising around who still wanted to ram into her, or maxing out her credit cards for a rental.

"Is the rental insured?"

"Yes, and that's not funny." Matt eyed the grin on Nicki's face. "I'll get my things from Maxie's, and will sleep on your couch for the duration."

"You can use my desk. I'll set my laptop up in the kitchen." Nicki didn't mind. She'd feel better if she wasn't alone in the townhouse for the next few days, and Matt's offer was perfect. This way she wouldn't need to fend off Jenna or Maxie when they insisted that she stay at one of their places. Which she really hadn't wanted to do. And now wouldn't have to.

The whole gang walked back into the room, and a noisy confusion ensued until each had found a good spot to occupy in the small space.

Jenna looked over at Matt. "So? Did you talk her into letting you crash at her place?"

"Yes, I did. She's going to put up with me in exchange for using my car."

"Good bribe, Dillon." Jenna nodded in approval. She turned her attention to her friend lying in the hospital bed. "Is it true what the chief told myMason? Did someone try to run you off the road?"

"I'm afraid so. Someone in a big white pickup truck."

"Whoever this someone is, you must be making him very nervous about our investigation, dear." Maxie looked at her husband when he tapped her on the shoulder.

"It's Chief Turnlow's investigation, honey. You need to let him do his job." Mason inclined his head when his wife opened her mouth to protest. "But he is a little short-staffed, so we could help him out here and there."

"Excellent!" Maxie leaned over and gave him an affectionate kiss on the cheek. "What do we do next?"

"Whatever it is, Nicki has to be able to do it from the comfort of her bed or couch for the next few days. That's not negotiable." Alex looked slowly around the room, her gaze lingering on each of them in turn. "Doctor's orders, or she isn't going home tomorrow."

"Good idea." Matt gave Alex a grateful look as his shoulders relaxed. "We have at least one phone call we need to make."

"To Drew Weston." Nicki said. "I can make that call from here."

"You can make that call tomorrow." Alex's tone was firm. "What you need now is to settle in, have some food and get some rest." She nodded to the far corner. "That's a sleeping chair for Matt. I'll ask the nurse for an extra blanket."

Within minutes everyone had said their reluctant goodbyes and filed out, leaving Matt and Nicki alone to stare at each other.

"I'm too exhausted to ask you what that kiss was all about," Nicki said. Which was the truth. Suddenly she could hardly keep her eyes open.

"That's good. Because I'm too tired to get into it." Matt looked around. "That chair doesn't look too bad."

"You don't need to stay here, Matt. I don't think anyone is going to come sneaking into the hospital in the middle of the night. And I'm sure your bed at Maxie's is more comfortable than that chair."

He walked over to the corner and started yanking the heavy chair forward. He didn't stop alternating between pushing and pulling until it was next to the bed.

"There. That works." He shoved a piece of hair off his forehead and readjusted his glasses on his nose. "I'm staying. And we aren't going to get into a debate about that either."

CHAPTER EIGHTEEN

IT WAS APPROACHING NOON THE NEXT DAY WHEN MATT stopped his rental car in front of Nicki's townhouse. He set the parking brake and glanced over at her. "Can you walk into the house? You didn't look too comfortable getting into the car."

She shrugged. "I'm just stiff. The doctor told me that was to be expected, and I'd have to work through it."

Matt didn't voice an opinion on that piece of advice as he opened his door and stepped out of the driver's side. He'd sprinted around the front of the car by the time she got the door open. He slipped an arm around her waist to help her get to her feet on solid ground. She tried not to grimace when each step had her whole back issuing a sharp pain of complaint, but set her mouth and started to hobble along the flower-lined walkway. She'd barely gone five steps before Matt scooped her up.

She squeaked in surprise, throwing her arms around his neck. "What are you doing?"

"Getting you into the house. I'd be filing for retirement

by the time you got there at that speed. Besides, it was painful to watch."

"I'm just a little stiff," Nicki repeated and then gave up. She really didn't want to walk that far either, and it was kind of nice having Matt carry her around.

When they were in the small entryway and he kept going, bypassing the opening leading into her living room, Nicki raised a questioning eyebrow. "Where are we going? The couch is back there."

"I'm going to make you something to eat. Which you won't let me do unless you can supervise my every move, so we're going to the kitchen."

She laughed. "I'm not that bad, am I?"

"When it comes to your kitchen and cooking? Yes, you are." Matt walked over to the counter and pulled one of the stools out with his foot. He set Nicki down and made sure she was steady before strolling around the island and facing her from the other side. "Now, what would you like, Ms. Connors? Eggs sunny-side up, eggs over easy, or eggs scrambled?"

"Well, let me see." Nicki furrowed her brow and pretended to consider the matter. "How about poached?"

"Nope. Can't do that."

"I have an egg poacher." She pointed to a cabinet next to the stove.

"So do I. Still can't do it. You'll have to choose from the list I gave you."

Nicki shook her head and did her best not to laugh. "You have an egg poacher and you still can't poach an egg?"

"It was a gift, and it's still in the box." Matt shrugged. "So what will it be?"

"Scrambled might be best." Nicki gave in and laughed. "And a piece of toast if it's not too much trouble? Or is your toaster also still in a box?"

"I can do toast." Not sounding the least offended, Matt went to the refrigerator and retrieved a carton of eggs and a loaf of bread.

"Two eggs, one piece of toast."

Matt stopped midway to the counter. "To start."

"And finish." Nicki decided she'd have to point out the obvious to the well-meaning-but-sometimes-blind Matt. "I can't eat the way you do. You're what, six feet tall and male?"

He chuckled and set the food next to the stove. "Last time I checked."

"Well, I'm a five-foot-two-inch female." She threw her arms out to the side. "It doesn't take as much fuel to keep me going as it does you."

Matt leaned against the counter and considered it for a moment. "I suppose that's true. But it takes more than it would to keep a bird alive."

"Well, when you show me a bird that's downed two eggs and a piece of toast, I'll consider eating more. But until then..." She trailed off and gave the food a significant look. "That's all I want, nurse Dillon."

"Okay. You win. But I get to win the next argument." He picked up the carton of eggs, took a skillet down from the overhead pot rack, and walked over to the stove. "And I prefer to be called Dr. Watson. That's a lot more dignified."

Nicki smiled. "Would it hurt your dignity if I got you an apron?"

Matt cracked two eggs into the skillet and turned around, a spatula in one hand. "Yes. Yes, it would."

"All right, Watson. Breakfast and then a phone call to Dr. Drew Weston, English professor and serious stamp collector."

LESS THAN AN HOUR later Nicki was sitting on her living

room couch, with Matt right next to her and her cell phone on speaker.

"Hi. My name is Nicki Connors. I'm a friend of Sam and Ben, the stamp collectors who live in California. Is this Dr. Weston?"

"It is. And Sam told me you might be calling." The voice sounded friendly and relaxed. Nicki tried to fit it to the picture of the gray-haired, portly man with the goatee that she'd found online. It turned out that since Drew Weston was indeed a professor and a prominent stamp collector, there was quite a bit of information about him floating around the internet.

"Oh good. I'm here with Matt Dillon. He's the editor for *Food & Wine Online* and a good friend."

"Is this also an interview for the magazine?"

"No, Dr. Weston," Matt quickly spoke up. "This is solely about Eddie Parker's murder."

"I see." The professor sounded disappointed. "Sam told me what happened. Such a tragedy. I liked Eddie and enjoyed talking to him. And both of you, please call me Drew."

"Thank you. And I'm Nicki and he's Matt."

"Well, I need to get my most pressing question out of the way. Was Eddie killed because of the stamps?"

"We don't know." Nicki paused, considering her words. "It could be, but there may have been another reason, or maybe it was a random act. The police are still investigating."

A loud snort came through the speakers. "Since his office and apartment were searched, I doubt if it was a random act."

Nicki wasn't surprised that Drew Weston already knew about the office and apartment being searched. "When was the last time you saw Eddie?"

"*Saw* him? Well that would have been the night all four of us, Sam, Ben, Eddie and myself, had wine in the basement of Eddie's diner, and then hamburgers and fries later on, when we went back upstairs. It was the same night that Eddie showed us his full sheet of the non-inverted Jenny. So over two weeks ago, going on three weeks now."

"And the last time you spoke to Eddie?" Matt prompted.

"A week after my visit to California. I got his telephone number from Sam. I wanted to make another try at persuading him to sell me those stamps."

"But you weren't successful?" Nicki looked over at Matt who was busy taking diligent notes of the conversation. He also had his cell phone lying on the couch between himself and Nicki, and the recording icon was flashing red. The former engineer was certainly thorough.

"No I wasn't, more's the pity. Especially now that the stamps are missing."

Nicki shook her head. Sam had certainly wasted no time in keeping his friend back East up on every detail of Eddie's murder.

"If he turned you down that night in his wine cellar, why did you call and try again?" Nicki had wondered about that ever since Sam and Ben had both claimed that Eddie had always been adamant that he would not part with his stamps.

The professor chuckled. "Because I'm a dealer as well as a collector, Ms. Connors. We never stop trying to improve our inventory. And when it comes to buying stamps, a collector's 'no' doesn't always mean 'no'. I got a niggle of a feeling that Eddie might be willing to let go of the stamps. I have a good internal radar for picking up on that kind of thing. But when I asked him, he said he couldn't sell them to me."

Nicki frowned. "Is that all he said? That he couldn't sell them?"

"Well, we talked a bit longer. Eddie had dreams of being part of a franchise. He'd mentioned that to all of us when we were enjoying our wine in his basement. And he had a big project coming up that he wasn't too detailed about, but he seemed very excited." There was a short moment of silence. "He didn't say much more than that. Our conversation barely lasted ten minutes, as I recall."

"And you didn't talk to him at any time after that phone call?" Matt leaned forward, his pencil poised over his small notebook.

"No, I didn't. I'm sorry I can't be of more help." There was a sound of rustling papers. "I have a message here that a Chief Turnlow from Soldoff called. I imagine he'll be asking the same things?"

Nicki sidestepped his question by giving him an indirect answer. "I'd call him as soon as you have a free minute, Professor. He can be persistent."

"Yes, well. I returned his call yesterday but was told he was out in the field."

"Weren't we all?" Matt said under his breath.

"I'm sure he'll be in touch today," Nicki said quickly, hoping to cover up his comment. She certainly didn't want to have to explain yesterday's events to a curious stamp collector who was also a college professor. "We appreciate your time, Drew."

"Not a problem at all. Sam told me that you're doing a little investigating of your own, and that you're pretty good at it. He said you've already solved two murders."

Nicki wondered what the Soldoff's Chief of Police would say about that. "Well, I was only helping our police department. Thank you again. Bye."

She politely waited for the professor to say his goodbye and click off first before she pushed the disconnect button. Leaning against the cushy back of the couch, she folded her hands in front of her and stared at them, going over what the professor had said in her mind. One thing leaped out and danced around in front of her.

"So what do you think?" Matt's quiet voice broke into her thoughts.

"I don't know." She shrugged. "We didn't hear much that we didn't already know."

"Not much?" Matt set his notepad on the coffee table in front of the couch. "Which implies we'd heard much of what the professor said already, but not everything. So what is it that he said that we haven't heard before?"

Nicki glanced at the mini recorder. "Can you replay when Eddie told him about selling the stamps?"

"Sure." Matt fiddled with the buttons on his phone until he came to the part of the conversation about the stamps. He replayed it several times until Nicki sat back again, a satisfied smile on her face.

Matt set his phone aside. "What? Eddie refused to sell him the stamps. We already knew Eddie wouldn't sell the stamps."

"But that's not what the professor said, Matt. He's an English professor, so I'd bet he's pretty precise about the language." She looked at Matt's phone lying on the coffee table. "He didn't say Eddie wouldn't sell him the stamps. He said Eddie *couldn't* sell them to him."

Nicki grinned at the dumbstruck look on Matt's face. It was the same way she'd felt when she'd realized what the professor had said when he was relating his conversation with Eddie.

"Then you think Eddie said that he couldn't sell the stamps because he'd already sold them?" Matt rubbed his chin before he picked up his phone. "We should call the chief."

She nodded her agreement. "Yes. And before he makes his own phone call. Ask the chief to find out if the professor uses the same word when he's describing what Eddie said."

"And verify the word." Matt lifted his phone to his ear. His conversation with the chief was brief and to the point.

When he'd hung up, he smiled at Nicki. "The chief agreed to let us know what the professor says."

"Great." Nicki winced when she stretched out her back.

"I think you should lie down for a while."

"I think I'd rather go take another look at the murder board." When Matt started to protest, Nicki added, "it will take my mind off these few minor aches and pains."

"Uh huh. Minor." He crossed his arms over his chest. "Your face isn't calling them 'minor'. I say you stay right here and rest."

"Fine. If you'll sit with me for a few minutes and give me your best expert opinion on how Eddie would have gone about quietly selling that sheet of stamps."

Matt gathered up his notebook and phone. He fluffed out one of the decorative pillows and grabbed the colorful throw Nicki kept over the back of the couch. "Lie down while I mull it over."

With a resigned sigh Nicki scooted into a prone position as Matt arranged the throw over her before taking a chair on the other side of the coffee table. Nicki thought it looked as if he was getting pretty comfortable in it.

"You aren't going to sit there and watch me sleep, are you?"

"Maybe." When she frowned, he grinned at her. "But I was thinking of going into your office and doing some work, after I answered your question of course."

"Okay. Answer away, Watson."

"A private party or an auction house."

"An auction house?" Nicki shook her head. "Hard to keep it quiet if you sell something at an auction house."

"If he was trying to keep it quiet, and that's a big 'if', Sherlock, he probably only wanted to keep it quiet in Soldoff. So he could have used an auction house. Sam and Ben might have picked up on a sheet of the stamps being sold, but it isn't the only one in existence. Eddie could have told the auction house to keep the source anonymous."

Nicki considered it. "Since Eddie wasn't a big-time collector, it might have been hard for him to quietly connect with a private buyer."

"Especially if he needed a quick sale," Matt added.

"But then the question would be, why? Why would he need a quick sale? And even if he didn't, why sell the stamps now?" She looked over at Matt. "Do you have any connections at one of the well-known auction houses?"

"You mean like Christies?" Matt shook his head. "But I am friends with a guy who works at Heritage House."

Her interest immediately piqued back up. "The one in San Francisco? Ben had one of their business cards on his desk. Can you call your friend?"

Matt dutifully held out his phone and scrolled through his contacts. "Calling right now." Matt tapped on his phone before he held it up to his ear. Several seconds of silence rolled by before he smiled.

"Hey, Ryan. It's Matt Dillon. Yeah, fine man. How about you?"

Nicki threw the cover off and managed to sit up. She waved away Matt's frown and mouthed the word "coffee" before walking stiffly across the room. As much as it hurt, she was sure moving would be more help than lying down all day, so she gritted her teeth and limped her way to the kitchen to make them a cup of coffee. She'd managed to get the drip process underway when Matt walked in.

"Why don't you go lie down, and I'll bring that out to you?" His expression set into a stubborn look that Nicki was beginning to recognize as his I'm-not-going-to-budge face. "Go lie down or I won't tell you what Ryan said."

Nicki started to make a comment about his blackmailing

skills when she thought better of it. That really was enough moving around for the time being.

"You know where the coffee mugs are," she said as she made her way slowly around the island and into the hallway. Matt caught up with her, a mug of coffee in each hand, just as she reached the couch. Carefully lowering herself onto the cushions, Nicki managed to get comfortable again. She propped her shoulders on a pillow she'd shoved up against the couch's arm.

"Okay. I'm lying down." She smiled her thanks when Matt handed her a mug of coffee. "What did your friend say?"

"Ryan didn't know of any valuable stamps coming up for sale in the last month or so. But he's going to check the catalogs. We're going to meet him for lunch the day after tomorrow."

"We are?"

"The outing will do you good, and according to Alex, who I called this morning, most of the muscle pain from being banged around in your car should be gone by then. But don't do any jogging."

"I hadn't planned on it," Nicki said dryly.

He laughed. "It's nice when we agree on something."

Nicki smiled and closed her eyes. She heard Matt walk across the room, his footsteps fading away, and thought he must have gone into the office to get his work done. But moments later he came back and settled into the chair again. It wasn't long before she heard the soft click of a keyboard. *Checking his email.* She snuggled beneath the blanket. It was comforting to know he wasn't far away. She was just drifting off when the sharp ring of a cell phone cut through the air.

She glanced over at Matt who gave her an apologetic look.

"Sorry. I should have put it on mute." He lifted it up to his ear and said a soft "Matt Dillon", followed by "hello, Chief."

Nicki raised her head and propped it in the crook of her

elbow, staring at him as he listened to whatever the chief was telling him.

"Yeah, that is interesting. I don't know. Uh huh. Well, thanks for letting us know, I'll pass it along to Nicki. She's doing fine. Resting, per the doctor's order. Okay. Thanks." He lowered the phone and grinned at her.

"Well, it looks like visiting my buddy at the auction house is a good idea after all."

"Is it?" Nicki's smile grew wider.

"Yep. The professor is absolutely certain that Eddie said he *couldn't* sell him the sheet of stamps. The chief said that might mean that Eddie couldn't bring himself to sell them, or that he'd already sold them. Since you like the second explanation, then I guess we'll be making that trip into the city."

CHAPTER NINETEEN

THREE HOT BATHS, TWO GOOD NIGHTS OF SLEEP, AND A constant stream of visitors to cheer her up, had Nicki feeling human again by the time they left to visit the Heritage Auction house in downtown San Francisco. Nicki was looking forward to the trip. She'd spent the day before catching up on her blog and novel writing, while Matt had moved his few belongings back to Maxie's house where he'd spent the day working in the genealogist's well-equipped and spacious office. By the time Matt picked her up for their appointment in the city, she was happy with the sizable dent she'd made in her backlog of work.

It took them just over an hour to reach Battery Street where the auction house was located, and another fifteen minutes to find a parking garage with an empty space for the car. Nicki winced at the posted rates and made a mental note to buy their lunch today. After all, she'd dragged Matt into another murder, and she didn't want him to pay for that dubious privilege. When they reached the sidewalk, Matt turned right.

"It's a couple of blocks down."

"How long have you known this friend of yours?" She was always amazed at the number of people Matt knew all over the country. "And is he a friend, or more of a business acquaintance?"

"Definitely a friend. We go back a ways. I met him in college."

"Oh? Is he another engineer who fled to the arts?"

Matt grinned. "Hardly. He majored in Art History, or something like that." He winked at her. "We met because he plays a mean game of basketball."

"That's a sport, right?"

"Nicki, I live in the Midwest. I can't be seen in public with someone who doesn't know that basketball is a sport."

She laughed at the exasperation in his voice. "All right, all right." She held her hands up in surrender. "I *do* know something about basketball, and I confess I've even been to a game or two."

"Really?" Now he sounded skeptical.

"Really. My mom was a Knicks fan."

Matt looked at her and his eyes softened behind the lenses of his glasses. "I wish I could have met her."

Nicki slipped an arm through his. "I do too. She would have liked you."

"Do you think so?"

"Uh huh. She liked the bookish types."

He frowned. "Bookish? Is that a compliment? Because it doesn't sound like one."

They kept up their easy banter for the entire two blocks to the offices of Heritage Auctions. Matt stopped under the signature green awning shading the front entryway.

"Here it is." He opened the door with a flourish, ushering Nicki inside.

"Hey, Matt! It's good to see you."

Nicki smiled at the man in the neatly tailored suit and silk tie, who was coming toward them with his hand outstretched. He was the opposite of Matt. Ryan Bevins was shorter and much stockier than his college friend. Nicki thought he looked more like a football player rather than a basketball player.

His blond hair was neatly styled, and he looked every inch a successful businessman, right down to a neatly folded kerchief in his breast pocket. But his blue eyes shone with a bit of mischief that was charmingly at odds with his formal attire. Matt stepped forward and clasped his hand as the two men gave each other a friendly swat on the back.

"It's been a while, Ryan," Matt acknowledged as he stepped back next to Nicki. "This is Nicki Connors. We work together. Nicki, this is the friend I told you about, Ryan Bevins."

"Well aren't you the lucky guy." Ryan took Nicki's offered hand and tucked it between both of his. "I should have gone into publishing."

"You'd have to learn how to read and write," Matt said. He looked at the hand Ryan was still holding and then back up at his friend.

Nicki withdrew her hand before Matt said something, and widened her smile. "I'm pleased to meet you, Ryan. I hope we aren't interrupting your day."

"You're not. And I'm glad you could make the trip into town. Why don't we go up to my office?" He gallantly offered Nicki his arm and strolled off, leaving Matt to trail along behind them.

Fully aware that Ryan was only pulling Matt's chain with all the attention he was lavishing on her, Nicki decided to do what she always did when faced with male egos colliding. She'd let the two men hash it out.

So she relaxed and walked along, her arm securely tucked inside of Ryan's, listening to his explanation of the various treasures on display. Many of them were noted as available for immediate purchase, and sporting price tags that made her eyes water.

"Here we are," Ryan declared once they'd exited the elevator. "I'm a couple of doors down on the right." He opened one in the row of look-alike doors and stood aside so she could precede him into a very tastefully decorated office. Muted watercolors adorned a wall painted in a light gray. A black mahogany desk sat under the window, with two leather wing chairs positioned in front of it. Ryan led her to one of the chairs, but when she gave a slight wince as she slowly sank into it, Ryan's friendly smile turned into a look of concern.

"Are you all right?"

"I'm fine," Nicki assured him. "Just a little sore is all."

Matt took the chair next to hers and fixed his own worried gaze on her face. "She was in a bad car accident a few days ago."

"Clearly not that bad, since I'm sitting here and I'm fine," Nicki protested.

"Let me get you both some water." Ryan stepped over to a small refrigerator in the corner of his office and withdrew two bottles. He took a glass from a shelf and filled it from a small bucket of ice before pouring the water into it. He carried the glass and a second bottle across the room and handed the crystal glass, along with a napkin he'd also grabbed, to Nicki. She murmured her thanks and took a sip to keep both men happy. Ryan tossed the other bottle in Matt's general direction before he took a seat behind the desk.

"Now then. You were asking about stamps?" He reached into his desk drawer and pulled out a thin file. "Specifically a sheet of uninverted Jennys issued in 2013 by the U.S. Postal Service?"

"That's right." Nicki looked over at Matt who added a

curt nod. "We were wondering if anyone had approached Heritage House to sell them?"

Ryan shook his head. "Not to sell. I checked our catalog, and also with our offices in Dallas and New York City, and none of our locations has made such a sale as far as I could find."

"Oh." Slightly deflated, Nicki leaned back into the chair.

Matt glanced over at her. "It was a long shot." He shifted his gaze to Ryan. "But thanks for taking a look."

"Not for sale," his friend continued. "But a colleague of mine here said that a gentleman made an appointment several months ago to have his stamps appraised. He brought in a sheet that matches the description of what you're looking for."

Nicki once again scooted to the edge of her seat. "He did? Did he give a name?"

Ryan flashed an apologetic smile. "He wanted to remain anonymous, and we're committed to respecting his privacy."

Now Matt leaned forward. "Well if his name was Eddie Parker, then he isn't worried too much about his privacy anymore. He was murdered over a week ago. And the stamps are missing."

The auction house employee's smile faded away. "Murdered?" Ryan opened the files and looked at his notes. "Then I'll go as far as to say that I agree. Our potential client won't be worrying about his privacy."

"So it was Eddie Parker who came here?" Nicki asked.

"I can't confirm or deny that." Ryan smiled as he nodded his head. "Now I have a question. Was this man murdered because of the stamps?"

Matt ran a hand through his hair. "That's the million-dollar question. Or rather the fifty-thousand dollar one. We don't know. It could be he was. Or, he could have sold the stamps before he was murdered."

"Or the man who said he would buy the stamps murdered him," Nicki said.

Ryan shot the dark-haired editor a curious look. "Why are you interested in this Mr. Parker and his stamps?"

"He was a client of a friend of ours, and she was unfortunate enough to have discovered his body," Matt explained.

"I see." Ryan's wide hand rubbed the back of his neck. "He might have sold them on his own. I have a few connections within the private market, both dealers and collectors. I could put out a few discreet inquiries for you."

"Thank you. That would be a big help." Nicki smiled. "Especially since we weren't sure where to go from here."

Ryan beamed back at her. "Well, let me dig around, see if anything floats to the surface. And if it does, I'll be happy to come up your way to tell you whatever I find out."

"That's why the telephone was invented, Ryan." Matt drummed one finger against the arm of the chair.

Ryan looked like he was trying not to laugh. "It's a nice drive. I don't mind making it. By the way, buddy, when did you say you'd be returning home?"

"Stuff it, Bevins."

Ryan stood and came around the desk, grinning at Matt. "Congrats, Dillon. I always knew you'd take the fall first."

The two men shook hands, once again acting like long-lost friends, while Nicki mentally rolled her eyes. It didn't take a rocket scientist to figure out what they were talking about, and she wondered if either of these alleged grown-ups intended to ask her what she thought of this whole thing. She waited politely through another five minutes of catch-up talk before smiling at Ryan.

"We're having lunch near Fisherman's Wharf. Can you join us?"

She pretended not to notice Ryan's sideways glance at Matt before he shook his head. "I have a heavy day in front of me and sent out for something earlier." He looked at his watch. "It should be here any minute."

"We don't want to keep you from your lunch." Matt held out his hand to help Nicki out of her chair. "I'll order us a ride to the marina."

"No you won't. It's only a few blocks, Matt. And I'm fine. The walk will do me good after sitting for a while." She smiled sweetly. "Unless *you're* too tired to walk."

Matt snorted and took her arm. He and Ryan flanked her on either side as they walked to the elevator.

When the doors opened, Nicki held her hand out to Ryan. "Thank you again. If you find out anything else, please give me a call."

"I will if Matt will send me your cell number," Ryan grinned.

"Shut up, Bevins," Matt said without any real heat behind it. "You can call me, and I'll relay the information to Nicki."

The door closed on Ryan's laughter as Nicki turned an exasperated stare on Matt.

"We aren't in junior high any more, Matt Dillon. What was that all about?"

He sighed and ran an agitated hand through his hair. "Honestly? I have no idea."

She maintained her silence and smiled at the staff in the showroom as they strolled through the first floor and out to the sidewalk. Once they were no longer within earshot of the auction house staff, she shook her head at him. "Can you behave for the rest of the day?"

Matt reached over and tweaked a lock of her hair. "I'll do my best, Sherlock."

Thinking that was as good as she would get out of him, Nicki pointed in the direction of the bay. "The water is that way." After walking along in silence for several minutes, she glanced over at him. "Do you believe Eddie sold those stamps?"

"He went to the trouble of getting them appraised. And somewhere between then and when Dr. Weston saw them, he must have found a buyer. So yeah. I think he sold them."

"Me too." Nicki kept her head bent as they walked along. "I wonder why?"

"Why he sold the stamps?" Matt shrugged. "I assume for the usual reason. He needed the money."

"For what? He didn't own a house, or a car for that matter. And according to myMason, the only money Eddie owed on the diner was the loan from him."

"Just another piece of the missing puzzle, I guess." Matt pointed to the large Fisherman's Wharf sign that had come into view. "Do you know where you want to eat?"

"Of course. It's right on the pier."

Two hours later they were walking off their delicious seafood lunch and enjoying the ocean air. Matt had declared a moratorium on the topic of murder, so they'd talked over possible articles for *Food & Wine Online*, and favorite places they'd traveled to.

Matt was astounded that she'd never been to Mexico, and she was equally astonished he hadn't yet made it to Paris. An oversight, she argued, that he should correct at once, since he was so knowledgeable about French wine and Champagne. They'd moved on to discussing the best car for her, with Nicki sure she'd get another compact, while Matt pushed for a sturdier SUV.

"Nice thought, Dillon, but a pricey one," Nicki said after he'd finished pointing out all the benefits of several of the newer models.

"Maybe so. But they won't fold in half at the first impact like those compacts do."

"But you have to consider the gas mileage too. And the insurance..." Nicki broke off when she heard her name. She turned around and came face to face with Rob. And a tall brunette who was pasted to his side before she took a quick step away.

Nicki blinked at her boyfriend, and mentally adjusted to the fact that he wasn't out of town the way he'd claimed he'd be. Didn't he break a date with her because he said his business trip had been extended... again?

"Hello, Rob. This is certainly a surprise." While Rob sputtered without managing to get out an intelligible word, Nicki smiled at the woman standing next to him, her large brown eyes blinking rapidly. "Hi. I'm Nicki. And you are?"

"Tricia. Rob and I work together." She unwound her arm from Rob's and took another step away from him. "You're his girlfriend, aren't you?"

Tricia's face was beet-red. She was very obviously so embarrassed, that Nicki felt sorry for her. She gave the uncomfortable-looking woman a friendly smile.

"Don't let this bother you."

"Nicki. My trip was cut short at the last minute, and I..."

"Rob." Nicki cut him off. "Maybe we can discuss this when you aren't out on a date?"

"That's not fair, Nicki. You're standing here with another guy. And I don't remember you telling me that you were coming into the city."

"Why would I, when you're supposed to be away on business? Why don't you give me a call when you decide you're back in town? Because right now, you're embarrassing Tricia." Nicki gave the red-faced woman another smile. "It was nice to meet you."

She turned around and walked in the opposite direction,

her back stiff and her chin up high. She'd gone a dozen steps before Matt caught up with her.

"Are you okay?"

"Thank you," Nicki said.

"For what?"

She kept her eyes straight-ahead. "For not getting into a sparring match with Rob the way you did with Ryan."

"I wouldn't have done that. I like Ryan. I don't like Rob. But you can thank me for not giving him a pop in the mouth."

Nicki stopped dead and turned to stare at him. "You wouldn't."

Matt shrugged. "I would, because he hurt your feelings, and because I don't like him." He ran a hand up and down her arm. "What do you want to do, Nicki? Go somewhere and have a drink and talk about this?"

She would. But certainly not with him. He was her editor, for goodness sakes. And a guy. What she wanted was a good glass of wine and a girl-talk session with Jenna and Alex. She forced her lips into a smile and shook her head. "No. I'm fine."

"Okay." Matt didn't look like he believed her.

"Since we have all the information we came for..." She gave a short laugh. "And some we didn't come for, let's go home."

Matt heaved a big breath and looked back in the direction where they'd left Rob and Tricia. "Okay. That's a good idea."

CHAPTER TWENTY

WHEN MATT HAD DROPPED NICKI OFF AT HER townhouse, she'd told him that she was tired and intended to call Jenna and then go straight to bed. Something in her face or tone must have alerted Matt that she wasn't in any mood to get into an argument, because he'd simply nodded and walked her to her front door before turning around and heading back to his rental car.

Now she stood in her doorway and gave him a short wave before closing herself inside. She wasn't even halfway to her kitchen before she had her cell to her ear, telling Jenna to come over right now. Nicki was pouring out two glasses of wine and talking to Alex on the speaker phone when her front door slammed shut and the slap of flip-flops sounded in the hallway.

"What's up?"

"Exactly what I'm waiting to hear." Alex's voice floated out from the phone Nicki had propped in its little stand on the counter.

Nicki slid the second glass of wine over to Jenna. "Matt

and I took a trip into San Francisco today to talk with a friend of his who works at a big auction house there."

"Okay." Jenna took a sip of her wine. "Nice day for a drive into the city."

"It turns out that Eddie Parker had taken his sheet of stamps there just a few months ago to have them appraised."

"Why would he do that?" Alex's disembodied voice asked. "Unless he wanted to insure them?"

Jenna frowned. "Or sell them." She looked over at Nicki, her eyebrows raised halfway up her forehead. "Did he sell them? Like, at that auction house maybe?"

"Which would leave us with no motive for him being killed," Alex pointed out.

"Well, shoot." Jenna drained a full quarter of her wine glass.

"You're both getting carried away." Nicki raised her voice to be sure Alex could hear her. "He did have them appraised, but he didn't sell them. At least not through the auction house."

Her tall computer-whiz friend pounced on that. "So you think he did sell them? Who to?"

"Do you think that's who he was meeting the night he was killed? And whoever the stamp-buyer is, that's who killed him?" Alex's voice had risen a whole octave by the time she'd finished speaking.

Nicki held up her hands. "All we know is that he had the stamps appraised and now they're missing." She picked up her wine glass. "And before you ask, yes, I think he sold them. Or at least intended to. But that isn't what I wanted to talk to you both about."

"Uh oh." Alex's sigh came through the phone. "If you don't want to talk about murder, whatever you *do* want to talk about must be pretty serious."

"You went into the city with Matt?" Jenna looked around. "Where is he?"

"At Maxie's, I'd imagine."

"Don't tell me you broke up with Matt?" Alex demanded.

"How can she break up with Matt?" Jenna laughed. "According to Nicki, he isn't even her boyfriend."

Nicki blew out an exasperated breath. "This isn't about Matt. It's about Rob."

"Rob?" Both her friends said in unison.

"Matt and I had lunch at Fisherman's Wharf, and we ran into Rob."

Alex groaned. "And he wanted to know what you were doing there with Matt?"

"Well I hope you told him it was none of his business. He's never around anyway," Jenna sniffed.

"No. He didn't want to know what I was doing there with Matt. At least not at first. He was too busy trying to get out an explanation about Tricia."

Jenna set her glass on the quartz top of the island. "Who's Tricia?"

"He was with another woman?" Alex sounded floored.

Nicki nodded at the phone. "Yep. A very pretty, very tall, leggy brunette who was draped all over him."

"Well. That's a first for you, and thankfully the last of lover-boy." Jenna lifted her glass in a farewell salute.

Nicki smiled. Trust the straightforward Jenna to say out loud what she'd been thinking during the ride back to Soldoff. And with more than a little guilt.

She should have been angry with Rob. Instead what she mostly felt was relief. Which is why she didn't want Matt around at the moment. She'd been dating Rob for almost two years. Surely their relationship deserved a bit more inner contemplation than a simple "see ya later"? What was bothering her was the temptation to do exactly that and call it a day.

Not nice, Nicki Connors. Not a nice way to treat him at all. She sighed as she halfway listened to the debate her two friends were having on what she should do next. Her thoughts came fully back to her surroundings when Jenna said, "lousy boyfriend".

"I wasn't the best girlfriend either," Nicki cut in.

"You are not going to tell me that him stepping out on you was in any way your fault?" Jenna demanded.

"No. It certainly wasn't my fault. But I'm not blameless in this... well, whatever this is. I love you both for feeling that way, but Rob and I both contributed to the downfall of our relationship."

"All you need to do is let him know," the ever-practical Alex said. "That the relationship is done, I mean. Not that you contributed to its downfall."

"The old, 'it's me not you' line, still works pretty well." Jenna grinned at Nicki. "If it works, I say go with it." Her grin widened. "I take it that Matt was standing right there when Rob was caught with good old Tricia."

Alex laughed. "If he was, I'll bet Matt was smiling from ear to ear."

"You two are impossible. Rob's a nice guy. Tricia would be lucky to have him."

Jenna shrugged. "Well good. Because she can. Have him, I mean." She drank the last of her wine. "Okay. What's the plan?"

The three friends had a short debate about what Nicki should do next, finally settling on waiting for Rob to call.

"And if he doesn't," Nicki concluded, "then I'll call him next week. We really should talk."

"Closure is a good thing," Alex agreed.

"As long as it ends in a 'goodbye', I'll go with that." Jenna put her hands on her lower back and stretched upward. "What's the next step with Matt?"

"He, Maxie and Mason will be by first thing in the morning. We're going into the police station for myMason's interview with the chief." She smiled at Jenna. "I know that's not what you meant, but it's the next thing I'm doing with Matt, and that's as far as I'm going to think about it."

"I CAN'T BELIEVE he might have sold those stamps." Maxie kept her voice low as she looked around.

The four of them, Maxie, Mason, Nicki and Matt were standing on the sidewalk, just outside of the Soldoff Police Department. Since it wasn't yet ten in the morning, the square was fairly deserted. The only places showing any signs of activity were Sandy's restaurant and the Starbucks Coffee directly across from it.

"The fact Eddie had them appraised doesn't mean he sold them," her husband said in his usual calm and reasonable voice.

"But if he did, we don't have a motive for his murder," Maxie complained.

"And if he wanted to sell them, our stamp collectors just became our best suspects. Ryan called me this morning and said none of his contacts knew about a sheet of those stamps being for sale. So that leaves Ben and Sam." Other than "good morning", it was the first thing Matt had said since he'd knocked on Nicki's door.

"Why is that, dear?" Maxie's frown showed that she clearly didn't like that idea.

Mason put an arm around his wife's shoulders. "Why don't we go in and hear what the chief has to say? We all have

our opinions on the case, but in the end, only his matters."
He winked at Nicki. "Isn't that right?"

She smiled at the former head of the Soldoff Police
Department. "That's what Chief Turnlow keeps telling me."

Matt didn't say anything as he stepped aside to let Nicki
precede him into the station. She wondered if she should
have a talk with him, as well as with Rob. An entirely
different talk, of course, but a talk nevertheless.

She wanted to be sure he knew there were no expectations
that he would be stepping into Rob's "boyfriend" shoes. She
really wasn't looking for the next one in line, and was worried
Matt might believe she was. After thinking it over the night
before, she concluded that the reason Matt was so protective
was simply his negative reaction to the fact that Rob wasn't.

Matt was definitely old-fashioned in some of his notions,
like who should pay for a meal, or opening doors, and Rob
had never met her editor's expectations for how a boyfriend
should act. That was all there was to it. No matter what her
friends thought.

Satisfied that she was right, Nicki glanced over at Matt
who quickly dropped his eyes to the ground. Yep. They definitely needed to have that talk.

"Nice everyone could make it." Chief Turnlow sounded
more amused than annoyed as he looked over the crowd
standing on the other side of the counter. "Since my office is
too small to fit everyone comfortably, why don't we have our
little chat out here."

"Suits us." Mason looked back at the chief. "What do you
need to know, Paul?"

The chief walked over and leaned against the counter
right across from Mason. "Your wife said you went on a last-
minute fishing trip with Charlie Freeman."

"That's right." Mason nodded. "And the night before I ran

a couple of errands. The last one was at that Stop2Shop right outside of town." He reached into his pocket. "Here's the receipt. I went home after that."

Chief Turnlow didn't even glance at the receipt in Mason's hand. "Yeah. I know. I dropped in there to see what cars their security cameras had picked up driving along the highway a couple of hours before and after the time of death. Saw yours pull in, and then out again ten minutes later. You turned toward home." He smiled at the other three faces lined up along the counter. "The opposite direction from the diner."

"Why didn't you call and tell me that?" Maxie demanded. "I've been worried sick over this whole interrogation thing."

"And now you don't have to worry," Mason told his wife with a smile before turning back to the chief. "See any other interesting cars driving along the road that night?"

"Jake Garces. He said he had dinner at his mother's place, and she lives out that way."

Mason frowned. "That's his alibi? He was having dinner at his mother's house?"

The chief nodded. "He was at his mother's. He could have sneaked out, or she could be lying to cover for her son. Roberta had dinner with Gordon Twill, who was thirty minutes late because of car trouble, or so he says. But that's not enough time to kill Eddie, trash the office and get over to the apartment and trash it as well. Roberta was at the restaurant waiting for Gordon. Sam Moore left his shop at six and went home, so no alibi there, and Ben Caulkin was in the city with friends. But he left about four, and even with rush hour traffic, he could have made it back in time to meet Eddie and kill him. That leaves Dr. Weston. He claims he was in Maryland at the time, but he's on a sabbatical this semester so he wasn't teaching. He could have flown back out here without anyone knowing it."

He paused and looked at the countertop. "Or it could be

someone else who simply came upon the diner and was looking for an easy mark. If Eddie was going to sell those stamps, it could be he was meeting with the buyer that night and things just went wrong."

"I feel like we aren't any closer than when we started." Maxie sighed and leaned her head against her husband's shoulder.

"Well whoever it was, took the cell phone so we couldn't see who Eddie had been talking to." Matt glanced at the chief. "Can we get the cell phone records?"

"Already asked for them," the chief said. "But it will take time. I've also asked for bank records and balances. None of the persons of interest here have anything unusual in their balances. Neither did Eddie. None are over two thousand, but I haven't received the full records yet."

Nicki frowned. Something about that didn't seem right.

The former police chief nodded at the current one. "It's looking like a business deal that went south is the best bet. Maybe those stamps will turn up somewhere."

"That would be helpful," Chief Turnlow agreed. "In the meantime, I'm not sure there's much else we can do folks but wait for the bank and cell phone records. It might take another week."

He turned his gaze on Nicki, interrupting the elusive thought about the bank information. "I've checked out the vehicles registered to all five of the persons of interest, shall we say, who live here. None of them owns a white truck. But Danny is still searching."

"Thank you, Chief. I appreciate it. And please thank Danny for me too." Nicki glanced at an unhappy Matt and smiled. "Maybe I'll get a pickup truck."

The big man standing across the counter laughed. "Maybe you should." He looked at Matt. "Not sure what's going on, but fish or cut bait, son."

Matt snorted. "Thanks, but I'm not the only one with the hook in the water." He stuck his hands in his pockets. "I guess we can get going."

Nicki looked over at Maxie who rolled her eyes. Once the four of them were out on the sidewalk again, Nicki latched onto Matt's arm and started pulling him toward the path leading to the bronze statue of a grapevine. "We'll be right back," she called over her shoulder to Maxie.

She'd barely set foot on the walkway that cut through the center of the square when her phone rang. As the ringtone she'd set for Rob floated out into the air, Matt stopped dead in his tracks.

"I'll catch up with you later."

Nicki adjusted her grip on the sleeve of his shirt. "Oh no you don't, Matt Dillon." She grabbed her phone with her free hand and pressed the connect button with her thumb. "Hi, Rob. I can't talk long. Yes. I think that's a good idea." Nicki continued to listen while her gaze stayed fixed on Matt. He stared back at her, his eyes narrowed and a stubborn set to his chin. "All right. I'll see you then."

She slid her phone into her back pocket, letting go of Matt's sleeve as she turned to face him, her hands on her hips. "Before you ask, and with the complete understanding it really isn't any of your business, I'm not going to break up with a boyfriend over the phone, or by sending a text message. It takes a discussion. Between two adults."

She continued to stare at him as Matt blinked rapidly and then adjusted his glasses on his nose. "Um... Okay. I can understand that."

When he started to grin, she held up one finger. "And if you're thinking that now you've suddenly become stuck with me, I am not expecting you to step in and take his place. So if that's what's put you in such a bad mood, you can stop worrying about it."

Matt's grin faded. "Okay."

"Okay." Nicki gave a firm nod. "Do you have anything else to say that does not include my personal life?"

Matt shook his head. "Nope. Not a thing."

"Good. Then maybe we can get back to solving this murder, so you can go home to your regular job." She glared up at him. "Unless you'd rather go back to Kansas City right now? I can call you if anything new comes up."

Matt's easy grin was back. "No. I'll just hang here for a few more days."

"Fine." Nicki whirled around and marched back along the path.

Matt caught up with her before she reached the sidewalk and fell into step beside her.

"Any ideas about how we're going to solve this?"

"Not yet." She kept walking with her eyes straight-ahead. "But there's something in all these dots that we just aren't connecting. Once I've had time to clear out my mind, it might come to me." She finally glanced up at him. "MyMason called it the missing piece of the puzzle."

"Well. Dumping one hundred and seventy pounds of dead weight should help clear your mind."

"Matt." Nicki stopped and crossed her arms, glaring up at him. "Enough."

He took a quick step to the side and held his hands up. "Changing the subject." He stuck his hands in his jean pockets and looked up at the sky. "Nice weather we're having."

Nicki managed to tamp down the urge to pull her hair out and kept on walking.

CHAPTER TWENTY-ONE

NICKI MARCHED INTO HER TOWNHOUSE AND SHUT THE door. She'd firmly told Matt to go home with Maxie and her husband. She'd ignored his protest, and Maxie's frown. Nicki had not been happy to see a quiet upset Matt, but she didn't want to put up with a smug, I-told-you-so one either. Jenna had used up all her patience the night before with her gloating about the demise of poor Rob. Despite what her longtime friend thought, Rob did have a number of good qualities.

She threw her purse onto the hallway table and walked back to the kitchen, heading straight for the wine refrigerator. At this point, she didn't care that it was completely out of character for her to have a glass of wine before noon.

The cork was still in her hand when her front door opened and slammed shut. Nicki sighed and poured a healthy amount of wine into a glass. First she'd apparently made Matt's day for all the wrong reasons, and now she was going to have to tell Jenna that unless something else turned up, or she suddenly had an unexpected and brilliant insight, Eddie Parker's case might go cold.

"Hey. I saw you get dropped off. How did the interview with Chief Turnlow go?" Jenna walked over to the kitchen island, her gaze landing on the full glass of wine in Nicki's hand. "Um. I guess it didn't go too well?"

"The chief says we have to wait."

Jenna frowned. "Wait? Wait for what?"

"The detailed bank statements to arrive, the cell company to release Eddie's phone records, for the sheet of stamps to turn up somewhere, or whoever Eddie met with that night to raise his hand and say, 'it was me, it was me'." When Jenna raised her eyebrows, Nicki sighed. "Both the present and the former chief feel it's a good possibility that Eddie was going to sell his stamps that night, and whoever was going to buy them ended up killing him." Nicki swirled the wine around in the glass. "Which of course makes no sense."

"Why not?"

Nicki set the glass aside, deciding she didn't want wine at this hour of the morning after all, and headed for the pantry. She emerged a minute later with a bag of chips in one hand, and a jar of chocolate-covered peanuts in the other. She set them on the counter just as her phone rang. Retrieving it from her back pocket, she looked at the caller ID and handed the phone to Jenna.

"It's Alex. You talk to her while I get some bowls."

Jenna took the phone and held it up to her ear. "Hi. No, she's right here."

Nicki waved as she dumped the entire jar into a metal bowl.

"Oh, that was the sound of chocolate-covered peanuts hitting the sides of a metal bowl. Nope, the whole jar. She's putting it on the counter. Next to her very full glass of wine." Jenna listened for a long moment, not saying a word. "Okay. I'll tell her."

Nicki looked over at her friend while she pulled open the bag of chips. "Well?"

"Alex said to tell you she has three days off and was planning on wedding dress shopping with her mom, but now she's going to call and tell her she has to make an emergency trip here. So no wedding dress shopping. Again."

"Great." Nicki closed her eyes. "The wedding date has already been put off once. If it's delayed again, Alex's mom will blow a gasket."

"The first time wasn't your fault. Ty wanted to save up more money so they could honeymoon in his latest choice of exotic places. I think it was Bali this time."

"I know that. And you know that. Even Alex knows that. But her mom thinks it was my fault because Alex was busy helping solve what she called 'Nicki's murders'." Thinking some wine sounded pretty good after all, Nicki picked up her glass and took a sip.

"That's true." Jenna nodded. "Alex's mom does think it was all your fault."

Nicki sighed and took a second sip. "She's going to hate me."

Jenna shrugged. "Also true. But not for long because you know she adores us both. Now that we've settled that, why do you believe this mysterious stamp-buyer didn't kill Eddie?"

"Because if he was there to buy the stamps, then either Eddie already had them out of their hiding place, so there was no need for the killer to search the office or his apartment, or if Eddie was waiting to get them out until he was paid, then the stamps would have still been in their hiding place." Nicki popped a chocolate peanut into her mouth.

"Which leaves us where?" Jenna asked. "If it wasn't the mysterious buyer, and everyone else either didn't know enough to steal the stamps or had an alibi, then who was it? Someone we've completely overlooked, and so has the chief?"

"I don't know. I haven't had time to think it through."
Nicki winced when Jenna deflated right in front of her.

"Well, like you said, maybe you'll get a brilliant insight."
Jenna looked at the floor. "And if you do, I want you to tell it
to the chief and then back away from this." She looked up at
Nicki with troubled eyes. "Someone ran you off the road and
almost killed you. Getting justice for a client who happened
to make great burgers is not worth risking your life for, and I
can't live with that. I want us to just forget the whole thing."

Maybe she could walk away and leave Eddie's murder
behind her, but Nicki doubted if Jenna could. She knew her
friend. The computer whiz always helped anyone, even her
clients, whether they could pay her or not. And not being
able to help Eddie, either the night he was killed or getting
answers for him now, would bother Jenna forever.

As Nicki struggled to find something to say to reassure
her friend, Jenna turned and headed for the door.

"Jenna," Nicki called out. She came around the island and
chased after her. "Jenna, wait."

"I'll talk to you later." The tall brunette pulled open the
front door and almost ran over a startled Suzanne.

"Oh, hello, Jenna. I'm glad you're here. I wanted to talk to
you about Eddie's memorial service. It's next...." Suzanne
bumped against the door as Jenna walked right past her. The
older woman turned her head and looked at Nicki. "What has
her so upset?"

"Eddie's murder investigation has hit a wall." Nicki heard
Jenna's front door slam shut. Well, if she was still slamming
doors, then maybe all Jenna needed was time alone to sort
through things. Nicki hoped so. And despite the wrath of
Alex's mom, she was very glad Alex was on her way here.

Knowing that waiting for Alex to arrive so they could talk
things over with Jenna together was the best idea, Nicki
headed back to the kitchen with Suzanne following after her.

"That's too bad. But Maxie asked me to arrange a memorial service for Eddie since he doesn't have any family in the area."

"That we're aware of," Nicki said as she reached for her wine glass.

"Yes, well. Anyway, I've managed to squeeze in time to make the arrangements, but I need to know if Jenna was intending to speak at the service. I mean since she knew Eddie, worked with him, and found the body and all." When Nicki took a sip of her wine, Suzanne stared at her. "It's a little early for that, isn't it?"

"Not today it isn't. And I doubt that Jenna wants to get up and speak at the memorial service."

Suzanne took out her cell phone and tapped on the screen. "I'll put her down as a 'possible' and check back with her later." She set her phone aside and picked up a folder she'd laid on the counter. "I also came by to give you this."

"What is it?"

"With helping out at the diner and then having to arrange the memorial, I haven't had time to finish the planning for the cooking courses. Now I have done most of it, so don't panic."

"Why would I panic?" Nicki didn't like where this conversation was headed. It seemed to be a day for bad news.

"I have the whole checklist right here on the front," Suzanne went on as if Nicki hadn't said a word. She pushed the folder over toward Nicki. "Just go right down the list and you'll be fine."

Nicki looked at the multiple-page list attached to the front of the folder and did exactly what Suzanne had told her not to do — panic. She had a blog and a novel she was behind on, and if she didn't get those outstanding articles finished for *Food & Wine Online*, she wouldn't be able to pay her rent, much less buy a new car. She didn't have time for this. She really didn't.

"Suzanne, I can't..."

The middle-aged blond gave her a sunny smile. "I know we all agreed that you wouldn't have to do any of the planning, but that was before bodies started to pile up all over the place."

"One body, Suzanne. It was one body."

"Yes, well. Things have changed. I'm needed at the diner every day or Jake would be lost." She pointed at the folder. "Besides, you can see most of the tasks are already done. And if you need help, you can stop in at the diner and I'll be happy to explain anything to you."

"But I really can't..."

"And I'm late meeting Jake there. The reopening yesterday went so well. So much support from the community, it was absolutely wonderful! I hope you can stop in today and soak it all in." She looked at her wristwatch with the bright pink band covered in rhinestones. "I have to go. Now don't forget to ask about anything that you don't understand."

Before Nicki could lodge even a minimal protest, Suzanne was gone out the front door. Nicki looked at the folder. She didn't even have a car. How was she supposed to run all over the place to get this very long list of errands done, much less drop in at the diner and ask any questions?

When the doorbell rang a minute later, she was tempted to ignore it. When it rang a second time, she sighed in resignation. Picking up her wine glass, she took it with her as she trudged down the hall. She didn't know who else would be standing there besides Matt, and she had half a mind to give *him* Suzanne's insanely thick folder and tell him to deal with it. That should keep him busy while she was free from distractions to try to figure out that missing piece of the puzzle that myMason had mentioned. Because she was sure it was sitting right in front of them.

She grabbed the handle and threw the door open. "What is it?"

A startled Rob stood on her front step, staring back at her. "We agreed I'd come by?"

Perfect. This is just perfect.

"Is it noon?"

Rob smiled. "Actually, babe, it's twelve thirty. A meeting I couldn't get out of ran late..."

Nicki cut him off by waving him inside. "That's fine. It doesn't matter. Come on in."

She shut the door behind him and motioned for him to go into the kitchen. Once there, Nicki walked to the other side of the island and waited as Rob looked around before taking a seat on one of the high stools.

He looked good, but then he usually did. With his blond hair and classically handsome features that went right along with a natural flirtatious charm, Rob really could be a great date. What had kept Nicki up the night before was wondering if that was all she'd ever considered him to be. A great date.

When he finally met her steady gaze, she smiled and pointed to the open bottle of wine sitting on the counter. "Would you like a glass? Or something else to drink? I have bottled water, and of course coffee or tea?"

"Water would be fine, thanks." Rob glanced around again. "I like the way your kitchen came out." He nodded his thanks when she handed him a cold bottle of water along with a glass of ice. "You had it redone about a year ago, didn't you?" He smiled as if he'd won a crucial point in a tennis match. "But this is the first time I've seen it."

"You've never asked to see it, Rob." Nicki tilted her head and studied him. "I don't want to fight. And especially not over something like whether you've seen my kitchen, or who said what."

Rob leaned forward, his expression serious as he held her gaze. "But that is our problem, Nicki. You have something major in your life, like redoing your kitchen or getting tangled up in a murder, and you shut me out of it."

She shook her head. "We don't shut each other out, Rob. We simply aren't interested enough to get involved with the important things in each other's lives. We both found Catherine's body, but you couldn't wait to put it behind you, and never asked about it after you left Soldoff that night." She held up a hand when he started to protest. "And I don't ask anything about the company business dinners you need to attend, and didn't bother to show up at the first wine history lecture that your boss gave at the local college, even though you made it clear it was important to you."

"Maybe neither of us have given this a fair shot."

Nicki smiled. Every once in a while, Rob could really surprise her.

"We don't have to be an exclusive item, Rob. I can understand how dating someone who lives in the city would be great for you. Tricia seemed very nice."

He nodded. "She is. We've worked together for over a year. But we aren't really dating. We just go out to lunch sometimes."

She raised an eyebrow at that one. Somehow Rob didn't think he and Tricia were "dating" because he only saw her at lunchtime. And for Rob, that did not fall within his definition of a "date". She felt a sudden twinge of sympathy for Tricia.

"So we're agreed?" Nicki was relieved Rob was being so reasonable about breaking up.

He grinned and rose to his feet, holding his water glass out in front of him. "We're agreed. Not exclusive." He took a drink and winked at her. "At least not at the moment. After two years, we probably need a short break from being exclusive."

"Rob, what I meant..."

He set his glass aside and made a quick dash around the counter. He put a hand on both her shoulders and leaned in to give her a quick kiss on the cheek, followed by a brief swipe of his lips across hers.

"I have to go. I have a plane to catch, but wasn't going to get on it until we had our talk." He looked at his watch. "I can just make it."

"But I meant..."

He gave her another kiss on the cheek before stepping back. "I'll call you from Seattle, babe." He gave her a wink. "Try not to stumble over any more dead bodies while I'm gone."

"I really think..." Nicki trailed off again since he'd already disappeared down the hallway. She stood staring at the empty space where he'd been, and listened to the front door close. Still bemused by the whole conversation, or what there was of it, she refilled her wine glass, grabbed the bowl of chocolate peanuts and the file folder Suzanne had left, and went into her office.

She sat at her desk and stared at the blank screen on her computer for a whole minute. Maybe what she needed was to spend a few hours with someone she understood. Like Tyrone Blackstone, the superspy hero in her novels.

She reached toward the power button when her cell phone rang. The minute she saw the caller ID she groaned. It was Jane, Matt's very efficient, and completely terrifying, admin assistant.

Wishing she had the nerve to ignore the call, Nicki reluctantly tapped "connect" and put as much cheerfulness into her voice as she could muster. "Hi, Jane. How are you?"

"I'm fine, thank you. And I hope you're doing the same."

Before Nicki had a chance to agree or disagree with that, Jane plowed right on. "Is Matt there? He isn't picking up his calls."

"Um, no. He's staying with Maxie Edwards and her husband, so I'm guessing he's at her house?"

"When you see him, can you please tell him he needs to call his office as soon as possible? Several urgent issues need his attention." Jane paused and took a breath. "Do you know how much longer it will take you to solve this latest murder, so he can come home?"

"No, I don't," Nicki bit her lower lip to keep from stammering. Jane always had that effect on her. "But I'll give him the message. It's just that I'm..."

"Wonderful. If I could hear from him within the hour, it would be very helpful."

"... not sure when I'm going to see him, and it isn't my fault he's hanging around here until Eddie Parker's murder is solved," Nicki finished, even though Jane had already hung up. She set her cell phone down next to the file folder and shook her head.

What just happened here? She had no idea how she'd suddenly become the center of everyone's annoyance. She might be a little preoccupied with murder, but it sure was a lot less complicated than her life had become.

Drumming her fingers against her desktop, she finally gave in. Like her mother always told her whenever she'd complained about being overwhelmed, solve one problem at a time and before you know it, they're all solved.

She decided to start with the easiest one and deliver Jane's message. Reaching for her phone, she punched in Matt's number.

CHAPTER TWENTY-TWO

NICKI OPENED HER FRONT DOOR TO A GRINNING MATT.

She put her hands on her hips and glared at him. "If you're still being smug over the whole we-caught-Rob-with-another-woman thing, then you can just go back to wherever you went to hide from Jane."

Matt's mouth dropped into a frown. "I'm not hiding from anyone. If I were, you wouldn't have found me so easily."

"I didn't find you, I called you. And you answered your phone." She stood aside and made a sweeping motion with her hand. "Are you coming in or not?"

Much to her annoyance, he was back to grinning. "I'll come in. I want to hear how Rob took being dumped."

"He wasn't dumped," Nicki said over her shoulder. She went around the island but wasn't surprised when Matt stopped halfway into the room, his gaze narrowed on her face.

"He lies to you about being out of town, goes out with another woman, and you don't dump him? So he's still your boyfriend?"

"No, he's not." Nicki opened the refrigerator and considered what to make for dinner.

It would be helpful if she knew how many people she needed to feed. But at this point, she could be having a full dinner party, or be eating alone.

Matt walked over and stood on the other side of the island, his arms crossed over his chest. "Just to be clear, Rob's no longer your boyfriend?

"No, he's not."

"But you didn't dump him?"

"No, I didn't."

Matt scratched his chin. "Am I supposed to understand that?"

"Probably not." She looked over at him. "Are you staying for dinner?"

"Yes. Maxie and Mason will be over too. Maxie said she wanted to talk to you."

"Of course she does," Nicki said under her breath. "Doesn't everyone?"

"What?"

She raised her voice. "I asked how you felt about pork chops?"

"I'm in favor of them," Matt replied. "But back to this whole Rob thing."

Nicki raised her head out of the depths of her refrigerator and glared at him. "Not talking about the whole Rob thing. None of your business, remember?"

Matt adjusted his glasses but whatever he intended to say was drowned out by the slamming of the front door.

"Hello? Are you in the kitchen?" Without waiting for an answer, the sound of flip-flops headed their way. Within seconds, Jenna appeared in the doorway. "I saw Rob's car, and then it was gone. And now Matt's car is here." She looked over at the editor who'd taken a seat at the island counter. "And so is Matt. What's going on? Did you dump lover-boy?"

"Nope, and he isn't my boyfriend either."

Jenna nodded. "Ah. That's probably the best way to go. In gentle stages. You *have* invested two years in him."

Matt's mouth dropped open as he stared at Jenna. "You understood that?"

She laughed. "Of course. Didn't you?"

"No. Not a sane person on earth would have understood that."

"Well I did, and I'm pretty sane." Jenna walked over to the counter and took a seat next to Matt. "I thought you'd be packing to head back to Kansas City since we aren't going to be involved in Eddie's murder anymore."

"What?" Matt turned a startled look on Nicki. "When did we decide that?"

"*We* didn't. Jenna did." Nicki looked over at her friend. "Matt's in favor of pork chops, how do you feel about them?"

"Great. If you use that special rub of yours. And I want you to let the police do their thing with Eddie's murder. As Alex keeps reminding us, that's their job." She looked at Matt. "Whoever ran Nicki off the road, it's because of this whole murder thing. You can't want to go through a repeat performance of that."

"No, I don't," Matt agreed. "But..."

"Hello? We're here." Alex's voice echoed down the hallway.

We? Nicki took the entire jumbo package of pork chops out of the refrigerator and dropped it into the sink before she turned around to wave a greeting at Alex and Tyler.

"I left our bags in the living room," Tyler announced. "I have strict instructions from Alex's mom that we're to get this latest murder solved in the next day, so she can go dress shopping with her daughter." He grinned at Nicki. "Consider the message delivered."

Matt stood and gave Alex a brief hug and shook Tyler's

hand. "That's good, but Jenna has decided we aren't going to solve the murder, and Nicki hasn't dumped Rob but he isn't her boyfriend. That brings you up to speed on the latest crazy around here."

Alex nodded at Nicki. "That's probably the best way to go."

Nicki smiled at her friend and ignored Matt who threw his hands up into the air. "I think so too."

Tyler clapped a friendly hand on Matt's shoulder. "The trick isn't to try to make sense out of their mental telepathy, but to just get the information you need to know."

"Which is?" Matt asked.

The fireman glanced over at his fiancée and winked. "Is Nicki going to be dating other guys?"

Alex nodded. "That's what she just said, or weren't you listening?" She walked over and gave Jenna a hug.

Matt looked over at Nicki. "*That's* what you said?"

Nicki laughed. "Yes."

"But what about Rob?"

She raised an eyebrow at him. "Still none of your business, Dillon."

Tyler gave Matt a hard nudge as he passed by on his way over to take a look at what Nicki was unwrapping in the kitchen sink. "You have the information you need, man. Just go with that."

"Yoo hoo!"

"You should get an automatic lock for that door," Jenna muttered.

Nicki grinned at Tyler's huge smile when he saw all the pork chops. The happy chaos made her warm and happy right down to her toes. Maybe she never would discover the truth of Eddie's murder, but there were definitely worse things.

She rinsed her hands and reached for a towel as Maxie and her husband walked into the kitchen.

"Oh good." Maxie beamed at Nicki. "I wanted to talk to you before Matt gets back from wherever he's taken himself off to."

Mason put an arm around his wife's shoulders and turned her so she was facing the far end of the center island. "Matt's right over there, honey. And you shouldn't interfere in his private life."

Jenna reached over to the bowl Nicki had filled earlier and grabbed a chip. "Don't bother, Maxie. He and Nicki have worked it out."

Matt looked over at Nicki and then back at Jenna. "We have?"

Alex gave him a pat on the arm as she headed in the direction of the wine refrigerator. "Yes, you did." She glanced at Nicki. "What are we drinking?"

"We're having stove-top pork chops so one of the lighter reds would be good." Nicki patted her mixture of salt, pepper and thyme onto the surface of the meat before placing each chop onto the large cookie sheet she'd set on the counter, so they could rest until she was ready to cook them. "And Jenna's decided we aren't going to work on the murder any longer."

"That's nice, dear. But we can't let poor Eddie's murder go unsolved." Maxie frowned at the tenant of her other town-house. "And you would never be happy not knowing what happened."

"True," Jenna agreed. "But I'd be a lot unhappier if whoever ran Nicki off the road kept on trying to stop her from finding out who murdered Eddie."

"Even if Nicki stopped, that's no guarantee that the guy behind the wheel of that truck would stop too." Matt's mouth was set into a flat line as he ran a hand through his hair.

"That's right," Mason put in. "But if we back off for a while, the killer might relax enough to make a mistake that will lead Chief Turnlow right to him."

Nicki abruptly straightened up and whirled around to face Matt. "Oh good heavens! Jane is going to kill me."

"Who's Jane?" Mason frowned.

"My assistant," Matt said, keeping his gaze on Nicki.

"Why is Jane going to kill you?"

"You weren't picking up your phone, so she called here looking for you." Nicki could have kicked herself for not delivering Jane's urgent message sooner. "I should have told you the minute I opened the door. Jane said something was going on that needs your attention right now. I'm so sorry I didn't tell you that right off."

Matt shrugged. "There's always something that needs my attention right now." He pulled his cell phone out of his shirt pocket. "I'll call her. Can I use your office?"

"Of course." Nicki waved him away. "Go. Take care of whatever it is."

"My point exactly," Jenna declared. "We all need to take care of 'whatever'." She looked over at Alex who was calmly pouring out wine into a line of glasses. "You have a wedding to plan. If it doesn't happen on schedule this time, your mom will have a stroke."

Alex sighed. "Very true."

Jenna switched her attention to Nicki. "And you're supposed to be giving the best cooking classes in town, starting next week. I know that because there are flyers plastered all over the place. And Suzanne said the first five classes are already full."

"They are?" Nicki couldn't help the leap of delight, even as an image of the long task list attached to the folder in her office floated in front of her eyes. "We'll need to add one more student. I promised Jake he could attend."

"And speaking of Jake and the diner, with it reopening with cash-paying customers once again at the door, that gloomy bookkeeper decided to send me a check for the money Eddie owed me." Jenna smiled and popped another chip into her mouth. "Nice to have the bank account a little healthier again."

Nicki froze in the middle of patting spice onto the last pork chop.

"Something wrong?" Tyler, who'd been closely watching the whole process, frowned.

She slowly turned around to stare at Jenna. "What did you say?"

"I said it was nice to be paid and that it really helped the bank account."

"Because you got paid, and there's money in your bank account," Nicki said slowly.

Jenna leaned on the counter and propped her head in her hands. "That's how it usually works when you get paid."

"Yes." Nicki vigorously nodded her head. "Yes it does, doesn't it?" She abandoned the pork chops and raced around the island. "I should have listened to Matt, and the chief. They both said to follow the money."

"What money?" Maxie's eyes followed Nicki as she darted down the hallway. She turned a frown on the others, who were all staring in her direction. "What money?"

Mason grabbed his wife's hand and started to tug her along. "Come on, honey. We aren't going to find out by standing here."

The rest of the kitchen's occupants took one quick, puzzled look at each other and then scrambled after Nicki.

Nicki flew into her home office, startling Matt who was sitting at her desk. He took one look at her and barked, "I'll call you back", before getting to his feet and meeting her at the murder board. "What is it?"

"I should have listened to you." She nodded at his puzzled look. "Follow the money, you said. That's what we should have done."

Maxie came up behind her in a rush. "What money?" She leaned against her husband's arm. "I need a moment to catch my breath."

Matt turned as everyone behind them pressed forward. "Okay. Let's step back and give each other some breathing space." He waited until Mason took his wife over to sit on the sofa, and Tyler had pulled Alex back toward the desk. When everyone had found a spot, he looked at Nicki.

"We talked about this. We don't know who bought the stamps, so we can't follow the money "

Nicki did another quick scan of the board before turning around to nod at the expectant faces in the room. "But it isn't the killer who would have been paid. It would have been Eddie."

The former chief of police shook his head. "But he wasn't. You heard Chief Turnlow. The money wasn't in anyone's bank account. Not even Eddie's. So he was never paid."

"Then we would have found the stamps," Nicki said. "Unless the killer took them from Eddie before he handed over the money. But then why search Eddie's office and apartment?"

"And the money wasn't in the safe, because the safe wasn't touched," myMason said.

"None of it makes sense," Nicki declared. "Unless the stamps weren't the killer's real target. What if it was *all* the money, not just what Eddie might have sold the stamps for?"

"All what money, dear?" Maxie repeated.

"Remember what Roberta and Ben said? Eddie had sold his house, and his car. But the chief said there wasn't any more than two thousand dollars in anyone's bank account, and I'll bet there was a lot less than that in Eddie's." Nicki felt a tingle up and down her arms.

This was it. She was sure of it. She wrinkled her forehead as she concentrated on her train of thought. "And I saw a letter from the local bank addressed to Eddie. It had 'your loan information' stamped on the side."

"Loan?" Mason shifted to the edge of the sofa. "What loan?" His jaw hardened. "And if he took out a loan, where's *that* money?"

"He used it all for his dream," Nicki said softly. She looked at Matt and gave a decisive nod. "We need to talk to Chief Turnlow right away."

"My car's outside." He stepped aside so she could lead the way. "What's your plan?"

"I think I know why the office and the apartment were searched, and what they were looking for," Nicki said.

There was silence in the room until Alex finally gave out an audible sigh. "Did you say 'what *they* were looking for'? Who are you talking about?"

Mason stood and fished his cell phone out of his pants pocket. "I'll call Paul and tell him that Nicki's found that missing puzzle piece."

"We'll call from the chief's office and let you know what's going on." Matt threw a glance at the whole group staring at him before he followed Nicki out the door.

WHEN MATT PULLED the car into the parking spot in front of the police department, Chief Turnlow was standing on the sidewalk, his hands in the pockets of his jacket and his legs braced apart.

Nicki stepped out of the car and nodded to him. He inclined his head toward the station at his back and waited for her and Matt to walk ahead of him. Once inside, Nicki stopped in front of the long counter as Matt stepped up beside her. Danny was leaning with one arm on top of the lone file cabinet, and Fran was sitting at her desk, as the chief came around the counter and rested his elbows on its top as he faced Nicki.

"Mason called and let me know you were on your way," he said without wasting any time on greetings. "He seemed to think you've figured out something about Eddie Parker's murder."

Nicki took a quick glance around the open room.

The chief smiled. "If another good citizen comes through the door, we'll go into my office. But it's too small to accommodate all of us, and I'd like the other members of the department to hear this. So get started, Sherlock."

Nicki hadn't said a word during the brief ride into town, instead using the time to scribble into the small notepad she always kept in her purse. She was grateful that Matt hadn't peppered her with questions, but had kept quiet and let her finish writing out what she needed to give to Chief Turnlow. Now she set the small book on the counter and ripped out the two pages on top. Leaning over, she handed them to him.

He looked down and read in silence for a moment before lifting his gaze back to her. "What's this?"

"Will the bank answer a specific question you have about Eddie's account?"

"It's a small town, so I imagine they would if I put in a personal call." He looked back at the two small sheets of paper in his hand. "A cashier's check?"

"You and Matt always say to follow the money. And that's what we should have been doing." Nicki smiled. "It wasn't about the stamps. At least not just the stamps. Eddie sold his house and his car, and he took out a loan."

Chief Turnlow raised an eyebrow. "How do you know he took out a loan?"

"I saw a letter from the local bank that had been delivered to the diner. It had a stamp on the outside saying that it contained loan information. I didn't think anything about it at the time, and just left it for Gordon to deal with."

The chief frowned. "When I asked about the balances, the bank told me Eddie had less than five hundred dollars in his account." He looked over at Fran. "Can you get the bank manager on the phone for me?"

"One call to Lou Applegate coming right up." Fran lifted the phone to her ear and did a quick turn of the rolodex on her desk. "Do you want to take it out here or in your office?"

"My office, Fran."

As the chief strode off, Nicki turned a smile on the young deputy standing in back of the clerk, who was talking into her phone. "Danny? I need to see those business cards that Eddie had in his wallet."

"Chief, Lou's on line one," Fran called out before she put the phone back in its cradle and turned toward Nicki. "All that was sent over to Santa Rosa for safe keeping. But I made copies."

She reached over to a basket on her desk and pulled out a manila folder.

"Both the front and back of the business cards?" Nicki asked.

"Of course. I'm not senile." Fran stood up and walked over to hand Nicki the file. "What are you looking for?"

Nicki quickly flipped through the pages until she came to a copy of the card for Green 'N Go. She got out her phone and dialed the number listed on the front.

"Hello, Mr. Bridgeton? My name is Nicki Connors and I'm consulting with the police on Eddie Parker's murder. Oh? Really? Well, I'm sorry to say that it happened right in his own diner. Your business card was in his wallet, and I'm hoping you won't mind answering a few questions?"

CHAPTER TWENTY-THREE

GORDON TWILL STOOD UNDER THE AWNING OF THE DINER where he'd been the bookkeeper for over a decade, and where a friend from his childhood had died. He shifted his day planner and the client file he was carrying until he was clutching them both to his chest, before forming his mouth into his usual vague but pleasant smile and opening the door.

He'd barely taken a step inside before he pulled up short, blinking at the number of people occupying tables. He always tried to get to the diner before it opened. He frowned and checked his watch.

The bookkeeper took another tentative step forward, his gaze darting the service counter where Roberta stood, with Jake beside her. He tried a smile, but when neither one of them smiled back, he hunched his shoulders and looked at the big man standing in front of him.

"Hello, Chief Turnlow." He ignored Nicki who was standing right beside the chief. His eyes did a quick glance around the room as Danny quietly slid in behind him and blocked the door. "If you're having a private party, I can come back to do my work later."

The chief pulled a chair out from the table beside him. "Have a seat, Mr. Twill. There are a few more questions I need to ask you."

Gordon winced but his feet stayed right where they were. "I'd be happy to help, Chief. Maybe we could go back to the office and I can explain anything about the diner that you don't understand?"

"Just a couple of questions. This won't take long." The chief inclined his head toward the chair. "Are you sure you wouldn't like to sit down?"

The thin, neat, and tidy man shook his head and pressed his planner and file closer to his chest. "I'm fine. What do you want to ask me?"

Chief Turnlow shrugged and put his hands in his jacket pockets. "I understand you had car trouble the night Eddie Parker was killed?"

"Yes." Gordon nodded. "I had a date with Roberta. We'd decided to have dinner at Mario's." He looked at the stocky woman standing behind the counter. "Roberta will tell you that we had a date."

"But you were late?" the chief prompted.

"I had car trouble," the bookkeeper repeated. "I sent a text to Roberta. She said it was okay. That she'd wait at the restaurant."

"What kind of car trouble?" When Gordon blinked at him, the chief smiled.

"I'm... I'm not sure."

"Did you call for help?"

"No, Chief Turnlow." A note of irritation crept into Gordon's voice. "I didn't call for help. I didn't need to. It finally started up and I went on my way."

The chief raised an eyebrow. "It just started up? Where were you?"

Gordon was back to blinking. "What?"

"Your car," the chief clarified. "Where was your car when it broke down?"

"A few blocks from here. I don't remember exactly where." The bookkeeper frowned. "What's this about? I went to see a client and when I got back to my car, it wouldn't start. I waited a few minutes and it started up again. I guess I must have flooded the engine or something. That's all there was to it."

"What client?" the chief asked.

The bookkeeper shifted his weight from one foot to the other and then back again. "Should I get an attorney? It sounds like you're accusing me of something." He looked around at the faces staring at him and his lips pulled back across his teeth. "This is an odd place for an interrogation." He jerked his head toward the counter in back of the diner. "Roberta and I were having dinner at Mario's when Eddie was killed. Go ahead and ask her." He stuck his lower lip out further. "The last time you questioned me, you said Eddie died at nine o'clock that night. When I was sitting at Mario's with Roberta."

"I said that Mr. Parker died *around* nine that night," the chief corrected. "Our work isn't quite as precise as yours."

Gordon shrugged. "Fine. Around nine. But I joined Roberta just after seven, and we were still there at nine o'clock."

"The problem, Mr. Twill, is that the victim died around nine o'clock, but he was put into the freezer a couple of hours before that. Just about the time you were having car trouble."

"I... That's ridiculous." Gordon took a quick step backward. "I told you. I didn't know anything about that stamp of his, how much it was worth or where he'd hidden it. And I certainly don't know who killed Eddie and stole it."

"The sheet of stamps wasn't stolen," Nicki said quietly. The more she'd watched and listened to Gordon Twill answering the chief's simple questions, the more convinced she was that she was right. "Eddie sold the stamps and put the money into his bank account. Along with the money from the sale of his house and his car, and the loan he took out from the bank."

"I don't know anything about all that either," Gordon snapped out.

"You were Eddie Parker's bookkeeper, weren't you?" Chief Turnlow kept an unwavering stare on Gordon Twill.

"And you did tell me that you took care of Eddie's personal, as well as business, accounts," Nicki said. "You also told me that nothing unusual had gone on in his accounts."

"What's so unusual about money going in and out of a bank account?" Gordon demanded. "It happens every day.

"Didn't say that it went out, just that it went in." As the color from Gordon's face started to drain, the chief shrugged. "As it happens, though, the money did disappear from Mr. Parker's account. Almost two hundred thousand dollars of it."

Since she was watching him closely, Nicki noticed that the bookkeeper didn't show even a flicker of surprise at the amount the chief had mentioned. Instead, he drew himself up and stood a little taller, a triumphant look in his eyes.

"Well I didn't embezzle it if that's what you're implying. I couldn't have. I didn't have any signing power on any of Eddie's accounts."

"But you knew the money was there?" Nicki pressed.

Gordon shrugged. "I kept his books and drew up the checks to pay his bills. Checks, I would remind you, that Eddie had to sign. There was nothing strange about me knowing what his bank balance was."

"Then you must have known that Eddie withdrew most of that money. He took out a cashier's check the morning he was killed." Nicki glanced at the chief. "The bank confirmed it."

"How would I have known that? I didn't ask the bank about a cashier's check." Gordon shifted his gaze to the police chief. "You can ask around at the bank. I never questioned them about any withdrawals from Eddie's account."

"Except you stopped by that morning so Eddie could sign some checks. You said that's why you were here." Nicki took in a deep breath. "And you're a good bookkeeper, aren't you Gordon? Like any good bookkeeper, you checked on the bank balance to be sure there were enough funds available to pay those bills. So you knew the money was gone. Did you ask Eddie about it? Did he tell you he was meeting Mr. Bridgeton that night and would be turning that money over to him by a cashier's check that was in his office safe?"

"I don't have to talk to you." Gordon took another step back. He let out a yelp, and jumped a good foot to the side, when he backed into Danny. The young deputy crossed his arms over his chest and didn't budge an inch. Gordon whirled around again to face Nicki. "You aren't the police. You don't know anything. And I've never met this Mr. Bridgeton. I don't know what you're talking about."

"Oh, I think you do, Gordon." Nicki's hazel eyes leveled a stare at him. "Mr. Bridgeton arranges the franchise agreements for Green 'N Go. His business card was in Eddie's wallet, and he's confirmed that he was supposed to meet Eddie that night and finalize the contract."

Gordon's face was sheet-white as his eyes wheeled around in his head. "Then you should be asking this Mr. Bridgeton about Eddie's murder. I don't know anything about a franchise. And Eddie never told me the combination to his safe. He never told anyone what it was. He used to brag that he was the only one who knew it." The bookkeeper pointed a shaking finger at Jake. "Ask him. Ask him. He knows Eddie used to brag about that."

Jake nodded. "He's right, Nicki. The boss used to say that

all the time. Just like his burger mix, and where he kept the key to his wine cellar, or where he hid that stamp, Eddie kept things to himself. He's the only one who knew that combination."

Nicki smiled at the assistant manager. "Yes, he did. And you also told me he kept all of his important information on his phone." Her gaze went to the right and landed on the waitress standing next to Jake. "Isn't that right, Roberta?"

"What? Why are you asking me?"

"Because you knew that Eddie kept a lot of his personal information on his phone, didn't you?"

"So what?" Roberta's lips drew back into a sneer. "So did everyone who worked here. Eddie was always saying his whole life was on that phone, so ask them your stupid questions."

She threw the towel she'd been holding onto the counter and shoved her way past Jake. Matt casually stepped over and blocked her path. She glared up at him and did an about-face, only to see Mason Edwards standing at the other end of the counter.

Roberta whirled back to face Nicki, her eyes throwing daggers at the petite honey-blond. "I don't have to talk to you, and you can't keep me here."

"You knew he kept the combination to the safe on his phone," Nicki continued. "The phone that he accidentally left at home that day. The same day you left work early."

"Because I had a date. I wanted to look nice for my date." Roberta looked at the chief. "I don't have to stay here. I'm going home. Tell them to get out of my way."

Chief Turnlow kept his hands in his jacket pockets and shrugged. "I think we've had this discussion before. We either talk here, or down at the station." He smiled at her. "And I hope you didn't hang onto that phone, because I have a warrant to search your place and your car." He studied her for a moment longer. "And your mother's place. It seems she owns a white pickup truck. We'll be checking that for any damage too."

There was a gasp all around the room. Roberta went stiff and Nicki would have sworn the waitress had stopped breathing.

"Why, Roberta? Why would you hurt Eddie?" Maxie had a shaking hand on Alex's arm and held onto one of Jenna's hands with her other. Tears glistened in her eyes. "He was a nice man. And he never hurt you."

"Never hurt me?" Roberta choked out a laugh. "Easy for you to say. You get everything. Me? I put ten years into that burger flipper and what does he tell me? That we're through. He's moving to Santa Rosa, opening another place, and it's time for us to move on from each other." She stuck her chin out and cast a glare all around the room. "Ten years. And I got nothin'." She sniffed at the chief. "Maybe I trashed his place and took his cell phone. So sue me. But I sure didn't kill him."

There was a gasp and sharp squeak from Gordon who gave her a bug-eyed stare. "It was your idea. The whole thing was your idea. You even told me to mess-up Eddie's office, so it would look like a robbery that went wrong." He turned wide eyes on the chief. "*She* told me about Eddie buying that franchise, and that he was going to pay for it with a cashier's check. She said the franchise said he had to use their accounting service, and Eddie was going to take his business away from me. Just like he'd dumped her." He pointed a slim finger at the waitress. "She had a plan all worked out. But I wasn't going to go along with it. Eddie wouldn't do that to me. We'd been friends since grade school. But then Eddie started acting different, and I knew. Roberta was right." He seemed to collapse within himself. "I didn't mean to kill him. He wasn't supposed to die."

The chief walked over and put a heavy hand on Gordon's shoulders. They were shaking so hard the chief's hand trembled along with them. "Let's go to the station and sort this out." He nodded at Danny who crossed the room and took the trapped Roberta firmly by the arm.

"Shut up, Gordon," Roberta yelled at the now sobbing bookkeeper. "Remember who *did* kill Eddie and shut your mouth."

She was still screaming at all of them when Danny finally got her out the door.

After several minutes, Jake broke the silence. "I can't believe they killed Eddie." His eyes and mouth drooped together. "He was a nice guy. He gave them jobs."

Matt walked over and gave Jake a firm pat on the back. "And he had good friends, like you Jake. And Jenna, Sam and Ben. Just not those two."

Jake smiled but kept shaking his head as he made his way back to the kitchen.

Nicki blew out a breath of relief. The chief hadn't told her about Roberta's mom having a white pickup truck, but it hadn't surprised her. When someone touched her arm, she looked up into Matt's concerned eyes.

"Are you all right?"

She nodded but gave in to a sudden weakness in her knees to lean her head against his shoulder. He put his arms around her.

"You did good, Sherlock."

"Thanks, Watson." She raised her head and smiled at him. "You're a great sidekick." She kept her smile in place as she stepped back and turned toward all her friends who were clustered together around Maxie. "Well. I believe I still owe everyone a pork chop dinner."

"Which we'll have another night," Matt stated firmly.

"We're going back to your place for a glass of wine while I send out for pizza."

Tyler let out a whoop at that. "We'll stop and get some beer. I think the Raiders are playing tonight."

Mason frowned. "The Raiders? You're kidding."

Jenna stared at them. "Football after all of this? You've both got to be kidding."

"Football and beer to decompress from solving a murder. Sounds like a good plan to me." Tyler grabbed Alex's hand and pulled her out of her chair. "Come on, honey. We have to make a beer run."

Nicki smiled up at Matt. "I guess that leaves us the pizza run."

He shook his head. "They can deliver. Let's go home."

CHAPTER TWENTY-FOUR

"Now that Mason has arrived, we can call this meeting to order, and get on with the official erasing of the murder board." Jenna grinned at everyone crowded into Nicki's office and raised her glass of orange juice. "Since the case is solved, thanks to our number one investigator, Nicki Connors."

Nicki blushed at the cheer that went up around the room. "The police solved it, we only helped."

"By 'we' I assume you mean 'you'," Jenna insisted along with a roomful of accompanying nods.

"But I'll be sure to let the chief know that you were happy to share the credit with the department." Mason smiled. "You did an incredible job of putting it together."

Alex raised her glass of sparkling water and tilted it toward Nicki as well. "Yes, you did. Taking a step away from the stamps and looking at the whole thing from a different angle was brilliant."

"I agree, dear. I'd love to know what made you do that." Maxie smiled before turning toward her husband. "But first we have some very good news." Maxie beamed at her husband. "It seems that Eddie's nephew doesn't care at all about owning the diner, and he's agreed to sell it for a very reasonable price, part of which will go to pay any outstanding debts, including the loan Mason gave to Eddie."

"That's great!" Jenna grinned back at the smiling Maxie.

"Thank you, dear. But we aren't going to get the money right away. Mason has agreed to lend it to Jake, so he can buy the diner. He was a little intimidated to take it on without Eddie, until Suzanne agreed to help him. The two of them are very happy about the whole arrangement." Maxie winked at Nicki. "Suzanne thinks they can arrange the hours to hold your cooking demonstrations there too."

Nicki did a double take at that news. Gourmet cooking classes at a burger diner?

"But of course we can discuss that later. Right now, we all want to hear what my Mason learned from Paul this morning."

Mason had just returned from the Soldoff Police Department, and everyone wanted to know what Gordon Twill and Roberta Horton had had to say. Especially Nicki. There were still a few missing pieces to the puzzle, and she was hoping Mason would be able to put them into place. When the former police chief simply smiled at his attentive audience, his wife wagged a finger at him.

"Mason Edwards, if you don't start spilling the beans now, I'm going to march right to that town square and start making a gigantic bouquet of all those flowers you spent hours and hours planting. Not to mention that Matt has a plane to catch, so we need to get right to it."

Nicki grinned. Now that was a threat that she was absolutely sure would have myMason talking as fast as he could. Matt was right next to her, leaning against the desk. They exchanged a smile as Mason held his hands up in mock horror.

"Anything but that, honey." Crossing the room, he placed a kiss on Maxie's cheek before draping an arm around her shoulders and nodding at the faces turned in his direction. "Roberta hasn't said much other than constantly repeating that she didn't kill anyone. But Gordon can't keep quiet, according to Fran."

"Did Fran know what he was saying?" Jenna clasped her hands in front of her and leaned slightly forward. "Did he really kill Eddie for the money?"

Mason nodded. "He did. It seems Eddie was his only regular client in town, and losing his business to the corporate accounting office for Green 'N Go would have been a major blow to him. He thought the money that he and Roberta were going to split between them was a kind of severance pay."

"How did they even know Eddie was going to have that cashier's check in his safe?" Matt asked. "That couldn't have been an incredible coincidence in timing."

"It wasn't." Nicki glanced at the chief. "Gordon said that Roberta told him about the money. And I'm guessing she also told him about Eddie's plans, including paying for his franchise license with a cashier's check, so all he had to do was keep tabs on his client's bank account balance. When it dropped, Gordon knew Eddie had taken the money out."

The retired chief smiled at her. "You're right again. Gordon saw that drop, and paid a visit to Eddie, who told him about a special meeting he was having that night. It didn't take much for Gordon to put two and two together. So he went to Roberta to put their plan into motion. Except there was one glitch."

"The cell phone." Nicki pushed away from her desk and walked over to look at the murder board. "I'll bet she only intended to get the combination to the safe off his cell phone, but then discovered he'd left it at his apartment, which Jake said he had a habit of doing."

Matt came up behind her and adjusted his glasses as he also studied the board. "So she stole the apartment key, left work early, and went to Eddie's place to get the phone. And while she was there, trashed the apartment for good measure."

"There's no wrath like a woman scorned." Ty nodded. "She probably trashed the place to get back at him for dumping her."

Alex slipped her hand into his. "Which was Eddie's downfall. He must have told her about his move to Santa Rosa for his franchising plan, and the cashier's check, as his reason for the break-up."

Maxie frowned. "What I don't understand is why that representative from Green 'N Go didn't show up for the meeting that night?" She turned a wide-eyed look on Nicki. "Or did he, and he left when he might have been able to help Eddie?"

"No. He never came to the meeting," Nicki said. "When I spoke to Mr. Bridgeton, he told me he'd received a text message late that afternoon from Eddie, canceling the meeting."

"Which was sent by Roberta." Mason gave his wife's shoulders a gentle squeeze. "The chief found the cell phone and Eddie's apartment key, along with a white pickup with a dent in its front grille, at Barbara Horton's house. Roberta's mom has been out of town for the last two weeks, so she didn't have any idea what her daughter was up to. But she did confirm that Roberta had a set of keys to the truck."

There was a long moment of silence before Ty stretched a muscular arm over his head. "Well, that wraps it up, I guess. Let's erase the board and get a proper breakfast."

"Except for one thing." Matt smiled at Nicki. "You never

answered Maxie's question. Why did you suddenly start looking at this from a different angle?"

"Watching you sort the groceries into their proper food groups." Nicki laughed when Matt gave her a blank stare. She glanced over at the rest of the group. "He was unloading the grocery bags, and he separated all the items into groups."

"Groups?" Jenna gave Matt a strange look.

"Yes. He put the canned goods together, the meat together, and so on."

Ty snorted and rolled his eyes. "That's just anal, man."

"It's efficient," Matt shot back.

"Which," Nicki interrupted in a loud voice, "made me start separating everything we knew into their groups until three things stood out." She raised a finger and pointed at the board. "A neatly folded jacket and a methodically trashed office, lots of money besides the stamps that wasn't accounted for, and a violently ransacked apartment." She stared at the board. "Two separate events connected by money."

"Which instantly brought to mind the tidy Gordon and angry Roberta." Maxie pursed her lips and nodded. "Very clever, dear."

"He said he didn't mean to kill Eddie." Jenna's soft comment had everyone going quiet. She tore her gaze from the board and looked around the room before settling on Nicki. "That's what Gordon said. That he didn't mean to kill Eddie. Do you think he was telling the truth?"

Nicki held her friend's gaze. "I do. Eddie was hit from behind, so he probably never got a look at his attacker. I think Gordon wanted to be sure he had enough time to join Roberta at the restaurant, and the freezer was the only place he could lock Eddie up, since he didn't know where the key to the basement was. Gordon must have thought that Eddie would wake up and someone would let him out in the morning. Which is why he left Eddie his 49ers jacket, folded up on that shelf next to him. So he could keep warm while he waited to be rescued."

"But Eddie didn't wake up before he ran out of oxygen, thanks to the dry ice he kept in that freezer," Alex put in.

Jenna let out a huge sigh before she straightened her shoulders and lifted her chin. "I need to call Suzanne and let her know that I'll be taking care of the flowers for Eddie's memorial."

"And I'll be bringing cookies and pies." Nicki smiled. "Suzanne wrote that in on my list of things to do for the cooking classes. Which fits in perfectly with the goodie basket I want to put together for Mrs. Sorenson. It was so nice of her to stop and help when I was run off the road. And to climb into that ditch to check on me at her age, was a remarkable act of kindness."

"Yes it was, dear. But I'm sure the flowers were enough if you're too pressed for time. I ran into Mary in town the other day, and she was thrilled with them."

Flowers? Nicki blinked in confusion. "I didn't send her flowers."

"Matt did, of course. And he should have." Maxie beamed at the red-faced editor standing beside Nicki.

When Nicki looked over at him, Matt hunched his shoulders and stuck his hands into the front pockets of his jeans.

"I appreciated her climbing into that ditch too."

"Ahh." Jenna's wink only made Matt's face go redder. "As long as you're making confessions, you might as well tell her the rest of it."

"Rest of it?" Nicki gave the suddenly smiling faces around the room a wary look. "What rest of it?"

Mason checked his watch. "Might as well get it over with, son. You have a plane to catch. You have ten minutes to get your explanation done, so you'd better go on out and do it."

"The rest of us will wait here." Alex grabbed onto Ty's arm and pulled him back onto the sofa.

The fireman grinned at Matt. "Too bad. I wouldn't have minded watching."

Nicki narrowed her eyes on Matt who was now glaring at Tyler. "Watching what? And go out where?"

He turned his annoyed stare on her and grabbed her hand. "Come on. I have something to show you."

Since her curiosity was now running high, she allowed herself to be pulled along as Matt headed to the hallway and then out the front door. He kept right on going until they were standing on the sidewalk in front of her townhouse. Parked at the curb was a shiny new SUV, its pearl-white paint gleaming in the morning sun. Nicki took a quick indrawn breath. It was beautiful. She turned a dazzled and questioning look at Matt who was watching her closely.

"It's yours."

"What?" She glanced over at the car and then back at Matt. "Mine? Matt, I can't afford this."

His jaw hardened, and he took on that stubborn look she was getting to know pretty well. "You don't have to. It's a gift."

When she started to protest, he raised a hand and covered her mouth. "Two things. First, a guy has to be able to sleep at night. I can't do that if I'm worried about you getting stranded in some weird place, and I'm sitting eighteen hundred miles away."

Nicki pushed his hand away as her lips twitched upward. "Eighteen hundred miles?"

"Eighteen hundred and thirty-two, to be exact, and I don't want to hear about it."

"Okay. And what's the second reason? You said there were two."

"When we were arguing about how much you don't eat,

you won that argument, and we agreed I could win the next one." He pointed to the car. "This is the next argument."

Her eyes followed the direction of his finger. "It is? You're comparing a car with another egg and an extra piece of toast?"

Matt dropped his hand as his expression turned serious. "Take the car, Nicki. Please. I need you to have something safe to drive around in."

Nicki stepped closer and put her arms around his neck. "I'll consider it a loan and pay you back whatever I can each month. Deal?"

Matt's hands went to her waist, but he still frowned at her. "Well, I don't know about..."

He was stopped in mid-sentence when Nicki rose on her toes and pressed a long thorough kiss onto his mouth. When she finally leaned back, she smiled. "Thank you."

Behind them, someone loudly cleared a throat. "I guess she liked the gift, son, and we need to get going if you want to make that plane."

Maxie slipped her hand through her husband's arm. "Unfortunately, he's right." She winked when Matt glanced over at her. "But I'm sure you'll be back soon."

Matt smiled at Nicki as she stepped away from him. "You can count on that."

There was a flurry of 'goodbyes' as everyone piled into cars. Ty and Alex had decided to make a beeline for Santa Rosa to placate Alex's mom.

Once he was in the Edwards' car, Matt rolled down his window and motioned to Nicki. She leaned over and met brown eyes that were dancing with amusement.

"I almost forgot. I left you something near your computer. It's supposed to help you get over being mad about the car."

She laughed. "I am mad about the car. Kind of." She

looked over at it. "But it's so beautiful, it's really hard to stay mad."

Matt grinned. "The keys are on the hallway table."

She stepped back as Mason put the Mercedes into gear and slowly pulled away.

"Well, pal. I need to get to work. Hopefully the next time our little club gets together, it will only be to enjoy a good meal and an excellent wine." Jenna gave Nicki one last hug before she headed for her own place right next door.

Nicki watched her go with a smile. Half a minute later she walked into her house with a definite spring to her step. She should also get to work. But not before she took a short spin in her new car. She scooped up the set of keys on the hallway table and then looked over at the door to her office. Curious, she made the detour to her desk and spotted the small box with a red bow around it. She cradled it in her hand for a moment. It was light, and her mouth curved up when she saw the name of Ben's shop imprinted on a sticker on the back. Lifting the lid, her eyes grew soft. Nestled against a bed of white tissue paper were the silver earrings with the red beads. Only Matt would remember how much she'd liked them.

Removing the earrings she'd put on that morning, Nicki replaced them with the gift from Matt before walking over to the murder board. She gave it one last look before she picked up the eraser. Taking a long swipe across the flat white surface, she hummed as she continued the small chore.

She'd just get this board clean and then take her new car, and her to-do list, over to Eddie's Diner and go over it with Suzanne.

She stepped back to admire her now-clean whiteboard as she jingled the keys she'd stuck in her pocket.

Life was good.

AUTHOR'S NOTE

To My Readers –

I hope you enjoyed following Nicki and all her friends as they raced to solve the puzzle in A Special Blend of Murder. There's something about a mystery that keeps us reading into the night. And it was fun writing about Jenna having a "Nicki" experience and being the first to find the victim!

I want to take this opportunity to thank you, the reader. Time is precious, and I so appreciate you spending some of yours to read my books. I enjoy writing, and am very lucky to be able to do just that. And even luckier to have someone read my stories.

Thank you, and happy reading!

Cat Chandler

You can pick-up the any of my other mystery novels on Amazon, or read for free with your Kindle Unlimited membership!

Be the first to receive notification of the release of the next novel in the Crimson Rose series. **Sign up** today at:

http://eepurl.com/dhGQYr

If you'd like to know what my latest projects are, and how they're coming along, drop by my website at: www.CathrynChandler.com

Follow Cathryn Chandler on your favorite media:

Facebook:
https://www.facebook.com/cathrynchandlerauthor/?fref=ts

Twitter: @catcauthor

Website/blog: www.cathrynchandler.com

All authors strive to deliver the highest quality work to their readers. If you found a spelling or typographical error in this book, please let me know so I can correct it immediately. Please use the contact form on my website at: www.cathrynchandler.com Thank you!

And finally: If you like an occasional romance, I also write those under the pen name: Cathryn Chandler, and they are also available on Amazon.

Made in the USA
Monee, IL
04 June 2022

97473591R00134